The River Baptists

# Belinda
# CASTLES
## The River Baptists

ALLEN&UNWIN

First published in 2007

Allen & Unwin
83 Alexander Street
Crows Nest NSW 2065
Australia
Phone:     (61 2) 8425 0100
Fax:        (61 2) 9906 2218
Email:     info@allenandunwin.com
Web:       www.allenandunwin.com

National Library of Australia
Cataloguing-in-Publication entry:

Castles, Belinda.
    The river Baptists.

    ISBN 978 1 74175 193 2 (pbk.).

    I.Title

A823.4

Typeset in 12/15pt Granjon by Midland Typesetters, Australia
Printed in Australia by McPherson's Printing Group

10 9 8 7 6 5 4 3 2 1

*For Brad and Ellie, with love*

Lord help me …
Because my boat is so small,
And your sea is so immense.

*Medieval French prayer*

# Prologue

Danny Raine contemplated the scene before him, his stomach shifting, watery. His father faced him on the bench at the stern of an eight-foot aluminium dinghy, his once-white T-shirt spattered with blood. The gore of grey prawns and worms was spread across his lap and seat and the metal floor in front of him. His bulk was hunched, focused on threading a worm onto a hook. There was a decent chop out here at the heads. Danny had watched him put away a six-pack so far this morning; he'd dropped the worm at least four times, sworn passionately with each of them.

Danny felt the pull of sleep, wished for bed. Not his bed, someone else's. Anyone else's. Someone soft and smiling. He'd been awake late, listening to the sounds of the house.

He sent himself through the walls, slipping through the levels of noise: a car with its motor idling on the next street, a cat and a possum wailing in battle, the mysterious rumblings of the hot water system. He probed through the ordinary sounds for a sign of trouble. But there was nothing. He'd lost a couple of hours' sleep for nothing, again.

Danny lifted his eyes to the horizon, trying to ignore the stench of the bait. Beyond the boat lay the island's blunt, rocky escarpment, blackening against the grey sea. An unpredictable current tipped the tinny around on the increasing swell. His stomach lurched and he tried to put breakfast from his mind. The eggs had been a bad idea. As he watched his mother fry them, then scrub the pan while he and his father ate, he could see she was working up to saying something. Her hand trembled for a moment as she cleared the plates. 'I'll get the barbie going at six to cook your fish,' she said, eventually. Then there was the scrape of his father's chair as it flew back, and his finger was a centimetre from her face. 'I'm going fishing with my boy. We get back when we get back.' I have to leave here, Danny had thought. I can't watch out for her anymore. But if he hadn't left by now, a grown man, who could believe he ever would? And she wasn't the only one he stayed for, the good it did him. The hooks were in him, sharp and deep. If he struggled, they drove in deeper.

'Look after him,' she whispered in the doorway as his dad loaded the gear into the car, in preparation for the hour-long drive to the river. 'His knee's playing up. Makes him cranky.' He'd almost laughed.

Behind his father, the motor lifted free in the chop, the screws loose from slack maintenance. Danny watched him stand, prawns cascading from his gut, turning to force the prop back under the water. One little shove, Danny thought. No one would be any the wiser. Or sorrier. He let himself see it for a moment, his arms reaching forward across the little boat, hefting the clumsy old goat overboard. The thought of touching his filthy clothes, the bulky, softening body beneath, kept his hands where they were, plaiting and unplaiting an old length of rope in his lap. He hadn't touched his father since he was a boy. He remembered hugging him when he came home off a run on his rig. There were still flashes then: days, weeks, of an ordinary man, a father you could touch without thinking. His dad brought home a puppy once and wrestled with the boys and the yappy little lab on the patchy lawn. They were all filthy afterwards, and starving, but his mum laughed and fed them and washed the boys and the dog. There was something between them then, the males in the family, that wasn't tainted or shaming.

As his father turned back to face him, the tinny tipped steeply into the river and Danny pitched forwards, grabbing onto his seat to arrest his slide. His father managed to stay in the boat through broad ballast—his wide backside—and the slowness of his body, sloshing about in counterbalance to the waves until he got a decent hold on his bench. Then, as the boat levelled, Danny caught a glimpse above his father's shoulder of a white-crested wave, bigger than any surrounding it. Before he had time to react a surge of water slammed into the side of the boat, and Danny slid across the bench until he was half-standing, gripping the side of the boat with his body clenched, almost horizontal. 'Dad!' he shouted—all he needed was a good yank on his jacket to overcome the force of the wave—but his father was glancing about, panicky, trying to tell where the next wave would come from. As Danny finally began to right himself another wave hit, and he grabbed for anything that would anchor him to the tossing boat. Then his foot slid on a gristly mass of prawns and bilge slime, and he was overboard; ears, mouth full of salty water, submerged in the cold, churning liquid, a frenzy of thrashing limbs.

There was no way to gauge how long he was under. It was like being dumped when he went bodysurfing as a kid, his whole body tossed about like a toy in a washing machine. Back then he'd wait to find a smooth bank of sand beneath him, get on his feet and lift his head free so he could start clearing his sinuses of ocean and beach. There was nothing for his feet to find here; the whole world was moving around him, but at last an upstretched hand reached a place above the water for part of a second and he forced his head in the direction of air, gulping it like a fish on the floor of his father's tinny.

Grey water rose and fell around him, surging into his nose, mouth and eyes, making it impossible to see for more than a second or two at a time. He swivelled as best as he could in the swell to find the boat, kicking furiously to stay afloat. As the water dipped he sighted it, distant and small already, past the island, headed seaward. He felt something large, sinewy, inhuman, brush by his leg and shrank into himself, thrashing away from that spot. Slow down, he told himself. Think. Where are you? Amid the peaks and troughs he forced himself to find his bearings. He was drawing closer to a bushy point, maybe fifty metres downriver. There was a sheltered bay beyond it, he was pretty sure, a fishing village, a kids' rec centre. If he could make land, he could pick his way through the bush and walk there along the rocks. Lightning forked out to sea, crashes of thunder following a second or two behind every flash. The strikes seemed close to his father's boat, a tiny figure attacked by an angry, alien sky.

He slowed his kicking for a moment, trying to figure out what he needed to do to get to land. The surge was pushing him towards the point. A piece of wood, a slimy plank almost a metre long, nudged his cheek. At first he pulled back from it, but seeing what it was, he took hold with both hands and began to kick for shore. As he grew closer, the swell ducking him under, he glimpsed sharp-looking rocks, smashing surf. But then he drew level and saw that there was a gap, a short sandy beach beneath the trees. His legs felt as though someone was holding onto them from beneath, pulling him under. He stopped pushing for a moment, trod water, then kicked hard across the rip with everything left in his exhausted limbs. After a few more maddening dunkings he was dragging his sodden body across the narrow beach to the dank shelter of the bush.

When he reached the first stand of eucalypts, he laid his cold, wet head on the damp earth. He blinked away the mist of saltwater in his eyes and looked back towards the mouth of the river. Beyond the beach, just visible in the darkening afternoon amid the greys of the churning water, the dark island, the blackish shore, was his father's little boat and the hulking figure that occupied it. Danny felt as though he had been down, down to the bottom of the river, down through the layers of silt and had emerged somewhere else, in a new world. The tiny boat, the grey ocean, were beyond an invisible, unbreachable border, in the world of a film or a dream. Danny took deep swallows of air; water ran from his nose. You can look for me forever you black-hearted son of a bitch, he thought. As far as you're concerned, I'm dead. And as far as I'm concerned, from now on, so are you.

# Chapter 1

Rose sat at the desk beneath the open window in the smallest room in the house, watching the green marker on the wide black river blink in the dark. Beyond the glow of the open laptop lay the night, and all the people in it. The black turtle shell of the island was dotted with lights, but between these she knew were more houses, their inhabitants moving and dreaming in the dark. She closed her eyes and imagined that they were some heat-sensitive, X-ray device that saw across distances, through walls, to the shapes within the houses, seeing the things that people did in secret to make themselves feel loved.

She lifted her hair off her sweaty neck and tied it in a knot, forcing herself back to her work. Her days were spent in a dream, floating around on the silver river. She could only work at night. All the busyness of the world must end so you could sit in this little pool of light, the night dark around you, and imagine the ways that people wanted to touch each other, and themselves, if there was no one to answer to about it.

When she'd done her thousand words, she snapped shut her laptop and left the room, closing the door. Out in the living room she arranged herself carefully on her side on the sofa, settling her swollen belly on a cushion. From the corner of her eye she glimpsed a dark figure cross the gap in the verandah fence and she caught her breath. Soon she saw it was pissed, grumpy old Tom from next door stumbling about—she recognised the slight hunch, the spindly legs beneath his shorts. She sank back into the sofa. The silence here, when it came, was deep.

Even now, though, she heard the low increasing hum of a tinny approaching. Then its light appeared in the gap, growing larger in the dark, steady on the flat river. It was like watching her memories, coming towards her in the blackness. She imagined that if she kept watching, the light would slow as it reached her jetty and become a little boat, two figures climbing out of it, onto the ladder, laughing, drunk. She and Ben, people from a different time, eight months ago, before the year was severed, into the time before and the time after.

She closed her eyes. They'd been drinking at the pub. The ride back across was chilly, but the alcohol had made her immune, excitable. 'I love this place,' she'd said, gripping his arm for warmth, her backside cold on the seat of the tinny.

'I can see why,' he said. 'Sub-zero temperatures, mud, a pub full of guys who look like Cousin It . . .'

'But the river at night—look at it, Ben. It's magical.' The night was just black shapes, the moon thin behind a cloud. The mound of the island, the looming cliff on the opposite shore. A train rushed out of the tunnel north of the river and thundered across the bridge, a long snaking worm of orange lights sailing above the black water.

She could just make out his features in the glow from the tinny's light. He was shivering, his lips darkening against his white skin. 'Inspirational place to write your porn, I imagine. All those hotties at the pub.' She gave him a sharp nudge that rocked the boat. 'Steady, kid!' He gripped the bench.

'It's not porn. It's erotic fiction, for adventurous ladies.'

'Ha! The kind of adventure you can have with one hand.'

'I have to tell you, it's a damn sight better than working for *Wank Weekly*.'

'That I can believe.'

The cliff reared above them; they were almost at her jetty. 'I always have trouble finding it at night,' she said, slowing the boat to a putter.

'How *do* you find it?'

'Well, I usually find next door first. His dog starts yapping as soon as you get anywhere near his place. And there's a yacht that's often moored just out from my jetty, too.'

'Your jetty. How long's he letting you stay here? Hasn't your sister dumped him?'

'Yes, well.'

'Yes, well what?'

'I'll tell you when we get inside.'

'This doesn't sound good.'

She giggled, and pointed the tinny at the ladder, bumping the pillars of the jetty twice as she tried to get the nose into position so Ben could jump off. 'Look, I can just grab hold of it now,' he said.

'No, no. I'm going to put you in the right spot. Have faith.'

When she'd finally tied off and they'd staggered along the narrow, rotting jetty to her verandah, she pulled back the screen door noisily and the dog began to bark. 'There he goes,' she said.

'Fucken shut up, Dog!' a voice snarled from the darkness.

'Delightful neighbours, too,' Ben murmured as they stepped inside. 'This is nice,' he said as she turned on a couple of lamps, illuminating the old sofas, the bright rug. 'Sort of slum chic.'

'I like it.' She emerged from the tiny kitchen at the back of the living room with a bottle of white wine and two tumblers.

'No, it's nice. I mean it. Are we really going to drink a bottle of wine?'

'Well, we can start it. Put the rest away for later.'

He laughed and threw his coat on one sofa, flopped on the other. She wedged herself into the small space he'd left. 'So, what's the scandal?'

'Oh, God.' Her face was hidden behind her hair as she worked the corkscrew.

'What, Rose?' She looked at him. She'd known his face all her life—his curly hair, his huge brown eyes, the mouth that seemed too small, insignificant in comparison. She had pictures of him as a kid—he looked just the same in them as he did now. She concentrated on his eyes for a moment. The teasing in his voice, his eyes, had disappeared. She didn't want to tell him, now, but he was looking at her, waiting.

'I've kind of got a thing going with James.'

He stood suddenly. 'You're kidding, right?'

'No, I'm not kidding. It's not that big a deal. Sit down.'

His hands were on his hips. 'What did Billie ever do to you, Rose? Are you getting your own back for something?'

'No.' She poured the wine, her stomach turning over. 'No, it wasn't deliberate. She dumped him. What does it matter? She can have anyone she wants. It's just a bit of fun. I'm not planning to tell her about it, actually.'

He began to say something, then sat down. 'Rosie,' he sighed. 'You're a disaster.'

'I know,' she giggled. She put a hand on his arm. 'Do you forgive me?'

'What's it got to do with me?'

'But if you forgive me, then it's OK. I can sleep at night.'

'I forgive you,' he said, holding her hand against his leg, drinking his wine. 'Oh my God. This wine is fucking terrible.'

They'd been on this sofa. Right here. They drank the awful wine, all of it. They crashed together in her bed, in T-shirts and undies, the way they always did. He faced away from her; she hugged his back. They'd slept like that since they were kids, through uni. She couldn't imagine they ever would again. 'I wish you were my brother,' she'd whispered in his ear. He shook his head into his pillow.

It was seven months now since she'd last seen him. She couldn't call him; couldn't imagine breaching the gap. She'd seen him one more time after that night, and had a feeling, even then, that he'd only come because, when she rang him, she'd been crying. It was a month after the night she told him about James, and she'd heard nothing in the meantime. They usually talked every few days. When she could speak, she asked him to come to the funeral.

He came, of course. His eyes were wet as he walked along the track towards where she was attempting to tie off the boat. She couldn't hug him; she was ankle-deep in mud, down in the riverbed. She'd woken to thick fog clinging to the river, the end of the jetty not visible from her bedroom window. There was no ferry for two hours, so she'd had to take James's boat. As she edged forward into the mist, she felt she was entering a cloud she would never leave. She eased the boat slowly in the direction of the opposite shore, and knew she would only find it by chance. Sounds came to her through the cool white fog: a train's ghostly wind as it whipped from the tunnel, a voice sailing through the cloud from another boat. She slowed almost to a standstill; the boat must be near. Eventually, little gaps began to clear in the fog and she caught glimpses of the island, the railway bridge, and navigated slowly towards the shore. By the time she reached it, her black suit was clinging to her and she was sweating with a mild panic in spite of the cold. She fought the urge to be sick.

In the channel that ran alongside the rail tracks she killed the motor and took off her shoes, stepping carefully into shallow water and foul-smelling mud. As she unlooped the rope from the bottom of the dinghy, she saw immediately that the boat wasn't close enough to the rocky bank for her to tie off around the post at the top, and glutinous mud gripped the hull. She gave the boat a fruitless push, and felt another prickle of sweat break out on her forehead and under her arms.

She took off her jacket and laid it carefully on the rocks, above the watermark, next to her black, heeled shoes. Looking at her feet, she saw they were covered with thick mud. As she approached the boat for one last try she felt like climbing inside and lying down on the bench, drifting out onto the silent river in the fog. Where was Ben? Where was his train? Like he'd get down in the mud and help, anyway.

She couldn't think about the day ahead. She needed to

tie off the boat, that was all. Pulling her skirt high around her waist to keep it out of the icy water, she waded back in and leaned against the stern. She heard the growl of a large boat behind her, roaring into the channel, ignoring the speed limit. She felt its wake surge up her legs, wetting her skirt, lifting the boat free of the mud, and pushed again. When the wake calmed, the boat was a metre further into shore. That was when Ben appeared. She dropped the anchor in the mud and scrabbled up the rocks to tie off. When she'd finished, he took her hand.

'Haven't seen you in a suit since graduation,' she said quietly.

'It's the same one.' He looked like a rock star at a wedding, his mad curls at odds with his clothes. 'You're drenched.' He looked her up and down. She nodded, and fought back the urge to cry. She carried her jacket and shoes in one hand and held his arm as she walked with muddy feet down the dirt road towards the car park. A train emerged from the gloom on the tracks above them, rushing into the mist that enveloped the river, lights gleaming in the fog. It left a wind that chilled her wet legs.

'I saw Billie the other day,' he said. 'With James.'

'It's all right. You know, he's really a bit of a tosser.'

'You don't say.' He put his arm around her. 'What are you going to do about your feet?' They both looked down. Mud gleamed all the way up her long shins.

'I think there's a towel in the car,' she said.

There was glass on the ground as they approached her

car, a green Hondamatic, and she peered carefully around her feet, trying to avoid it. 'Bugger,' he said quietly. She looked up and saw that it was her windscreen that was broken. She put a hand to her face and took a breath.

'It's all right, mate,' he said. Again that urge. She wanted to lie down on the ground and sleep, wake up in summer and all this be gone. 'We'll get the train,' he said.

'No, we're going to have to drive. There won't be another train for an hour.'

In the back seat was an old towel. She dried her feet before brushing the glass off the front seats. They'd done a thorough job, anyway. The windscreen was entirely gone. So were her CDs and her stereo. 'Wankers,' Ben muttered as he eased himself into the passenger seat.

They took the old highway; she couldn't get on the freeway without a windscreen, especially not in this weather. She took it as fast as she dared, the mist making it hard to see even to the next bend, the dense bush looming, uncanny. Occasionally the highway came so close to the freeway that the rumble of trucks was almost deafening, though she couldn't see them, and shafts of light appeared then vanished as the traffic blocked out the weak sun between the trees above. It was strange to drive with the air directly on her face, and she concentrated on that: on the cool wetness of her skin, her hair damp against her neck, her glasses fogging and needing a wipe every few minutes.

'What happened, Rose?' he said eventually.

She heard herself tell him, but her voice seemed remote, unnatural. 'A truck rear-ended his van on the freeway.

I saw the smoke, from my verandah. I was having dinner with James. Didn't know what it was, till later. It seemed— beautiful at the time.'

He put his hand on her knee and she trembled for a second. They said nothing on the long descent through the bush until they reached the glaring stretch of suburbs that lay between the national park and the ocean. The mist had lifted and the sun was growing hot on their faces. Outside a bungalow, a table of paintings was propped up next to a sign on which was daubed '$60'. 'Doesn't change, does it?' he said.

She shook her head. They were passing the browning oval of the high school, the one they'd both attended, where her father had been the music teacher, until the week before. 'The bay does, though. You been back lately?'

'Saw Mum a couple of weeks ago. There's some crazy money down on the beach. She reckons she'll sell up, eventually.'

'Oh, no. Where would she go? She's been there forever.' He shrugged. 'She coming today?'

'Yeah. She liked your old man. Everyone did. Between you and me, I think she had a bit of a crush on him.'

'No!'

'I reckon. Then I could have been your brother,' he laughed. She blushed, and stared straight ahead at the white- and yellow-brick houses, the orange roofs, peeling away towards the ocean.

When they reached the little blue church, a block back from the beach, there was a sea of shining cars, baking on the grass verge, on the street, on the path. Must be people from school, she thought. He'd known so many people she didn't. All those children—not just the ones he'd been teaching now, but all the ones that had grown up, and remembered him, and had heard somehow. He'd been a presence in so many lives, and now she had to share her grief with them, give up a little of her claim to each one.

The door was still open, but the pews were full. She made for a space in the back row, but an elderly woman— tiny, hunched, a distant relative she recognised but could not immediately place—ushered her forward firmly, gripping her still-damp arm. 'There's a place for you next to your sister, Rosie dear, at the front,' she whispered. 'And your friend,' she said, glancing up at Ben. 'Go on, love. It'll start soon.'

As they passed the crowd in the back rows, she spotted three of her dad's on–off girlfriends—the hot chickas, she and Ben always called them. He always brought home stunners, but none as beautiful as the portrait of her mother he had once painted—so like Billie now she was an adult—that leaned against the wall at the back of the garage, dusty and wrinkled with moisture. She'd always felt sorry for the chickas and intimidated by their sleek womanliness all at once. Always was a sucker for a pretty face, her dad.

In the front row was her sister, her wide silk ribbon of blonde hair clinging to the back of her suit. Next to her was James, and it was beside him that there was empty space. 'Can't we sit at the back?' she said under her breath as Ben guided her, hand on her back, down the aisle. She could feel heads turning towards her, as though she were a bride.

'You've got to be at the front,' he said. 'I'll stay with you.'

She tried to duck past Billie quietly, nodding hello, but her sister threw her arms around her and pulled her close. 'We were so worried about you! Where have you been?' Rose drew back. Billie put her hand on Ben's shoulder. 'Bless you, Ben.' She was as fresh and lovely as ever. Her eyes shone moistly from an unlined face. If she was wearing make-up, you couldn't see it.

'I see she hasn't lost any sleep,' Rose whispered to Ben as they sat down.

He put his hand on hers. 'Shhh,' he said gently. 'Not now.'

Rose dared herself to look at James; he was as handsome as always. It was a shock when you hadn't seen him for a while. His eyes were fixed firmly on the casket. She took it in, the impossibly long box that held the body of her father, and sat down quickly. 'Christ,' she breathed. A tear slid down Billie's beautiful cheek.

Rose didn't listen to the pastor. He hadn't known her dad, who hadn't been even faintly religious. The wool of James's suit grazed her elbow. She glanced again at his profile. The last time she'd seen him he'd been naked, in the house on the river, passing Rose her mobile across the bed. He'd dressed in another room when he saw who was calling, left when she whispered the news. That was just under a week ago. She'd heard nothing from him since, but Billie had told her she'd rung him. He'd gone round, when he heard, and stayed. Rose had taken it with grim resignation. Of course he did, she thought. Of course.

'Where's the wake?' Ben whispered to her when it was finished. She was staring blindly at the curtains behind which the coffin had disappeared.

'What? Oh God, the wake. I don't know. Our house, I suppose. I'm not going.'

'Rose—'

'You go, if you want. I'm going back to the river.'

She made her way quickly down the aisle while Billie was talking to the pastor. She caught James's eye quickly as she passed but kept moving. His eyes had already slid off her face, down her body and away. 'People will want to see you,' Ben said, as he hurried after her. The house, it would still smell of him—cigarettes, the reheated junk he brought home from the school canteen, his home-brew. The house of a man without a wife.

An aunt, her father's sister, grabbed hold of her arm as she picked her way through the cars to her own. 'Rosie,' she began, but lost her words in a constricted sob. Rose watched her from another place. Her eyes were Rose's father's to the closest detail: pale green, so pale they seemed almost blind. Rose put a hand on hers and lifted it gently from her arm. 'I'm sorry,' she said quietly and turned her back on her aunt, walking quickly to her car. Ben took the passenger seat, saying nothing.

She drove, limbs rigid, to the nearest garage, where she paid a small fortune to have the windscreen repaired while they waited on plastic chairs in the warm sun, blinding against the white wall of the garage and the pale brick houses all around. One of the mechanics made phone calls at the counter in the workshop and stared at her legs. After a while, Ben noticed, put his hand on her thigh. She longed for the space to cry.

Back at the village, he spoke, finally. 'Let's go to the pub, mate. We'll have our own wake. Talk about him, if you want.'

She shook her head. 'I'll have a drink. But I don't want to talk about anything.'

'All right, Rose. Come on. I'll shout you.'

She attempted a laugh. 'Since when? You robbed a bank?'

'I'll shout you the first one, anyway.'

They sat on the terrace outside the pub in the winter sun until it grew chilly and Ben told her stories about work. He worked in a bar in a leather club at night; he was studying for his Masters in the day. He always had something new to tell her. But then he'd always had something new to tell her when he worked in the weigh station on the freeway in their uni holidays. He was like that. Reckoned some of the truckies from those days turned up at his leather bar, but he'd tell you anything for the sake of a story. She drank slowly, was still on her first as he started his third. Halfway through it, she felt sick and knew she had to stop. 'I'm not up to this,' she said.

'Don't tell me Rose Baker is off her beer.' For a moment she thought she would tell him. His face, though, when she said she'd been seeing James. And she wasn't certain herself yet. 'Do you want me to help you get home?'

She looked at him. He would never have asked, before. He would have just camped out at her place until she kicked him out, tomorrow or the next day.

'I think I just want to be on my own for a while.'

He nodded. It felt like the end of something, but she couldn't think about that now. He hugged her at the train station. 'I'll call you,' he said.

She looked at his face. As though she knew this was it, that she'd be alone on this river from now on, she said quickly, 'He was my favourite person in the world. When I was a kid, I spent whole days planning tricks to make him laugh.'

Ben bit his lip, took her in his arms. 'I know.' He smelled as he always did, slightly dirty hair, tobacco—like her dad, beer.

The light was fading as she walked along the muddy road by the train tracks, thinking of nothing, watching the ferry chug in and a boatful of junkies circling recklessly at the fish co-op, yelling and shoving each other. 'Want me to break your fucken nose again, Angie?' one of the women shouted. When she reached her mooring, she had taken her shoes off and hitched up her skirt for the scramble down the rocks before she realised the boat—James's boat—was gone. Stolen.

'Unbelievable,' she said quietly. Down by the marina,

the ferry was approaching. She ran along the muddy path to the wharf in her heels. 'Come on, wait,' she whispered. 'Give me something.'

She made it, just, found an empty plastic seat at the back among the tired, sullen commuter crowd and watched the shore pulling away. Beyond the narrow windows of the ferry the short winter day was ending, the grey-blues of the river and the sky deepening, the wooded hills turning black, pinpricked in clusters with the lights of the houses.

Rosie lay on the sofa, her hand on her large belly. The winter seemed so long ago. It was like a serious illness, from which you recovered, restored but changed. She seemed like a convalescent to herself, a shadow wandering the gardens of a high-walled hospital in a foreign country, easing herself off painkillers, nervous of life without assistance. Out on the river, the silence had deepened to nothingness. Her body brimmed with solitude and the dark.

# Chapter 2

Danny woke to a clear island morning, the air fresh, eucalypt-scented after two days of rain. The sun flickered through the trees outside his window, making patterns on the thin white curtains of the shed. As he stepped outside to pee in the bush behind his shed, the air was crisp and cool. The river below, down through the leaves of the spindly gums past the main house, was a blue mirror.

His shift started late today, so he made a coffee on his camping stove and sat on the sun-warmed flat rock outside his door. The gums were bone-white against the blue sky, and it was a great thing for it just to be morning, to be drinking coffee, to feel the sun on his face. It was still new to him, though he'd been on the river for a little more than seven years now.

An urgent whisper came from behind him, in the shed. 'Where's the toilet?' the girl asked. He turned and smiled. For a moment he couldn't remember her name. You wouldn't forget that hair, though, long and red and wavy and thick. He'd spent most of the night with his arms buried in it. Warm, silky, alive.

'You're looking at it,' he said.

'You're joking.'

'Afraid not, April.' How could he forget? Month he was born. He brought the camping stove outside and got some more water going while she looked for a spot where neither he nor the neighbours would catch her out. The river sparkled through the trees below and the summer opened up in front of him. He'd be working almost every hour of it, but he'd be out on the river—who in their right mind could call that work?—and this would be the last summer he'd be working for someone else. Big Alf was going to sell him the taxi service so he could buy out his partner in the chandlery. He'd worked for two men in the eleven years since he left high school; Alf had been a damn sight better than the old man, but after this summer, he'd never let someone else be his boss again.

On the way down the track to the beach he let the girl walk ahead a little so he could watch her hair some more. Sunlight fell in shafts and dapples through the trees and it shimmered like a liquidambar in the breeze. When they emerged from a short overgrown path onto the beach his dory was sitting on the mud. 'You hop onto the jetty over there,' he said. 'No need for you to get covered in mud.' He watched her walk along the beach—the slight sway of her hips in the little white sundress she'd showed up in at the pub last night, her long, skinny chalk-white legs, her hair. Come on, Dan, he told himself. Get a move on.

The tide wasn't too far out; he rolled up his jeans and waded in. The water was cool though the sun was warm, and the seaweed and mud seeped between his toes and around his ankles. He clambered into the dory, hanging his feet over the side, sloshing them about to rinse off the mud, then pulled the boat free of the bottom with his running line. It stayed shallow all the way out to the end of the jetty, and he tapped the bottom with his oar until he was alongside the pontoon. She peered at the narrow boat, the mud beneath it, uncertainly. 'Hang on a sec,' he said, and tied the boat off. He jumped up onto the platform next to her and helped her in. She climbed down unsteadily, gripping his shoulder. She had her own smell. There was the usual stuff—clean hair, the faint tang of sweat after a night with him and no shower, but something else, too. Nuts. Salty, buttery, good. Once she was seated, he was in front of her in one smooth movement and untying the rope.

He barely had to row to clear the bay. The tide was still pulling strongly. Once past the point, though, he had to turn almost 180 degrees, back upstream against the tide. She relaxed once they were moving. Touched his knee a few times. Asked him about his job. He had to row hard; she had a train to make. By the time he reached the channel his skin was glistening and liquid gathered on his top lip, but he could feel himself grinning, his whole face stretched in a way he couldn't control.

Alf was waiting for him on the wharf of the chandlery, his vast gut poking out above his waistband despite the fact that he was wearing a T-shirt you could have made a decent sail out of. Behind him was a thin, pale young bloke with longish hair and a goatee, dozing against a backpack in the sun.

'Late, Danny,' Alf said. 'Need to pick up Sue over at the beach. Young fella Kane's going over that side. Gonna be working on the Durham place. Take him on the way.' He handed him a bunch of keys and shuffled back along the jetty and into the chandlery.

The sleeping man opened his eyes—a startling blue, they seemed to reflect the river—and watched Danny help the girl from the boat. Danny climbed up after her. 'Well, catch you,' she said and reached up to kiss Danny on the cheek. He laid a hand on the hair that fell down her back. He whispered in her ear. She laughed, turned away, her long legs striding along the jetty. Behind her, Kane followed her movements, rising stiffly to his feet. Danny, too, watched her till she reached the shop at the other end of the marina. Her hair blazed for a moment in the sun at the doorway and she was gone.

He turned to Kane, on his feet now and taller than Danny by a good ten centimetres, muscular in the chest and shoulders, though slender. Danny would never lose this habit of sizing men up the moment he met them. Didn't even notice it anymore. 'Sorry, mate. Let's go.' The bloke looked nervous, uncertain. 'Well, come on. Do you want a lift or don't you?' Kane gave him another wary glance and then made his way down into the Quintrex. Danny followed him and started the motor. Once clear of the channel he opened her up and the boat bounced across the glassy water.

'Beautiful day,' Danny ventured as they raced towards the opposite shore. The man gave him a sideways glance and said nothing. Funny bloke, Danny thought. Skittish as a crab. Everyone on the river lived their lives out in the open. Couldn't just get into a car and hide your worries from the world. From the corner of his eye he glimpsed a new pallor creep across his passenger's face as he gripped the bar. The sandstone cliff above the long strip of houses on the near bank loomed above them. Best get him over there quick and off the boat before he threw up. 'Where do you need? Durham's?' he shouted over the motor. 'Or you dropping your gear somewhere first?'

'Mancini's,' Kane said quietly.

'What's that?' Danny called.

'MANCINI'S!' he shouted, too loudly, then looked away, out over the river, embarrassed.

Danny wondered whether Kane was the full deck. He slowed the motor as they approached the row of wharves and curved to the south. He knew the place—it was a little beyond the centre of the row. You couldn't miss it because it was next to Tom Shepherd's and everyone knew his place. Looked like a scrapyard—every spare inch of land surrounding the house crammed with tyres, old fridges, tinny hulls—with a wharf that seemed ready to fall into the river on the next big tide. A bit further along on the other side was Durham's, a wooden frame mid-construction, the old house gone in the last bushfire, several years back. Mancini's was a nice little place, a wooden house set back from the water with a broad jacaranda that kept off the worst of the afternoon sun. It was just losing the last of its purple flowers now; they spread in a carpet in the shade. Couldn't imagine what this bloke wanted here. The house was let to that girl, Rose, the quiet, pregnant one with the big bush of blonde hair. This guy looked like he was moving in.

He brought the rear of the boat round to the ladder at the end of Rose's jetty. 'That's fifteen bucks, mate.' The notes the bloke fished out of his jeans looked like they'd been living down the back of a couch. Danny shoved them in his pocket and hefted the backpack onto the jetty. Not much reason to hang about and chat. Didn't figure this one would be a regular user of the water taxi. You got one-offs this time of day; ferry didn't stop at the beach for a couple of hours after peak hour. People got stuck.

He was about to slip the motor into gear when he saw the girl coming down the wharf towards them. She was very tall, as tall as Danny, and had a serious face, long, curly dark-blonde hair tied back at her neck. Looked like she was wearing her nightie—a long shapeless white shift that hung unevenly around her knees. She wore glasses, little rectangles that reflected the light and obscured her expression, though she scowled slightly into the sun. She walked a little strangely, cautiously, as though there was something slightly wrong with her legs or back, but that'd be the baby. She gave Kane a little wave and nodded at Danny. He wondered again what the connection could be. You could spend your life wondering about those things, the stuff you saw on the river, he thought, yet you were almost always wrong. He took the boat out clear of the jetties and the moorings of big old wooden boats, the sleek yachts with names like *You Beaut* and *Aurora*, and headed south towards his pick-up at the far end of the beach.

Rose watched the tenant climb out of the water taxi and make his way along the jetty towards her. Billie had told her to expect him. After eight months' free run, James was putting a tenant in the boatshed. What could she say? Maybe he'd be company. Someone to notice if she fell in the river one fine morning, at least.

He was tall and slightly bandy-limbed. She thought of a cowboy as she watched his figure approaching, the front of his body cast into shadow by the western sun at his back, winking and glaring between his legs as he drew closer. She shielded her face with a hand so she could see him more clearly. He was young, scruffy, soft-faced. He dropped his backpack at the foot of the stairs to the verandah. 'G'day,' he nodded. 'You'd be my landlady, would you?'

'Not really,' she said. 'Your neighbour. I'm a tenant, too. My sister's boyfriend owns the place. Want a cuppa?'

He peered at her. 'OK. If it's all right with you.'

'Sit down.' She nodded towards the cane chairs on the shaded verandah. 'I'll be back in a sec.'

When she returned with the tea tray she could see him more clearly. Bamboo blinds shut out the worst of the afternoon sun, allowing a filtered light onto the verandah. His eyes were as blue as the river on a still, cloudless morning like this one. It had been so long since she'd had a cup of tea with someone. Who was her last visitor? Billie, that was it, when she'd come to tell her she'd sold their father's house, back in the winter. She'd gotten rid of her as quickly as she could; said she had to work. In fact she had felt overwhelmingly nauseous, needed her sister to leave before she could no longer hide it.

'Nice place,' he said.

'Yes,' she said, looking at the river through the gap between the blinds. 'I haven't been here that long myself. I'm Rose, by the way.' She turned to him, held out a hand.

He took it, tentatively. 'Kane.' His long, dry fingers trembled for a moment and he withdrew his hand quickly, wiped it on his jeans. 'Husband at work?'

She smiled. 'Husband?' He nodded at her belly. 'Oh, no,' she said. 'There's no husband. Where do you get one of those?'

'What's the deal with that fella on the water taxi?'

For a moment Rose couldn't follow his train of thought, but then realised he'd changed the subject. 'Oh, Danny? I don't know. What do you mean?'

'He was laughing at me, over at the marina. Made some joke to his girlfriend. This one of them places they don't like outsiders?'

'Oh, don't worry about that. You need to baptise your firstborn in the river and then sacrifice a goat every full moon for a year before they'll say hello to you in the pub around here.'

He grinned briefly, but seemed unsure. 'Hard to fit in, is it?'

'They're all right. I think they check you're staying before they waste too much energy on you, that's all.' She leaned forward. 'Watch this one, though,' she gestured towards the house to their left. 'He's a miserable old bugger. Neighbour from hell.'

'Yeah? What's he do?'

'Leaves his garbage on my jetty. Lets his dog crap in my yard. Just a charmer, you know. Drunk, mostly.' She noticed he'd finished his tea. Must have downed it fast enough to scald his tongue. His left foot was jumping around on the decking. 'Come on, I'll show you the shed. Hope you're not expecting too much.'

She set her cup down on the table and led him off the front of the verandah along to the boatshed. It was an ugly brick thing, built long after the little wooden house, but it had tinted glass sliding doors that let you look out at the river from the bed. As she slid back the door a smell escaped, a faint odour of damp. She'd tried to air it out the day before but it persisted. 'You can probably leave it open. Most people do round here.' She watched him take in the narrow room, the concrete floor, the single bed, the bench on the wall opposite with a bar fridge underneath, a camping stove and a kettle on top. 'Will you be all right, do you think?'

He stared into the room for a few seconds more, then looked into her eyes. He was a fair bit taller than her, tall as she was. His mouth opened. He seemed lost for a moment. Then he lowered his eyes and grinned. 'It's great, mate,' he said. 'A waterfront mansion! I've come up in the world.'

'OK,' she laughed. 'Let me know if you need anything. I don't have a boat but the ferry stops at the public wharf if you need to get over the other side.'

He took his backpack inside, dropped it in the middle of the floor, sat on the bed. She waited for a moment to see if he would say anything else, but he was looking at the floor. She withdrew, quietly, and made her way back to the verandah.

He felt like the world was playing tricks on him. A girl like that, right next door, not married, no bloke anywhere in sight? When he'd seen her standing on the steps, he'd almost turned around and got back in that arrogant clown's boat. Her hair, honey-coloured, glowing in the sun, her beautiful belly. And so tall, almost as tall as him. He couldn't look at her at first, but when he did she was smiling, kindly—at him. And then making him tea. It made him nervous to sit and chat to a girl like her, as though that kind of thing happened to him every day. Every second he sat there, on her verandah, right next to her, seemed to bring him a second closer to being discovered. In the shed he could relax a little, though he was sorry when her figure at the glass door, blocking out the sun, finally disappeared. He'd driven her away, he knew, but he needed time to think.

He wasn't sure how things were going to go here. He was getting confusing signals. He tried to read the world, tried to get a glimpse of what was coming, avoid the old mistakes, but it wasn't easy. That bloke on the boat, he'd been a bad sign. The trophy girlfriend, the whispering behind his back. Rose seemed to balance things out—there was something about her, like she wasn't just being nice for the sake of it—but some people were put there to trick you, catch you out. You had to be careful.

He lay back on the bed and watched the dazzle of the river through half-shut eyes. His thoughts slowed, his jumping leg stilled, out of the sight of others. This was a new place, his place. Back up the river it was a bad scene. He'd only been up there for six months and there was a double shooting—some old couple borrowed money off bikies—and a knifing every other week at the back of the pub. And then that other business. Round here, he'd heard, it was wall-to-wall doctors and lawyers and advertising people with weekenders. They looked normal, out fishing in their tinnies, drinking tap beer at the pub, but it was Paddington on the water—he knew that. Well, except for the junkies, he'd seen a few of those already. That was all right. Made him feel at home.

No, he thought. He let himself believe in the future, in himself, in new beginnings. He'd been reading a book; his mum had given it to him when he'd visited. Christ knew where she'd got hold of it. It was about being your best self, about deciding to be something and then being it. 'That's all right for him to say,' he'd told his mum. 'Look at him, look at the guy's teeth. They're worth more than your car.'

'No, Kane,' she insisted, putting his dinner in front of him. 'He came from nothing, like you. If he can do it, why can't you?'

The book seemed cheesy, American, until he got into it. When you got past the talk-show host thing, it made sense. No one was going to do it for you; you made your own destiny. His problem was, he'd always hung around with losers and he'd let them tell him what he was worth. He wasn't sure how he'd managed it, but he'd wriggled out of trouble up the river like an eel. That was another thing in the book: you had to recognise gifts. It was a sin to waste them. Here was a gift if ever he saw one. He had a place to live—a beautiful place—a lovely, kind girl next door and the job on the Durham place that his mate in town had hooked him up with. A new start, that was his gift—he knew how hard they were to come by. All he needed was a boat—maybe he could get his first couple of weeks' pay in advance—and he'd be the freest man that ever lived.

# Chapter 3

It was just on dusk and the water was cold. The tide was coming in, fresh from the sea, and old Tom Shepherd was hanging onto a marker. He'd had more than a few, and had sunk his barge, again. He'd been there twenty minutes or so. He could see Dog on his wharf, and Dog could see him; he was on the edge, barking for all he was worth. No point in fighting a tide like this, though, Tom thought, just on the turn. The ferry sauntered past, not fifteen metres away. Bastard Steve, he muttered. He'd been wondering whether it was worth the effort of hanging on, but after the ferry soaked him in its wake he decided he'd keep going just to spite him.

Then, not five minutes after the ferry had left Tom for dead, Danny Reynolds came tearing across from the island in the water taxi. He was a good boy, that one. Danny slowed as he approached, and helped Tom scramble over the side and onto a bucket seat, wet and limp like Dog after an overenthusiastic fishing trip with the old man. 'Steve radioed me,' Danny said. 'What's that, third time this month?'

'I've kept out of the drink for a good stretch now. I'm to be congratulated, if anything. Better take me where the beers are cold, young man.'

'Want to go home and get into some dry clothes first?' Danny asked as the engine idled. 'I'm OK to wait.'

'Christ no, mate. Late for the boys already. They'll be running up my tab as we speak.'

'All right, Tom. Marina?'

'You'll go to heaven for this, Danny boy.'

Danny dropped him at the petrol bowsers just as the last of the day's light drained from the cliffs across the water. 'Join the boys for a drink, Danny?' Tom called after him as he began to motor away slowly towards the chandlery.

'Beer's good. I'll just drop the boat.' After he'd tied off he posted the keys through the locked door of the chandlery. Alf must already be down there with the others. As he reached the little crowd of men gathered outside the marina shop, beers in every hand, someone handed him a cold brown bottle. He looked up and there was Rob, looking like he'd just come off a shift himself, still in his yellow trucker's vest. 'Thanks, mate,' he nodded.

'Seen the show, Dan?' Rob said, nodding towards the water. 'Some bright spark's started the season early.' Down on the track that ran along between the channel and the railway line, maybe fifty metres away, was a car in flames. It hadn't been going when he came across, so someone must have just lit it. Liquid fire poured in sheets from the bonnet, and the shape of the car disappeared for seconds at a time inside the ball of beautiful yellow-orange flame. There was a series of sharp cracks as the tyres blew out, like someone thrashing a horsewhip on concrete. Behind the car the dark sky glowed.

Danny stared at the fire. It reached a part of him he hadn't known was there, that sprang up, perfectly preserved, from his memory. There was a night—he must have been seven or eight—when his father had set fire to a car in some paddock. There was a load of men, drinking, shouting, a couple of dogs on rasping chains. He'd sat in the cab of his dad's truck and watched, not knowing what he saw—the flames, the lurching silhouettes of the men under the trees, everything flickering as he plunged towards sleep and tried to keep his eyes open, failed. He wondered now where his brother had been. He had no memory of him being there, but he'd found that with memories. You erased people from them because they weren't what you were interested in at the time. Then they'd mention the same memory and you'd have to admit that the things you remembered so clearly were always a little bit skewed, so you could have no confidence in them.

'Let's go get the little shit,' said Steve, the ferry driver and island fire chief, scowling into his beer under a mop of wild ginger hair.

'Oh come on, mate,' said Rob. 'It's just kids. They can run a damn sight faster than us, and that car's been dumped there for weeks, anyway. Maybe the council will finally shift it now.'

Steve shook his head. 'No, bugger it. We've had no rain all winter and there's already people doing stupid things. I don't like it. Teach the little buggers a lesson.'

Rob thrust a beer into Steve's hand and slapped him on the shoulder. 'Easy there, Steve. Leave the police something to do.' The men laughed, and Danny swigged his beer quickly, watching the reflection of the flames on the water as the sky and the river grew dark.

Rose floated on her back in the inlet behind the railway line, the little channel the locals called the Gut, dusk bringing the mosquitoes buzzing around her exposed face and the long flanks of her arms and legs, finding herself strangely buoyant. It was her belly, and her swelling breasts. She could lie here for hours, finally cool. She felt hot all the time now—though it hadn't been a particularly warm December so far—and the relief was delicious. Could she sleep like this? She felt incapable of sinking.

A tap on her shoulder brought her out of it. When she stood on the oozing mud the water didn't reach her knees, though she thought it had been much deeper when she walked in. The sun had still been out then. Kane pointed behind him towards the tracks and the village beyond.

There was brackish water in her eyes, dripping from her hair, and at first she couldn't work out what it was she saw. There was a blur of hot light on the other side of the railway tracks. She couldn't tell whether it was small or large. She wiped her eyes. It was a car, burning up on the service road between the inlet and the river.

The water felt cold suddenly, and unclean. She clutched her belly and, in clumsy, rushed strides, sloshed towards the bank where she had left her clothes and began pulling them on over her wet swimming costume and skin, the mosquitoes attacking in noisy squadrons. 'Hey, wait up,' Kane called, lunging through the water after her. 'What's the problem?'

'I need to go home,' she said quietly when he reached her, dripping in the dark in his black underwear and nothing else. 'I don't feel too good.'

He stood and considered her for a moment. For a weird second it seemed to Rose that he was trying to work out whether she was telling the truth. 'OK,' he said eventually. 'Tide's going out, anyway. Get stuck on the mud if we don't go soon.'

The shallows were difficult to navigate in the dark— Kane had not brought his torch—and they ran into the muddy bottom a couple of times, the motor spluttering and cutting out as the prop clogged up. Rose kept her eyes steadfastly on the long, dark peninsula that separated the inlet from the main passage of the river, willing herself not to be sick, though the gorge rose with every lurch of the little dinghy and its inadequate motor. Kane seemed unsure of his new purchase, but she was no expert on boats herself and in no state to offer advice besides.

A good fifteen minutes had passed by the time they'd cleared the mud, rounded the tip of the peninsula and passed back under the railway bridge to draw level with the village. She dared herself to glance in its direction. The flames had died now, embers flying off the car into the night. Men's laughter drifted over from the marina. It's just a car on fire, she told herself. It has nothing to do with you. She fixed her gaze on the opposite shore, and soon the island was between their boat and the village as they laboured home, not speaking above the efforts of the motor pushing over the little caps of the river.

At last they pulled alongside her jetty. 'You get inside,' he said. 'I'll sort out the boat.' She nodded and climbed the ladder quickly, feeling every extra rung exposed by the tide, and half ran, half stumbled along the jetty and up the steps to her door. She was grateful to find she hadn't locked it. Inside, she ran across the living room to the bathroom and just made the toilet before the vomit rushed out of her mouth and nose.

When she'd finished she sat on the cool tiles of the tiny bathroom and rested her head against the space on the wall between the cistern and the bottom of the sink. She closed her eyes and in the blackness let herself feel what she had struggled against on the boat ride across the river. She had nothing left with which to fight it. It was him, her father, still, after all these months. His presence filled the space around her: the smell of his guitar, of rolling tobacco, the wool of his jumper, scratchy against her face as she leaned against his warm chest. It must have been an old memory, if it was real, because he was like a giant and she was little, wrapped up in his arms. She couldn't open her eyes. She kept them shut and tried to hold on to it for as long as she could, knowing it was fading, that every time she did this there was less of him there, that she was using up her memories too fast with the strength of her longing.

Tom watched the fire quietly, laughing when required, slugging his beer with the rest. He found himself out of sorts, despite the presence of a cold beer in his hand that he hadn't paid for. Steve was right. Little shits should be taught some proper respect for fire. He could think of a few good ways to instil it, too. He was wet, as well; should have taken Danny up on his offer to fetch dry clothes. More than these things, though, now that he was out of the water he was bothered by a dream from this afternoon, after his lunchtime beer. He'd been trying to recapture it right up to the moment when he sank his barge less than a minute out from his wharf. Now he remembered. Molly— the dream was about Molly.

It was all that activity over at Mancini's, after it being quiet for so long. When this stuff got stirred up it was like shit in the river—never see the end of it once the tide started washing it around. First that little wanker in a suit turning up after all this time, deciding to use the place as a weekender. Didn't he know what his old man had done? And he'd just stroll back in and make himself at home? Then, when you got yourself used to that, he installed the young chick who, it was getting more and more bleeding obvious, was knocked up. It had to be his, didn't it? Another generation of Mancinis sent to blight his twilight years. And now he'd let the boatshed to that wastrel. The boy was in and out at all hours, disturbing his sleep. And when the baby came there'd be the bloody infernal racket as well. He wouldn't be able to look at it without wanting to drown it. And she wondered why she got short shrift when she said hello.

He hadn't dreamed of Molly in a long time. Wasn't sure he ever had. He didn't know what happened in the dream, but she was in it. That moon face. Pretty curly brown hair like her mother's. Eyes that never knew what day it was. Figure like her mother's too, when she was a girl. Not that you're supposed to notice. How you'd miss it he didn't know. Old bastard Mancini hadn't, that was for sure. No clothes in the dream, like when they found her. He felt as though he needed a wash, a swim in the ocean. Mancinis. Always brought a stink with them. Never got what they deserved so you could feel clean again. He remembered the days before them. He'd been salty-skinned, ready for anything.

Now there was Alf with a face on. The old fella had been keeping a low profile lately. But here he was, wanting something, looking at Tom in that quiet way while he was trying to have a sociable drink with the boys. 'Need a word, Tom,' he leaned down and muttered in his ear.

'Not now, Alf. Having a friendly drink. Can't you see?

How's the chandlery going, anyway? Daft tourists keeping you busy?'

Alf nodded at the empty outdoor café along the boardwalk towards his shop.

'You fucken listening, Alf?'

But he was off, and Tom followed. When it came down to it, you did what Alf said. Even Tom didn't know the truth of the stories that had always surrounded him. Alf owned half the businesses this side of the river: the chandlery, the general store, the marina itself and all the moorings. Anything that opened up in competition lasted a few months then closed without warning, its owners moving quietly away from the river, never to be seen again. Maybe just the threat was enough with Alf. Maybe he started the rumours himself about what he'd done to people who interfered with his business interests. They loved those stories on the river. Occasionally a body, or guns washed up. Alf's name was always in the air, even though it usually turned out to be some Sydney underworld thing, nothing to do with anyone round here. Anyway, even Tom knew not to push Alf too hard. Supposed to be my shout, he was thinking. Maybe the others would forget and keep going without him. Then he could slip back in for the next round.

The café was a sea of empty plastic tables. Closed on weeknights, dark at this end of the marina. Full of bloody journos and architects on the weekend. He stayed home on Saturdays—when it came down to it, grog tasted the same wherever you drank it, and the boys knew where to find him. Alf sat down at one of the tables, huge back hunched over. Tom sat down next to him. It was almost dark now and Alf was quiet; his voice, when it came, was low, steady, all business.

'Heard a rumour today, Tom. That Mancini who's been back at the old place. They're saying it's his kid the girl's carrying.'

'Alf. Shut up. I know all right. What do you expect me to do about it?'

'I should have done him.' He fixed Tom with a stare. 'We both know what he did. I left it to you. Not another bloke's business to sort out your problems for you.'

'Christ, Alf, what are you saying? My wife—you know that. Edie wouldn't have that.'

'Now there's going to be another one of those little arseholes.' In the light coming from the shop Tom could just make out his massive expanse of face. It slackened for a moment. Alf sighed. 'This river. It's going to the dogs.'

This was as much fun as scraping the barnacles off his barge. Tom stood and tried to walk away. Alf grabbed his arm. His face was stony now. No glimpse of weakness. Nothing to say they'd been mates since school. 'You could have done it,' he whispered loudly, too loudly for Tom's liking. He tried to shake him off but Alf had always been a bloody big bloke. There'd be a bruise on his arm the next morning. He was starting to feel pretty ticked off himself now. Didn't know how much longer he could mind his Ps and Qs, Alf or no Alf. 'You knew what to do, Shep. If you'd sorted Mancini out, she never would have—'

'Get fucked, Alf,' Tom cut across him. 'Don't ever talk

to me about this again.' Alf let go then, and Tom brushed past the men drinking on the wharf, on his way to the pub to get stuck into the hard stuff.

# Chapter 4

A few days after he'd seen the burning car, his shift finished, Danny let himself into the chandlery, opened up the till, and from under the cash tray removed a yellow envelope with his name on it. He counted the notes; it hadn't been a bad fortnight, not too many days sitting around on his arse in the café, and there was a bit more than usual. He peeled off some of the notes, shoved them in his pocket, then crossed his own name out and wrote another name and address on the envelope before resealing it. He took a couple of stamps from the drawer beneath the till, left a few coins on the counter and let himself out.

The marina was quiet, but he glanced around quickly anyway before posting the envelope in the red box outside

the shop, then made his way to Rob's fibreglass dinghy
down on the jetties. It was just the little boat Rob used to
get between the shore and his yacht mooring, nothing
flash. It would be fine for tonight, even though he needed
to cross the river at a fairly wide point. Less work than the
dory, that was for sure. It was a calm night and he'd take
it slow.

He began to plough his way softly through the dark, a
cold beer in one hand, the tiller in the other. Rolled up in
his canvas satchel on the opposite bench was a free local
newspaper. There was an ad in it he wanted to show Rob,
for a piece of land upriver. Would he laugh? Danny didn't
want to seem all talk. That was the old man. I'm gonna do
this. I'm gonna do that. He wanted to be the one who did
the things he said he would do. Sooner or later you had to
confide in someone, though; you'd go crazy carrying it
around on your own the whole time. Rob was a good bloke.
He'd known him longer than anyone, the only one from
the past.

It took him a good half-hour before the lights on the
opposite shore turned into the windows of houses and you
could see the jetties with no moon. The motor failed a
couple of times and he had to restart her, patiently, trying
not to flood the engine, failing once and having to wait
five minutes before trying again. Rob's thirty-footer was
moored twenty metres out from the Mancini place. He
could see a lantern burning on deck, a little spark hovering
a couple of metres above the river. He puttered over and
grabbed hold of the other dinghy. 'You there, Rob?'

'Come up, Dan. Beer's cold.'

He found Rob sitting on a fold-up chair, smoking a cigar, feet on a little stool. He pushed a chair towards Danny and raised a beer bottle. 'Fridge is full, mate. Help yourself.'

Danny went below to the galley and emerged with a couple of bottles. He set them on the deck and reached inside his bag for the paper. 'Want to see something?'

'Sure. What is it?'

Danny passed him the paper and pointed to the picture. Rob held it under the lantern hanging from the overhang of the roof of the galley. The light illuminated his softening chin, his spreading belly straining a little against his T-shirt. Rob was a good fifteen years older than Danny; his older two were teenagers. 'Looks nice. You got plans to move?'

Danny dipped his chin. 'Maybe. It's not too far. Got a bit saved now. Build something maybe. Take a while. Just a shed first, probably.'

'Sounds good. Give you a hand when you're ready.'

'Cheers, Rob. Appreciate it.' Danny lifted his beer and they both drank.

'Been meaning to talk to you anyway, Dan. Glad I caught you.'

'I'm always on the mobile if you want to go fishing.' He watched Mancini's place. There was a lamp burning in the front room. He wondered about the girl. Just the quiet around her was a mystery. The girls round here were friendly and talkative; even the married ones flirted as easily as breathing. He'd seen her, though, talking to that

Kane over at the ferry wharf, laughing, alive to something in a way that seemed unusual for her. Starved for company, probably.

'Bloody mobiles. Always dropping out. Can't have a proper conversation on those things.'

'Well, I'm here now, mate. What is it?'

'Heard a whisper your dad's got a run to the servo.'

'Which servo?'

'Ours, mate. The marina.'

'What, petrol?'

'Not since that accident. Frozen stuff. Fish fingers and that. Works for Fast Freeze now. They've put him on a whole new route. Semi-retirement. Keeping him local-ish. He's finished with the big runs.'

Danny sat in silence in the lamp glow from the table. Not for the first time, he wondered why it was him that had to go over the edge of the boat rather than the old bloke. He'd never shake this feeling, this prickling at the back of his neck every time something to do with his father came up.

He studied the label of his beer, picking at the edges. As soon as he'd arrived on the river, he'd found out since, Rob had recognised him. Young bloke out of nowhere, it seemed, unless you knew a bit of his story. He went around haunted then, got himself some work helping out with deliveries at the pub, then on the ferry, eventually on the water taxi. Rob knew Danny from when he and his older brother Terry helped their old man out on his rig, doing some of the runs for him as they got older. Rob had driven a truck all his working life. Thirty years. He was involved with the local union, knew everyone in the area, if not by face then by reputation. He knew Dan's old man by both: a lairy, big old bloke that drank and had the odd prang, fewer than you'd imagine.

Rob had wandered over one night in the pub, early on, seven years ago now. Danny was drinking alone, miserable, unsure of his surroundings, of who he could trust. The local girls were checking him out, but he didn't notice. Different man back then. Drawn in, sitting in the shadows, trying to make himself invisible. Wary of the world. Rob took the stool next to him and ordered a drink, nodded at Danny. He leaned a little closer. 'I know your face, young Raine,' Rob said. Danny looked up from his beer, bristling.

'It's Reynolds.'

'OK, have it your way. It's all right, fella. If you want the quiet life, you'll get no trouble from me.'

'Who are you?' Danny said, his voice barely audible over the pokies and the six o'clock news. He searched Rob's face, grappling with faint recognition, fearing what the connection would be when he came to it. Was this one of those moments, when the air drew tight and snapped back, and then violence came? Whose violence would it be? He'd never hit anyone in his life.

'I'm in the union, with your dad. He thinks you're dead. But you've probably seen that in the papers, haven't you?' Danny said nothing. 'You can trust me, boy. We used to hear stories about your old man, what he did to you and your mum. Always wondered what'd happen when you and your brother got big. Just live your life and forget about him. You ever want news of her, I'll get it for you. The kiddie, too, if you want.'

Water stood in Danny's eyes. He abandoned his beer suddenly and shot out the back door. After that, he hadn't set foot out front of the pub for months; crept down to the marina after helping with the kegs, rowed quietly home.

A couple of months later, after Alf had given him the water taxi gig, he was passing under the freeway bridge when he came upon a woman and a young girl stranded in a broken-down tinny, bobbing about on a choppy night near the sandstone piers. The girl was crying. The woman shouted at her. 'It's going to be OK—just give me a hand!' But they were being pushed closer and closer to the massive pier with no control over the little boat, and the girl was immobilised in panic. The woman was doing her best with an oar, but the chop was strong, concentrated, in the little space between the pylons. When they noticed him pulling alongside, their smiles beamed at him in the dark. It took a bit of messing around to get them in the water taxi. The girl was still shaky and kept backing off from climbing over at the last minute. After a couple of goes, swearing under his breath, he saw that they were only a couple of metres from the sandstone pillar and he grabbed her waist and pulled her in.

He discovered as he chatted to them on the way back to the village that this was Rob's wife, Maggie, and his daughter Bronwyn. Since then, things like this happened to him every other week. He was owed more favours than he could keep track of—got a free beer or two most nights he turned up at the pub. But this was the first time, and it was Rob's family, sent to him like a gift. Since then he'd had some relief from worrying about his old man knowing where he was. It felt better, somehow, to have one eye on his dad, rather than never knowing where he was or what he was doing. Otherwise he could be standing right behind you and you'd never know.

'He's not gonna know you're here,' Rob said. 'He'll only be down once a month. Be pretty unlucky to bump into him.'

Danny nodded. 'Bit close for comfort.'

'Don't go taking off, Dan. You've made a life for yourself on the river.'

'Not my life, though, is it; it's the one I ended up with. Not that I'm complaining.'

'What would the girls round here do without you? They'd go feral.' Rob laughed, then said quietly, 'That bit of land. That'd be far enough.'

Far enough, Danny thought. How far is that? He always knew he should have gone further, but he loved this part of the world. The dark hills, the slabs of sandstone erupting from the gleaming water at every turn. Did he have to give up everything? He downed the rest of the beer. 'Thanks for the tip, Rob.' He stood to leave.

'Mate, have another beer. He's not here now, is he?'

'Early shift tomorrow, Rob. Another time.'

* * *

Ten metres out from the yacht Danny twisted the throttle sharply and the bow lifted out of the water. Almost immediately, he heard a shout from in front of him in the dark. He hit his kill switch and swerved to the right, narrowly missing a man in a little hull as small as his own. 'Nearly killed me!' the man shouted.

'Well, what are you doing? How about using a light, mate?' He turned his headlights on him. Kane, smoking a doobie. That figured. 'Dip shit,' he muttered as he put his engine back into gear and chugged across the river to the island. Who sat on the river in the dark? Couple of weeks back someone fishing before dawn without a light had been hit by the garbage barge. Lucky to be alive. His kind of bloke always shot through for some reason or another. Be good if he found a reason soon.

Kane drew on his joint to steady his nerves. Told his mum he wouldn't smoke anymore but he had to test it. Be no good if he sold dodgy stuff to some mug who came looking for him afterwards. He'd learned that lesson the hard way.

And it helped him out, calmed him. He'd been sitting here—beautiful night, stars out, most of the yuppies in bed, the night and the river all for him—just listening to the voices float across the water. Hadn't realised it was that Danny bloke. Hadn't been thinking, just enjoying the night, listening to voices, gleaning obscure gossip, wondering idly what it might be about.

Maybe it was just as well Danny had stirred him up

when he did. He needed to be up early for work. He'd missed today, called in sick then had to hide in his shed all day. Last night had been the first time he'd smoked in a month and he couldn't get out of bed till he'd had a quick cone, then he couldn't work. He was seeing things, shadows on her jetty, just some blokes fishing, drinking, but shadows. He knew they weren't there.

Tomorrow would be different, though. That was what the book told you: you slip back, you just keep going. He'd only got hold of the stuff in the first place because he needed that boat. You couldn't just wait for the ferry all the time; it was like being an old lady, like his mum, spending half her life at the bus stop, her old car on blocks, surrounded by graffiti and the stench of some scabby teenager's piss. Tam the foreman wouldn't give him an advance, said he needed to prove himself first, so what choice had he had?

Tomorrow. He'd turn up for work, moan about a stomach bug, shift the stuff at the pub in the evening, pay the dealer back his loan and he'd be square, ready to live his life, make himself someone he wanted to be, someone who was good enough for anyone.

# Chapter 5

Danny had been on for four hours already—long ones, only three fares —when he saw the woman wandering along the deck of the marina, somehow managing not to get her heels caught in between the slats without looking down. You got a lot of pretty girls on the river, especially in summer. Tourists from the city, people visiting friends on the island for a barbie. They were always fresh, loose, happy to be here. But this woman was out of the ordinary; she wasn't the kind you'd just notice if you got a smile from her or happened to be her mate. No one would walk past this one; she was like something from a commercial for a holiday somewhere exotic. You saw her hair first, slippery blonde, falling down the back of her singlet to her backside. Her arms and legs were long and lightly tanned with silver glinting at her wrist and ankle. He sat at the café table and willed her to face him. She drew level with the shop and turned, looking for something. Sometimes their faces let you down. Not her. She saw him and smiled, a wide-open beam of white teeth, smooth skin and green eyes, not a care in the world. She came back towards him and he smelled her perfume. She was a creature from another world—the one they lived in on TV or maybe in some suburb of Sydney where you saw American tennis players in the restaurants and actors at the markets.

'Hi,' she said. Who, me? he thought. 'Are you the water-taxi driver?' He nodded. 'Hold on,' she said. 'We'll be back in a minute.' He watched her sway back up to the entrance to the general store and speak to someone inside. He emerged a moment later, a guy from the same world: tanned, polo shirt, long shorts, smart backpack, just-cut hair, always just-cut hair. Danny touched the curls growing over his collar. Time for a backyard buzz cut. He'd been neglecting himself, taking his luck with girls for granted, settling for whoever seemed interested.

On the boat she took the seat next to his, her long legs taking up all the available space in the cabin, her presence absorbing the air around him. Her mate took the plastic seat behind him. Danny couldn't think of a thing to say for a few long seconds. She didn't seem in any hurry. These were people who didn't find silence uncomfortable. They had too much to be confident about for a bloke like him to even begin to unsettle them. 'Where are we going?' he eventually asked her as they approached the end of the channel.

Her eyes were half closed in the late morning sun. It took a moment for her to answer. 'Over at the beach. It's my boyfriend's place,' she said, nodding behind her. 'Mancini's. With the jacaranda.'

'Oh, right. Where Rose has been living.'

'That's the one. She's my sister.'

She is? he wondered. These women seemed to be from different species, never mind families. He had never really looked at Rose, he realised now as he studied this woman's face for as long as he dared before starting the motor. He knew her hair and height, the general outline of her, but couldn't bring to mind her figure or her face—just a feeling that there was something, some secret she carried. She was one of those people who just didn't draw attention to themselves with their looks, moved quietly through the world without asking anyone to see them. Perhaps she was as pretty as this, behind the glasses and the loose clothes and the pregnancy. But this woman, it wasn't just prettiness; the way she moved, the way she watched you, screamed 'Look at me', and she knew you would.

'You know her?' the woman asked.

'Not really. I just know who lives where. She's got that guy Kane in the boatshed, too. He's your tenant, I guess.'

'James's.' She gestured behind her again. He glanced behind her as they pulled out of the channel. The man had not said a word, watching the river from behind dark glasses, legs open and stretched out across the floor of the boat, an arm draped along the stern. 'James grew up here, when he was a boy,' she said, smoothing her hair as they picked up speed. 'He's really a local, when it comes down to it. Only started using the place again recently, though. His mother left it to him.'

Danny wondered why the man didn't speak for himself. It seemed odd to be talking about him while he was right there.

'I haven't seen you before,' she smiled. 'I've spent a bit of time here myself. I'd remember you.'

Once again, all words left Danny's head. He brought the boat round to face the opposite shore, stood up and pulled open the throttle. She stood, too, matching his height, balancing gamely on her heels. Gorgeous as she was, he was looking forward to dropping these two off at Rose's. He felt as though he was in a room close with unspoken words, everyone waiting for him to leave.

'Mind if I drive?' she asked. He looked at her. Was she joking? 'I'm pretty handy with a boat. Go on, I won't tell anyone. He taught me,' she said. 'He'll tell you.' Danny glanced back at the man. You couldn't even tell if his eyes were open, his glasses were so dark.

'She knows what she's doing,' he said, without moving.

Danny didn't know what to do other than stand aside and let her take the wheel. He shuffled behind her onto the passenger side, reaching around to grip the rail in front of her with one hand. The boat tilted for a brief moment in the handover, but then she was bouncing it confidently over the flat water towards the sandstone cliffs, smiling wholeheartedly, hair whipping around her face. He watched her, he couldn't help it. She was so full of life, and her boyfriend back there was so flat and dull. He'd always believed you could never know people's stories just from looking at them. You just couldn't tell what kept people together, what passed between them in a room while everyone else went about, oblivious. Here was a beautiful example.

He'd planned to take the wheel back as they approached the shore but she was slowing down, steering expertly through the moorings, her hair flat again now on her shoulders. Her exhilaration had passed, replaced by a quiet focus as she took them in to Rose's jetty. He thought for a moment he could see the similarity between them now, that quietness and absorption.

Rose was out on the verandah in a loose white shirt and pants, squinting out into the sun from beneath her hand, still, only visible because of the brightness of the cotton against the backdrop of shadows. She was waiting, but the shape of her body didn't seem happy, just patient. 'Oh my God,' the woman said. 'She looks—she's pregnant.' Danny gave her a sideways glance. The man sprang into action, galvanised suddenly, stepping on and off the boat with the ease of someone brought up on the water, to tie off to what was presumably his jetty, fetch bags of groceries, pay Danny, help his girlfriend launch herself off the bow and straight up onto the pier with one sure movement of her hips and legs. Danny was standing right behind her, down in the cabin, low enough for it all to be at eye level. It hurt to watch her gleaming, scissoring limbs; her lack of care. The whole time they were tying up, Rose stood motionless in the blaze of light at the edge of the stairs.

The woman turned back towards him as the man carried the bags along the rickety jetty to Rose. There was still a box of groceries sitting in the warm sun next to the ladder. 'Give me a hand with the shopping?' she said.

He nodded and stepped up onto the bow, and then the ladder. He followed her towards the house, his legs heavy. She hadn't known her sister was pregnant? What was that all about? But now he remembered something he'd overheard, in the island shop. People were saying Rose was having this guy's baby. He hadn't made the connection at first. They'd said it was the one whose dad left after all that old business with Tom. The kid had come back when his mother had left him the house. This was the kid. This was who they were saying was the father of Rose's baby. He wanted to be on his boat again and out of this. He couldn't imagine what these people were about to say to one another.

'Come in,' the woman said, just ahead of him. 'Bring the box to the kitchen.'

Danny stepped through the sliding glass doors after her. The man was in the kitchen with Rose, taking things out of bags, putting them on the bench and in the fridge. He'd never been inside this house before, though he knew the front of it well enough from sitting up on the deck of Rob's yacht. The living room was darkish—there were blinds on the verandah against the western sun—but big.

There was room for a dining table at one end and a couple of large sofas at the other, covered with bright throws. The kitchen was off to the back; he didn't want to go any closer to the silent pair in there, so he edged the box onto the bench and backed away. Next to him, the woman said, 'Rose! Why didn't you tell us?'

Rose wore a look of bewilderment. Her sister strode across the room and hugged her. The man backed out of the crowded little kitchen. Danny watched Rose's face above her sister's shoulder, trying to see the similarity between the women's features. It was there, in theory. They were the same structure: heart-shaped, with apple cheeks and pointy chins, wide mouths, straight teeth, green eyes. But there was something in the life behind each face that was totally different—in intent and feeling. Rose was watching, processing. The other one was glowing with her sense of herself, triumphant. Wherever it was she'd been headed, she was already there. Rose was looking sideways at the silent man. Could it really be true, what they were saying? He retreated from the room quietly, with a small nod to Rose. He had stepped into a stifling, private world and needed to get out again.

He took it fast on the way back over. Alf had tried to ring his mobile twice. The cabin seemed spacious, full of fresh air, with the woman gone. At first he caught her scent, clinging to the upholstery, but by the time he passed the island it had gone. He pointed the boat at shore, closed his eyes against the sun for long seconds at a time and breathed in the wind.

\* \* \*

Rose couldn't believe she'd actually had sex with him. And not just once. For a month, at weekends, regularly enough for it to be expected. Now part of him was lodged in her belly, kicking her. Perhaps it felt the presence of its other DNA donor in the room and was responding in some primeval way. His back was to her, out on the verandah. Billie was next to her, talking to her, at her, on the big, too-soft sofa. You fell into it and against whoever was sitting next to you. Billie's leg lay alongside hers. Not longer, not different in any tangible sense except that it was bare, and it held a mysterious power over men, over everyone, that hers did not. 'So you don't want to tell me who it is, this one-night stand.' She threw a hand in the air. 'It's not Ben, is it?'

'No! God no.'

'OK, all right. Be sweet if it was. There's so much to think about! You won't stay here, will you? You can't drag a baby all over the river. It's a shame we've sold Dad's place now; you could have gone there. My apartment is really too small, or we'd love to have you. When's it due, anyway?'

'Seven weeks.'

'Seven weeks! Oh my God. When were you going to tell me?'

Rose let out air. She watched James, unmoving, leaning on the balustrade. 'We were going to ask you to move soon,' Billie whispered. 'We need somewhere to take the boat at the weekends. Of course, there's no rush now. What are you going to do?'

Rose sighed. She'd stopped thinking about what was next when the tenant came, pushed it to the back of her mind. It didn't guarantee anything, though. She had no rights. Stupid, she thought. Stupid! She'd even gone so far as to imagine herself hopping on and off the ferry with the baby, painting the spare room pale purple—she had the paint chips—so it didn't matter if it was a boy or a girl. 'How long have I got?'

'Oh, Rose. Don't be silly. As long as you want. No one's kicking you out. I had no idea you were pregnant. How would I know?'

'Why mention it, then?'

Billie stared at her, then laid a hand on her forearm. 'You're tired, aren't you? What a time you must have had of it lately. James,' she called out to the verandah. 'Put the kettle on for Rose, would you?' She started to talk about her job, as a lawyer in the city—she'd been promoted recently. Her new apartment, paid for with her share of their father's money from the sale of the house. Rose's own share sat in a savings account. She couldn't bring herself to touch it. James placed a mug of tea in front of her. He knows how I take it, she thought. He should have asked. He caught her eye briefly. Perhaps he had realised his mistake. She watched him retreat onto the verandah, tried to retune to Billie. She thought about the old house as Billie talked, the things in it. She hadn't wanted anything to keep; she'd let Billie clear it out. But now something hit her. She felt breathless, suddenly, as though the baby had lodged itself against her lungs.

'Listen,' Rose spoke across her. 'I need to ask you something. When you sorted out the house, what did you do with his guitar?'

'I gave it to the school. They always needed things like that.'

'But why that one? We could just buy them a new one.'

'What's the big deal? He wouldn't mind the kids having it.'

'Not his kids, no, but then there'll be kids who didn't even know him. They'd be better off with a new one.'

'What's the problem? You've got a guitar. Why didn't you tell me if you wanted another one?'

'It's not just any guitar, Billie.' She couldn't say any more. Tears threatened.

'Well, look. I'm sorry.' Rose sensed that James was listening to them, in spite of himself. His body was very still. Billie spoke more quietly. 'Rose, I did ask you if you wanted to come and get anything. How could I know you wanted it?'

'It doesn't matter. Forget I said anything.'

Billie looked at her. 'I know it's hard on you.'

'What?' snapped Rose. 'What's hard on me?'

'Dad.'

'He was your dad, too.'

'I know. But everyone knew how you doted on him. It's all right to be sad. And now this.' She dipped her chin at Rose's stomach.

'Look,' Rose said, her hand held up, open-palmed in front of her. Stop, it said. 'I didn't dote on him, and I know it's all right to be bloody sad. It's all I do, all right.' How dare she? Billie had always been his favourite—she was the one who'd always worked on him to maintain her advantage. Rose looked out the window, blinking. James's back, dark against the sun, remained motionless. Rose wished they would disappear.

Billie paused for a moment. 'We've got to head off in a minute. I'll just go to the bathroom. I'll be right back.'

Rose watched her sister glide across the room to the corridor. She'd been watching her glide across rooms all her life. So had everybody else. She took her fury out onto the verandah.

'You guys seem to be going well,' she said.

He flinched a little; he hadn't heard her approach.

'What are you going to do?' he said, without turning.

'Well, have a baby, I guess. Why?'

He looked her up and down. 'You know what I mean. Christ, Rose, what a nightmare. Why didn't you tell me?'

'You're assuming it's yours,' she said through her teeth. 'Isn't it?'

She shrugged. He took his glasses off and peered at her in the shade. She couldn't believe she'd gone to bed with him. He looked like a doll. She hoped the child would be a girl; perhaps it would look less like him. 'Are you going to tell her?' he asked.

She shook her head. 'I barely think of it as yours, if it helps.'

'Whatever that means,' he muttered. 'Jesus.'

She sighed and looked away. 'Do you want me to move out?'

'Stay as long as you want. I've got that bloke paying rent.'

'Sounds like Billie wants it back to use at the weekends.'

'I'll sort that out. We can always rent something. This place shits me, anyway.'

She was about to speak—she couldn't remember afterwards what she was going to say, some protestation—but suddenly there was a dark blur of fur streaking up the stairs, a growl, and then it had hold of his leg, the mangy black dog from next door. 'Call this fucking thing off,' James was shouting to someone, off to the south of the deck.

'He does what he wants,' came a voice from the yard next door. It was old Tom, stepping out from under the strip of collapsing aluminium roof patched to his front door. 'He knows you, fella. That's all.'

The dog was growling and salivating, drool running down James's tanned calf. 'Bloody hell,' Rose said. 'Is he biting you?' She felt a snort of laughter threatening to escape.

'No,' James said. 'He's trained him to do this. I ought to call the pound.'

Billie let out a little yelp from the doorway behind them. 'What the fuck is that?'

'Just get some food and chuck it off the verandah,' James said.

Rose went inside and took some sausages from the fridge. She came back out, showed them to the dog and threw them over to Tom's yard, where they fell between a rusting stove and a pile of tyres. The dog relinquished his hold and was gone, leaving a film of bubbling moisture on James's leg. He went inside to wash it off.

'That man! He's out of control,' Billie whispered.

'He doesn't bother me,' Rose shrugged. She knew she was being childish, but she was in the grip of something.

'You get these people who've been here forever and they think they own the place.'

The little white ferry appeared around the point from the island. 'Let's get that one,' James said as he emerged from the house. 'Enough excitement for one day.'

'Oh, we could just call that Danny back. He was so nice.'

'The ferry's right here, Billie. I said I'd duck into the office this afternoon.'

'Well, can't stand in the way of a man's career when he's bucking for partner. It was lovely to see you looking so well, Rose.' Rose nodded, her throat sore, listening to the ferry approach. Billie reached up to hug her. 'It kicked me!' she said as their stomachs touched. She leaned down towards Rose's stomach. 'Hello! It's your aunty. I'll see you soon!' James was making busy noises inside, picking up keys, jangling change. 'I can't get over this. Look, there's the ferry. I'll call you.'

She raised a hand as they picked their way gingerly around the front of Tom's yard, looking out for the dog.

They just made the ferry, and as she watched it depart her sister waved from the stern. She waved with her whole body, like a child. Again, Rose raised a hand in the air, and turned to go inside.

She watched the ferry grow small as it rounded the tip of the island. What happened? she thought. She tried to look squarely at what she had done, at the situation they were in now, all of them. She hadn't meant James as revenge. Revenge for what, anyway? He had lent her the house to write in—or, really, Billie had—when she'd got the commission for her naughty books. Then Billie had broken up with him, and he'd arrived one night with the boat for her, just fixed after months on the slips. They'd smoked a joint on the verandah and kissed slowly, and laughed. It was delicious, and wicked, and it was nothing. But now it was everything.

She heard Ben's voice. 'What did she ever do to you, Rose?'

Nothing, she answered silently. Nothing, nothing, bloody nothing.

# Chapter 6

Tom couldn't say the words in his head. 'Say it again, mate,' he said to the young Eastern European doctor. Too young to know what he was talking about, surely. Too foreign.

'Cancer of the prostate, Mr Shepherd. I'm very sorry.' His accent would have made it sound almost glamorous, if it hadn't meant what it did. 'We can't tell yet how advanced it is, but you're in good health generally. The outlook can be very positive if we get to it in time, and if you look after yourself properly.'

Tom leaned across the desk and began pulling pieces of paper out of the doctor's file. 'No, Doctor. You've got me mixed up. This is someone else's information.' But when he'd finished shuffling the pieces of paper around the desk, he saw that his name was clearly typed at the top left-hand corner of each. 'You're not having me balls,' Tom mumbled into his chest. 'You can forget that right now.' The truth of it was, if it would rid his body of the disease, he'd let him take the pair of them, right now, on that bed in the corner. This was the last way he wanted to go. He'd witnessed Edie's pain until in his heart he'd wished her death on her, willed it to hurry up so he didn't have to watch her body fall apart, the smells, the moans anymore. And her bald head, it had frightened the life out of him every time he'd woken up next to her, right to the end. Had to remind himself it was still Edie, over and over again.

'That's not what they do for prostate, Mr Shepherd. It's the prostate gland, not the testicles. Listen,' the doctor said as Tom stood. 'Talk to friends, family. Try not to be frightened. It is likely you have many good years ahead of you. You need to go to the hospital for the tests. Irene can give you the details.'

He almost bumped into his neighbour in the corridor. She was shuffling around reception in a daze, big dopey bovine. 'For fuck's sake!' he shouted in her face. If you'd asked him about it, he was being restrained; in his head he called her a fat cunt.

'What?' She stepped back.

'Mr Shepherd!' the receptionist snapped. 'Do you mind? Miss Baker is pregnant!'

He was halfway out the door. 'Do it a favour,' he turned to face her briefly. 'Drown it at birth.' The screen door banged behind him.

\* \* \*

The next morning a northerly blew through the mesh nailed over Tom's bedroom window, the warmest yet this season. Christmas Eve tomorrow. Perfect. Behind his still-closed eyes pricked the beginnings of a headache. But there was a warmth in his belly, spreading through his body. That wind, the early heat—irresistible. He opened his eyes. The yellowing curtains were billowing in the strong breeze. An orange glow burned behind them. Must be later than he thought. Dog's chin lay on the cool tiled floor, mouth lolling open. 'Carn, Dog,' he said. 'Let's get a drink. I'm parched, too.'

From the kitchen he could see the river. There were little orange caps on the water, reflecting a sun discoloured by smoke. Someone had been busy. He could smell it now, faintly. A branch fell on his tin roof and made him jump.

As he filled Dog's bowl at the tap a movement on the Mancini jetty caught his eye. It was that Kane, disappearing into his shed. Useless bludger. Where was he coming home from at this hour? Tom had made the mistake of smoking a joint with the lad a couple of weeks back. Bad idea. Been years since he'd touched the stuff and he never would again. He'd sat on his front deck for two days unable to make a decision about going to the pub, feeding Dog, fixing the barge, anything. There'd been a feeling of something beyond the edge of the wharf, something floating in the air over the river that meant him harm, and he hadn't been able to shake it or move from his spot.

He had to row over to the village; his barge was still on the bottom. He left the side of a carton of VB tied to the post at the end of his wharf, a note for the woman who owned the big barge round at the Gut. He'd painted on it: 'Sharon, please pull up barge if you're passing. Owe you one. TOM. PS You put a hole in the side last time, had to weld it, be careful, thanks Sharon.'

It was a bugger of a row against the northerly and the little waves, his headache growing by the second. But he felt great, like he used to on his way out to sea for a proper fishing trip. Or when he'd helped build the Kennedy house on the eastern point of the island. That had made him happier than almost anything he'd ever done, to see its frame go up where nothing had been before. The rhythm of the hammer. The smell of the shavings as you planed the timber smooth. He knew something was going to happen today, there was going to be a bit of excitement. You could smell it in the smoke, see it in the churned-up river. It was going to be a long, long summer.

He passed Danny in the channel, taking the people who'd bought the island shop across the water. Blow-ins like everyone else these days. Like that blonde piece who'd turned up next door the other week. What was young Mancini up to now? Starting a brothel? He knew that one, seen her before. Something weird going on there, no question.

He pushed on to his wharf by the rail track and lugged his kit up the ladder shakily. It was heavy and he was hungry. Have to have a bacon roll before he went any further. Maybe stop in and see Alf. Sort out this business about Molly. They hadn't spoken for a good few weeks now; if Tom was at the marina in the afternoon, he'd go to the pub, and vice versa.

No sign of him at the chandlery, so he bought a longie at the marina shop and left it on Alf's wharf—they'd been mates too long for all this. Besides, his short-term memory was shafted and he was never clear on details the next morning, let alone a couple of weeks on. If you can't remember what you're pissed off about, no point in being pissed off. And there was the barge. It was going to need a new bilge pump when it came up. Wouldn't make any sense going all the way up the bloody river to find one. Some people you just had to stay mates with. Who else was he going to tell about what the doctor had said?

He had to admit, old Alf did love Molly. No kids of his own. No wife either. Face like that, who'd have him? Loved little kids and they loved him—that was the thing about kids, they didn't worry about reputations, just saw you for what you were with them. Molly especially. Other kids gave her a hard time, being a bit simple. They mostly gave up on school with her and she'd sit on Alf's lap over at the chandlery wharf, waiting for Tom's trawler to come back from a trip. He'd know it was her soon as they came around the point, tiny kid jumping up and down and waving next to a bloody big giant, still as a mooring post.

Alf didn't know Edie though, not like Tom knew her. Very religious woman. Wouldn't have put up with what he was talking about. And she was the one who had Molly in the first place, who had to identify her when they fished her out. Tom was adrift. Bastard motor had gone on a night trip and he was well out past the heads and drifting towards New Zealand. The coastguard picked him up in the morning and it was them who told him: a couple of young fellows who it was clear felt that being paid to go to sea was the best thing that could happen to a bloke. They weren't wrong. Anyway, they didn't know she was his daughter, they were just passing the time of day. Even made a blue joke about the 'touched river girl'. He hadn't said anything. Hadn't wanted to embarrass himself. This is twenty-five years ago now, Tom thought. Just wish people would leave it the fuck alone.

After he'd dropped off the longie he rowed back out into the channel—time to see what was happening with this fire—but coming out of the channel, the ferry swamped him in its wake. Steve was driving; he lifted a hand slowly. Fucking Steve, Tom muttered sharply. He vaguely remembered giving the frizzy-headed freak a dressing-down in the pub the previous night. He was in there with the brigade, feeding them a load of bull—as usual—about cleaning your gutters three times a week and never having a barbie in summer. Big help that was going to be on a day like today, when the firebugs got a feeling in their waters.

Tom could see the ferry full of the yuppies from the island pissing themselves. His dory was filling with water and his feet were soaked. It's OK though, he thought, as he watched the arse of the ferry chug off towards the island, tooting its horn—'cause there's Alf, coming into the channel now. He'll tow me back to the chandlery before I sink and fix me up there.

Alf pulled alongside him in his new Quintrex. The water was over Tom's boots now; he was having to bail fast. 'Hand there, Alf?' he called over his shoulder as he drew up level, but Alf kept right on past him. Tom looked up and all he could see was the back of Alf's fat head getting smaller as he motored off to the chandlery.

He could still just about manoeuvre the boat so he rowed back down the channel to Alf's wharf just as he was tying off, casual as you like. The beer was still there, so he paddled in behind him, retrieved his longie, smacked it on the side of Alf's shiny paintwork and took off down to the public wharf. It was slow going and a lot of bailing but he made it, just. Let it sink here and with a bit of luck Steve wouldn't be able to get the ferry in till he'd pulled it up. He scrambled onto the wharf, careful to keep his satchel dry, gave the dory a tap at the stern with his foot and watched it dive slowly to the bottom, the bow pointing upwards. Right in Steve's way, perfect.

His pants were wet to the knees and so was his backside. Couple of oldies gave him a funny look as he walked up past the station towards the pub. Didn't often pass the pub by, but at this hour it was closed, like the police station opposite, and he carried on up the hill and found himself a nice high flat rock at the top of someone's yard in the bush. From up here he could see where the fire was, at the south end of the ridge that ran along behind his place, back into the national park. There was a helicopter filling its little bucket from the river and making drops. Couldn't be that big or they'd have those American tanks up there, Elvis and the other one. They'd had Elvis out for one of his once, a couple of years back. A sight to behold, spraying tonnes of water on his raging wall of flame on a farm up the old highway towards the coast. Everyone stood back to watch; the volunteers, including him, called back out while the wind whipped the fire in every direction. They sat on top of the truck and watched the helicopter and the fire waging their battle. And the sound of the heat as the leaves and branches exploded, it reached some part of him deep in his gut.

The smoke was billowing back over the ridge and spreading across the sun in the east. A strange light hung over the river, and there was hardly anyone on the streets. He'd missed the flow of commuters herding over the railway bridge, and the early comings and goings from the post office and the café. He had no set time for rising in the morning. He could wake suddenly in his bed and haul himself out on the river at any time. He saw the early mists on the mirrored surface of the water and the full moon high in the sky. Kids coming home in the afternoon, roaring on and off the ferry, tiny hooligans. You could see in their faces what families they came from and how they'd turn out. Who'd go, who'd stay. It was about ten now on a Friday. No sense in hanging around, making himself conspicuous.

He slipped behind the rock and scrambled through scrub overgrown with ferns to the path he knew was above him, leading up to the old dam. Couple of tourists and their dog had drowned in it the summer before and now hardly anyone went up to swim in its cold green water. Usual thing, dog gets in trouble, husband goes in, wife goes in. Kid left crying on the bank until he has the sense to run down and tell someone. Tourists, he thought. Somebody tell me what they're good for.

It took him a good twenty minutes to get up to the dam. Felt better for the walk. Could have made it sooner but best to keep off the tracks as much as he could on a day like today. Place'd be crawling with National Parks and Rural Fire Service. Where were they the rest of the time? He was crunching over dried gum leaves and bracken an inch deep. Hadn't been a burn-off since the season before last. Disgraceful.

As he thundered through the undergrowth, breath so loud he wouldn't have heard someone walking next to him, the slicing blades of a helicopter startled him as it appeared suddenly over the freeway from the ridge beyond. Not the fire service this time. Channel Ten. He smiled, once he'd stopped for a moment and slowed his breathing down. Better give 'em something to look at then, now they're here.

He reached the dam and sat down on the high wall at its perimeter, his legs dangling above twenty metres of nothing. He pulled a tin mug out of his satchel and reached behind him into the water, poured cup after cup of icy liquid over his head. His blood charged through his body and his skin tingled, cool for a second in the hot air.

The bomb was in his bag. Liked to have one ready on a hot day, just in case. Mostly they sat there for weeks and he only remembered them when something had really ticked him off. Brown Bundy bottle, bright yellow dusting rag. He took a bottle of metho from the satchel and poured it carefully into the bottle through the fabric stuffed into the neck. Slapped the pocket of his pants for matches. 'Wouldn't you know it?' he said. But in his shirt pocket was a book from the pub with a couple left. He let the first one go out, his hand trembling. 'Come on, Shepherd, you goose.' The final match flared suddenly. A gust of wind rustled the leaves all around him and he quickly placed his body between the fragile flame and the source of the wind. He touched it to the rag and threw the bottle clear across the dam into the shrubs beyond.

He took a couple of steps backwards, watching the dark patch of undergrowth intently where his bomb had disappeared. There was an almighty bang and one low shrub was aflame, then two. 'Beauty,' he said quietly as he settled into a patch of clear ground out of sight of anyone approaching on the track.

Soon it blazed along the opposite side of the dam, hot winds coming off it, smoky orange and black fire reflecting in the disturbed waters. Tom finally began his retreat; big black embers were drifting across the dam, and there was already a small fire in the grass of the picnic ground a little further back along the track behind him. And now the news helicopter was back. He'd have to stay off the track altogether until they were out of the way. They'd have their telephoto lenses and whatnot poking around all over the place. Wankers.

Here came the first of the trucks. How long had that taken? Half an hour? Hopeless. He scrambled through the trees away from the fire to a cave above the track that he'd known some of the local homeless fellas to sleep in. None around at the moment. They'd had one of their clean-outs lately. Wouldn't give them their pensions without an address, shipped them all off to shelters for about five minutes.

It was cool and dark in the shade of the cave and he could stay close to the fire without being seen. He lay on the ledge and pressed his cheek to the cool sandstone. Ah yes, there was Steve, off the ferry already, pointing at the fire, shouting instructions, buggering about with the hose. Even with the wind and the fire and Channel Ten he could hear him clearly, he was so close. Call this lot fire fighters? He could see the yoga teacher from the island in her overalls and boots. Sixty-five if she was a day, rolling out the hose like it was the linen from her glory box. Lord help us. They got the water going but they might as well have been pissing on it. Then the fire helicopter came and emptied his bucket straight into the dam. Nice work, mate, Tom laughed. Another appeared soon behind him as he disappeared behind the ridge to refill from the river. There were too many trees crowded around the dam to get his bucket in up here.

It took them a couple of hours to bring it under control. Best morning's entertainment Tom had seen in a while. As he watched his fire his mind emptied of Alf, of Molly, of the Mancinis, of the thing that was eating away at him down there. The sound of the brush crackling, the smoky, scorching wind, the water pouring from the sky; all this filled his mind and spirit, and for those few hours in his cool cave, the bush around him flaming, he was at peace.

# Chapter 7

Rose woke in stages, trying to hold onto sleep, slipping in and out of a dream in which she'd had six babies, and she could never remember when to feed them or where they all were at any one time. But then something stirred her, some change in the air, in the light.

It was dark and cool in the little room, in spite of the thin bamboo blind in the window. The house faced due west, with a cliff at its back, and the deep verandah would help keep the sun out of the room for several hours yet. The room was furnished with old, mismatched furniture: a 1930s chest of drawers, a '70s tubular bed, an Afghan rug. On the drawers was a photo in a frame, a picture of a little boy—James, a beautiful boy. His mother had moved back to Sydney when he was a child. This was a time capsule. She shifted slowly from under the blankets, crossed the floor to the photo and placed it in the top drawer of the chest.

The baby rolled and gave her a sharp kick in the ribs. It was getting crowded in there. Her sister was right, she should have told her about the baby. It was a new sprout of their family, when it seemed everything was gone. But what was the point of telling part of the truth? Would she ever tell her all of it? If Billie and James broke up? If the baby looked too much like him? What is there to lose, really? she thought. But she'd told him she wouldn't say anything, and it was almost Christmas. She wouldn't do anything right now.

She'd been trying to avoid thinking about Christmas, but now she sat on the bed and massaged the baby inside her, and felt the fragments pushing their way into the room. One Christmas Eve, when she was very little, she knelt by her bed, squeezed her hands together tightly and prayed to Jesus to make her as pretty as her sister. The next morning she woke, electrified with excitement, and ran to the mirror in the bathroom. Everything was blurry; she had to put her glasses on. But Billie didn't wear glasses. When she saw it was just her—the same frizzy, dirty blonde hair, same freckles, same beanpole body—she burst into tears. Her dad found her sitting on the bathroom floor, sobbing. 'Hey,' he said, picking her up. 'What's this, on Christmas Day?' She told him what she'd prayed for between sobs. 'Oh, Rosie,' he said while her tears and snot leaked through his shirt. He pulled her away from him, looked her in the eye. 'I've told you, mate, there is no Jesus. Don't you go wasting your time on that old fraud.'

Rose peered at the water, glinting through the blinds. She pulled them up. There was a strange light on the river. The water looked orangey. And it was hazy out there. She padded along the dark corridor to the living room. Through the wall of windows along the front of the room she saw a man walk onto her wharf, stop and look at the hazy air, the water. Across the river she could see a tower of smoke, a helicopter buzzing around it. She stared; there was a momentary gulf between what she knew she was seeing and belief. The man rapped sharply on the front windows.

It was Kane. She hadn't recognised him in the shadows, the strange light behind him. 'Do you reckon we should get across now? I can take you in my boat.'

She pulled her dressing gown around her bump and nodded. 'Let me get dressed. I'll be right there.'

As she followed him down the wharf, she forced herself to look up at the ridge behind her. Black and red smoke billowed from a spot to the south of the strip of houses and in another above the village across the river. As she stepped into the tiny boat, she felt it dip a good twenty centimetres further into the water. 'I'll sink it,' she said. 'I'm getting huge.'

'No,' he shook his head. 'You're just right.' He smiled at her for a long time before busying himself with the motor.

She put a hand over her face for a moment, tried to breathe slowly. Last winter she'd stood here, watching the smoke from a fire on the freeway billow towards the village, not knowing he was in there, her dad, and that her whole life had changed and the news just hadn't reached her yet. It was a beautiful fire—like she'd told Ben—a column of black smoke with an orange core, shooting straight up into the cobalt sky. She and James were eating salmon and roast potatoes that he had cooked and drinking cold white wine on the verandah in the smoky sunset. The light was magical. 'You're the most beautiful girl I know,' he'd said, and what she heard was: You're more beautiful than your sister. She'd had a few hours to believe it, and then she was plunged into a deep, black hole there was no scrabbling out of. Stupid, vain idiot.

Crossing the river, she focused hard on Kane's eyes, bright and blue and distant as he watched the smoke rising from the trees on the cliff. The smoke cleared and ballooned in surges as the wind caught it. One moment he was clear as day, almost glowing in the strange light; the next the edges of him were blurry and unstable.

'Don't worry, mate. It's just fire. Bush needs it. Helps the regrowth and that.'

She nodded silently, tried a small smile. 'Seems like there's a lot of fires, here.'

'Guess this one's the drought. Or some silly bugger with a ciggie.'

'Easy to get cut off.'

'Get yourself a boat, Rose. You seen the mums round here, jumping on and off their tinnies with their bubs strapped to 'em? No sweat.'

'I had one but it got cut loose. Haven't bothered with another one. I found it a bit hard to handle, you know?'

'Just get a little one. That'll do you. Or borrow mine, when you want.' She smiled at him and he looked away quickly this time.

Over at the marina, the channel was full of people in boats, chatting, shouting to others up on the wharves. The ferry ploughed out into the smoke on the river, the deep growl of its motor opening up as it left the channel. She hoped the trains were running. As they pulled in, a couple of teenagers—a boy and a girl—shuffled about near the petrol bowser. They were watching the boat, eyeing her and then Kane. Kane nodded to them as he pulled in. 'I'll drop you here, mate,' he said to Rose. 'I've gotta check on a few things. Maybe you should go into town for a bit, till the smoke clears.'

'Thanks for the lift.' Behind her on the wharf and in the shop and in their boats on the water were a hundred people she didn't know, who didn't know her, who would have left her there, even when the flames reached her house. He was the one person who'd thought to check on her.

'No worries,' he winked, and disappeared into the fog.

She took the twenty-minute train ride to the suburbs, passing within metres of flame and heat in the bush. She looked around at the other passengers. Some watched the fire, but most were reading the papers, headphones on, tapping laptops. There was a thrumming of their thoughts, the air was crowded with them. The carriage seemed thick with frustrated energy, abortive plans, dreams falling short.

She spent the afternoon in the cinema, away from the smell of smoke, away from the possibility of it. She chose a romantic comedy, because you could cry easily and unashamedly. Every moment of sincerity, of clichéd intimacy between the man and the woman, every kiss, reminded her that she was alone, and that there was no possibility of being otherwise. Even the scenes when the characters were hanging out with their friends slapped her with her own solitude. She watched the credits through a blur of tears and a pain in her throat from trying to cry silently. She passed her hands gently one over the other, as though she was washing them, as though each hand belonged to a pair of lovers who could not believe the wonder of them. I need to touch someone, she said to herself. I need to be touched. In her head were the scenarios she invented for a living, for her adventurous ladies. There were the memories of the men she'd slept with: James, men in the city, old colleagues at the magazine, Ben one drunken, slightly embarrassing time. She missed Ben. And she could never ask him. They'd spent years keeping things light, funny—with that one lapse. She knew from the way he looked at her then, the way he still did when his face slipped, when he forgot the world might be watching, that his feelings for her ran deeper than either of them would ever say out loud. She didn't want tenderness, for anything to be asked of her. It was just skin on skin she wanted, warm breath in her hair, a kind presence as she slept.

* * *

The smoke finally clearing at sunset, Danny came off his shift with his skin smeared with soot and his throat dry and raw. He was exhausted from ferrying people, pets, kids from their homes over to the car park at the village. He'd have a cold drink and call it a day; his bed was calling to him.

At the marina café there was a new girl behind the counter. Dark hair, skinny, tired. 'You new?' he said as she handed him a lemonade and some change. That was all it took with some. She flashed him an enormous smile, an ordinary face transformed. Friendliness in her blood, he reckoned—a family of talkers and drinkers and dancers.

'New to here. Back up the river before this. Dad just took the lease on this place. Me and Mum moved down here to look after it. He stays on his nights off from the old place.' One of those girls who told you everything, straight off.

'Know anyone down this way?' he smiled. 'You'll meet plenty, working here, anyway. More than you want, probably.'

Before she had a chance to speak, a shadow fell on her face from behind him. Then came Alf's customary grunt, the announcement he was here. Danny felt the bulk of his presence. 'Girl at the tables. Waiting for you, I reckon.' Alf shuffled back into the shadows to tend to the mysterious mechanics of his business.

He turned to see a woman with her head laying on her arms, on the table, her back to them, hair pale in the glary light. He knew the hair; it was Rose. There was a little knot of resistance in his stomach. He'd been hoping to keep his distance from those people for a while. He didn't know what it was. Just trouble, sadness, things he tried to avoid. 'You should get her out of the smoke,' the girl told him. 'Bad for the baby.'

'Listen,' Danny said. 'I sometimes go up to the pub after my shift of an evening. Come and say hello, if you like. Meet the locals when you're off-duty.' She nodded, beaming. 'I'd better go. Don't work too hard.'

He walked towards Rose, the only person out here among the plastic tables and chairs. 'Excuse me?' he said quietly, but she was asleep. He tapped her lightly on the shoulder. She lifted her head, bewildered. He had brought her back from another place, and she was lost. Tears brimmed in her green eyes. 'Sorry to frighten you,' he said softly. 'I'll come back in a minute.' He went to the toilets and washed his hands, his reflection staring back at him from a discoloured, streaked mirror. He barely knew his face, saw it rarely—there was no mirror in his shed. His skin was dark and he looked older than he remembered. That girl, Rose, was a well of sadness. He would take her across the river where she could be alone, not stared at by strangers like him, and then he'd go to the pub and sink a few, and maybe the new girl would be there, and he'd think of nothing but good times and the next few hours, and taking her home.

# Chapter 8

Rose listened to his motor idling as she climbed the verandah stairs. He seemed a decent bloke, that Danny, in spite of his reputation as one for the ladies. He was scruffy and tanned, like everyone who worked on the water here. His hair was darkish, short, probably cut it himself with an electric razor. His eyes were grey, and though he was cheerful and friendly he always appeared to be thinking. He had that boaty middle-distance gaze, thinking his own thoughts or perhaps nothing at all, wearing a look that worked, ready for the next girl to appear on the horizon.

She dragged her heavy legs up the last step and smelled it before she saw it—three twists of light brown faeces on the decking. At first she thought of that half-feral dog next door, but something about it, the deliberateness, the neat spacing, looked human. She'd been trying not to think about what Tom had said to her at the doctor's. Now she could think of nothing else. It wasn't that no one knew her, that she could be abandoned here in a fire through lack of knowledge. They did know her, and they hated her.

She found a piece of bark on the grass at the bottom of the steps and did what she could to remove it. She threw the bark next door and hosed down the deck, then disinfected it. Afterwards, she scrubbed her hands for ten minutes. She felt the germs she could not see, making their way inside her, infecting her baby.

In the last light, she sat still—rigid—on a camping chair on the deck. If she didn't move, if even her breath made no sound, there would be no pain; there would be nothing of her to feel. The cicadas throbbed, and the light from the living room illuminated an enormous spider in her web across the deck awning. A train roared over the bridge and she heard a tinny on the water, its motor slowing as it curved into the bay over at the island. There was no moon tonight, and she could see the water to the end of her wharf and then nothing. Someone laughed, long and hard.

She stared into the blackness. James had told her that the river was addictive, that people found it hard to leave after only a few days. It was familiar to her now, but its mysteries seemed to go on and on, up the twisting creeks and into the endless little bays, drawing her further in with every day she spent here. The mist lay over the oyster beds early in the morning and you were in another world.

Pelicans spent hours lined up on the pillars of her wharf. From the ferry you caught glimpses of falling-down shacks—some with washing out, some abandoned—in still, dark places on the water.

Everyone seemed to rush around, unsurprised by the place. Perhaps she would become a local, too, but she doubted it. Before now she had only come to the river to cross it, travelling between her dad's place and the city. Then it had always seemed like a glimpse of a secret country, crossing low over the wide blue water, catching glimpses as the road wound up through the bush, of lonely gullies and wrecked trawlers. She thought of the city and dreaded the moment she would really be asked to leave. Maybe she should just rent something else. But it was this house too, in spite of Tom. It seemed full of memories; she could feel James's childhood here. The baby was growing in the place that its father did. It was a piece of continuity in Rose's life, just a little one.

She closed her eyes and let herself see for a moment the thing she fought. A couple of kilometres from where she sat, the truck had ploughed into his old van. It had burst into flames, the smoke sending her a signal that she hadn't understood until later. She'd grown up with that van. Her sister was always up front; Rose in the back with his band gear, staring at Billie's shiny hair, listening to her laugh and joke with their father.

She remembered drifting in and out of sleep on the hot vinyl seats, her hair wet at the back of her neck. They were on the way home from the city to the coast. She would have been thirteen, perhaps. They thought she was asleep. 'Rosie's quite pretty, isn't she? Bit chubby, though, don't you reckon?' Billie said. And she had been, at that age, compared to her sister, who'd been dieting since the age of ten.

'Billie,' her dad sighed. 'You got your mother's looks. Rose is a clever girl, and pretty enough in her own way.' Rose had kept her eyes closed for the remainder of the journey, unable to speak. When they'd pulled into the driveway, she launched herself out of the car and up to her room, only emerging when it was time for school in the morning. No one seemed to notice.

She remembered Billie's carrot sticks for lunch, her turned-up nose when Rose and Ben had giggling midnight feasts of chocolate, chips, lemonade. Have you ever been full, Billie? she thought. Have you ever given yourself a day off from being beautiful? I can't keep doing this, she thought. She didn't used to think about her, before her dad died. Lived her own life. Drank, worked, laughed, made friends. How did I get so alone? She wanted to change something—her life, herself. Recover something.

She closed her eyes, leaned back in her chair, withdrew from the world and its lack of sense, far beneath the surface of life into a dark, cool, silent place, a night-time river, a dreamless sleep.

'Rose,' a voice was calling to her, bringing her back through the layers of darkness. 'Rose,' it whispered. 'It's getting cold out here, mate. Wake up.'

There was a hand on her forearm. She looked at it, tried not to flinch. Wait, Rosie, she told herself, wait. She followed the hand, the arm, to a man's old, old white T-shirt. It was Kane. 'Oh,' she said. 'I fell asleep again.'

'No kidding,' he smiled. You'll get eaten alive by mozzies if you don't cover up.'

She rubbed her eyes. 'Thanks. I'll go in.'

He paused for a moment. 'I'm going over to the pub if you're interested. Fancy it?'

People, she thought. Noise. Distraction. 'OK. Why not? That'd be nice.' She rubbed her eyes.

'I'll let you wake up. Be back in ten.'

Rose wondered whether old Tom would be there. It was one of those pubs where they looked at you as you walked in. She felt her bump grow in the eyes of the locals—a mix of scruffy male-only groups and the odd slightly slicker-looking couple—as she made her way past the high tables and stools to the bar. There was tinsel draped haphazardly among the bottles, brightly coloured flashing bulbs around the mirror. It had been an age since she'd been in a pub, and the smell of the beer- and tobacco-soaked carpet hit her as though she'd been picked up and put back into her old life. Kane was right behind her as they walked in, but he stopped to talk to a group of pissed-looking young boys near the door so she caught the barman's eye and ordered. She bought him a schooner of tap beer and waited at the bar.

It was busy—there seemed to be a bit of a holiday crowd—and she could hear people talking about the fires;

maybe that was what had brought them all out. She stood up straight and dared anyone to judge her, then reminded herself that no one knew her and no one cared. Kane walked towards her at last, and behind him was Danny. She nodded at him and he joined her, just after Kane. He was the local version of dressed up—wearing a short-sleeved button-up shirt rather than a T-shirt. 'How's it going, Rose?' he asked as he leaned on the bar and made eye contact with the landlady. 'I'm sorry about startling you earlier. You OK?'

'Must stop passing out drunk in public.'

Danny laughed. Kane was standing very close to her, all of a sudden. Danny took his drink and noticed someone further down the bar. 'Have fun,' he said, glancing at Kane, and left them to it.

'I know something about that bloke,' Kane said quietly.

'Oh yeah?' she said, handing him his beer. She was expecting a tale of his latest escapade with some out-of-towner. She heard snippets on the ferry, saw how the blokes teased him at the marina. No one seemed to begrudge him.

'His mate owns that yacht out from our place.' She glanced at him. Our place? she thought. He took a quick gulp of his beer. 'I heard them talking.'

'Oh, maybe you shouldn't tell me, if it's private.'

Kane pushed on. 'He's hiding from someone. His dad, I reckon.'

'That seems a bit odd. Maybe you misheard.'

'Don't think so.'

She shrugged. 'Guess it's none of our business.' She glanced at Danny. She could see he'd had a haircut now his back was to her; he had a white stripe between his hair and the sliver of tanned neck showing above his collar. It made him look vulnerable, boyish. He was joining the girl from the café at a table. She looked thrilled to see him. Maybe Kane had taken a shine to the girl from the café, too. 'Can we sit down?' she said, rubbing her back. 'Come on, we'll boot some old lady out of her spot.'

There was the girl, sitting alone, beaming at him from along the bar. Bare shoulders, gleaming lips. Oh dear, Danny thought. Young. He smiled back. 'What are you drinking?' he asked as he took the stool next to her.

'Bourbon and coke, please.'

He ordered her drink. 'She old enough?' Doug, the grotty old landlord winked.

The girl laughed. 'Old enough for what, you old bugger?' Been here a while then, thought Danny.

After the first drink, a bit of chitchat about the fires, a body found at one of the wharves up at the point a few weeks back, he took her out to the poolroom, settled in on a table after a little wait. Nice night. A few people about, drifting over, getting themselves introduced to the new face. Her name, he found out, was Jesse. She laughed loudly and often, swore like an oysterman. Good bit younger than him. Still, she seemed happy to be here. He wasn't twisting any arms.

After four schooners, he was about ready for a quiet

row home, half an hour of his book and bed, unless Jesse had other ideas. She was touching him a lot. His hand, his shoulder. But she was that kind of girl. Shared her excitement at being her. He opened his mouth to say something, test the water—he never planned these things, said whatever came to mind—when there was a crash of broken glass from the front bar. The sound travelled along his arms from his fingertips, vibrated for what seemed like a long time before dissipating. Then, rather than the usual cheer, a moment of silence, and a drunken voice shouting: 'I won that meat tray fair and square, Shep.'

There was a swift migration of the twenty or so people in the poolroom through to the front bar; Danny and Jesse were swept along with them. The room was silent. Everyone was still, turned towards the bar. At a poker machine there was an electronic jingle and then a noisy spewing of change. 'Fifty bucks!' a young man with long hair shouted as he began to scoop it up, and then turned to see a room bristling with anticipation. One of the older blokes who had a permanent stool at the bar—Vern—was squaring off with a fellow from out of town. There was broken glass around his feet. Danny was hemmed in on all sides by an expectant crowd. He felt a strong urge to make for the door, the river, his boat.

Old Tom, a known enemy of Vern's from an incident from another age involving non-payment for some white-anted lumber, had been raring to go at the out-of-towner's shoulder. Shoving the stranger to the side, he threw a punch that caught Vern on the chin. For a few moments the room remained caught in a stunned pause, watching a series of punches and shoves between the two old fellas, and then the landlord broke the silence from behind the bar. 'Take it outside, you blokes!' A red-faced, meaty woman in a little knot of people close to Danny poked her finger into the chest of a large man next to her. 'You shoulda left it alone, fuckwit. Now look what's happened.'

Danny glanced around the room. There were similar stoushes erupting in three or four groups. Behind the bar the barmaid was shoving the landlord, and in front of it Tom was a blur of clumsy blows while Vern, the much bigger man, was pushing him in the chest every few seconds to try and fend him off without actually hitting him. Behind Danny, some of the boys who'd been playing pool in the back room until a few moments before were landing a few punches on each other, and suddenly he and Jesse were surrounded by jostling, shoving and shouting.

Beyond the group immediately in front of him, where the woman was now crying but still shouting, he saw a cluster of people who were still, a little island amid churning seas. He took Jesse's arm and steered her between the flailing bodies. Blood roared in his ears. He saw Rob in the little crowd at the centre of the pub; he was chatting intently to his wife and glancing around him, a look of amused astonishment on his face. 'Danny, mate,' he called to him as he approached. 'Come and be with the sane people.'

'What the hell happened?' Danny asked him.

'You wouldn't read about it. Weekender won the meat raffle. Vern reckoned he had the winning number but lost his ticket. Took the meat tray from out the back and stashed it at his place. Then Doug realises it's gone and starts having a go. Next thing Tom rounds up a posse and they go and get it from Vern's. Quarter of an hour later Vern's back and the rest you can see for yourself.'

Danny looked up at the bar in time to see the first stool flying through the air. It hit the optics in front of the mirror and there was an almighty crash. There was a pause, and a cheer, and then the room erupted again. 'Come on, Jesse,' he said. She was glowing, taking it all in. 'I'll walk you home.'

'Don't worry about me!'

'I'm going. You stay if you want.'

Her face froze for a moment, her eyes still glossy from the drink, the excitement. 'It's OK,' she said. 'I'll come too.' Then her eyes were back on the fights erupting like mines around her. He steered her towards the front door. Right next to it they almost stumbled over a couple of young blokes, one punching another repeatedly in the head. The one bearing the brunt of it went down—it was the Indian guy from the petrol station—and the other kicked him in the back. Danny grabbed the attacker's arm—it was sinewy, tough—and pulled him around to face him. It was Kane, the muscles in his jaw clenched, his face almost purple with adrenalin and exertion, wild at being stopped.

'Cool down, fella,' Danny said. Kane spat in his face.

'Fucken hell,' said Jesse behind him. He shoved open the door to the terrace and pulled her out after him. The hot night smelled of smoke. 'I know him,' she said as the door slammed shut behind them and the fracas in the pub dulled to a muffled roar.

He was marching her swiftly across the terrace to the road, wiping his face with his sleeve. 'What? How come?' he said. Behind them, the shouting in the pub surged into the street as someone opened the door.

'Listen!' Kane called. Danny kept going, propelling Jesse along by her wrist. 'I know something about you.' His voice wavered. 'I know what you're hiding from.' Then the door closed and the pub was quiet again behind them.

'What was that all about?' she asked.

'Christ knows. Listen. How do you know him? Not a mate of yours, is he?'

'No way. He was up the river for a while. He seemed all right at first—bit odd but people liked him, seemed to fit in OK. But he was dodgy.'

'What do you mean, dodgy?' He could feel the sticky skin where he'd wiped the spit off his face. The blood was pumping in his legs and arms. He wanted to punch someone.

'He had a girlfriend up there. She got bruises. And one of the kids said he gave them drugs for free, then the next time you had to pay. The story was, one of the dads went looking for him, but he must have caught on because he'd already gone.'

'Does he know you?'

'Don't think so. I only recognise him because someone pointed him out when he was hanging round school.'

'School. Christ. How old are you?'

'I've left now, OK. That was last year. Why'd you let him spit at you?'

Danny looked into her face. 'I don't fight.' If he'd been in front of him now, though, he felt like he'd hit him until he stopped moving.

'Fair enough,' she said. They reached the marina stairs. 'Coming up?' she smiled.

He paused. 'Another time, Jesse. Really, mate. Maybe I'll see you tomorrow? At the café?'

After leaving her at the stairs up to the flats above the marina Danny untied his dory from Alf's boardwalk and dropped into it. He rowed out hard into the channel, his breathing ragged. What was he talking about? How could he know anything? He asked himself these questions over and over again, in rhythm with his rowing, but beneath them lay an insistent answer that he could only ignore for a little while. Kane had been there, down in his tinny, when Rob had told him about his dad. He'd heard it all, or enough to make a pain in the arse of himself about it. What's he going to do? Danny asked himself. Who gives? But Kane was trouble. He couldn't tell himself he wasn't.

He stopped rowing and watched the phosphorescence disintegrate around his oar. The island was a black shape on the inky river. His heart slowed while he sat on the water. He picked up his oars again and kept on past the point that usually marked a left turn and the last push for shore—onwards to the beach beneath the sandstone cliff. After another ten minutes, in which he willed himself to think only of the next clean stroke through the milky water, he reached Rob's yacht. He tied the dory to the ladder and clambered on deck silently. He took a torch from his pocket and shone it down below, making his way down to the galley. Returning with a beer, he took Rob's chair, faced it towards the shore, and made himself comfortable.

He didn't know why he'd come; couldn't face the shed, wanted to be on the water, the air on his face, until he'd cooled off a bit. But he was right opposite Rose's place, and just off to the left was Kane's shed. Was this really going to calm him down? He'd have his beer and row home.

There was a lamp burning in Rose's living room. He hadn't seen her when the fight broke out. She'd either been in the toilet or had left early, caught the last ferry. He was on his second beer when he heard the low drone of a tinny behind him. He'd been close to dozing, but now he was wide awake, a guard dog growling low at the sound of the softest footfall. The noise of the motor grew as it rounded the yacht, then cut out suddenly as it reached her jetty. There was a half-moon, high in the sky. He knelt on the deck and inched forward to the balustrade, keeping his head low. It was two men; he could hear their voices clearly now the motor was off. The passenger was Tom. His gravelly voice sounded close, as though he was standing right beside him rather than twenty metres across the water. That was the way on a still night. The things you heard, when people thought they were in private. He'd made that mistake himself, hadn't he?

'They'll be taking our money again by the weekend, Kane. Don't you worry about that.'

Kane said something softly, too quiet for Danny to pick up.

'Don't see many like that these days,' Tom replied. 'Nice to see the river boys have still got it in 'em. Made my Chrissie.'

There was a silence, then Kane said, 'Night, Tom. You all right to use Rose's jetty? I'll just tie off here.'

'OK, young fella. Thanks for the lift. Appreciated.'

Tom's figure rose creakily up the ladder and along Rose's jetty, while Kane sat in the boat, his dark shape motionless. Next door, the dog began barking. Then there was the squawk of a screen door, a slam, and a light went on. At this, Kane left the boat and made not for his shed but for Rose's verandah. Oh, she couldn't, Danny thought. He heard voices again. It seemed she'd been sitting out there the whole time.

'Hi, Kane,' she said. 'How was the rest of your evening?'

'Bit of excitement. There was a fight over that meat tray business.'

'God, really? I'm glad I left. I hate fights.'

'Yeah. Got a bit out of hand.'

'You didn't get involved, did you?'

'Oh, no. Got sideswiped in the mess, you know.'

'You all right? Does it need looking at?'

'Nah. Just a bit of a bruise, I think.'

'Do you want a drink? I was just going to go in.'

'OK. Yeah.'

He saw their shapes—her tall, the round of her belly silhouetted in the lamplight spilling through the glass door; him appearing after her, wiry, angular, hesitant. Danny stood from his chair, as though there was a way to stop her. But there was nothing he could do. He went down below where he knew the bed was made and was his to use. He'd crashed on the yacht many a time on a stormy night when he couldn't get back to the island in his dory. Even shared the bed with Rob after more than a few beers; in the morning he'd wake up in a room barely bigger than the bed, the air stale with farting and socks, and take his hangover up on deck where he could breathe. He'd brought girls here, too, on the odd occasion, until the one time Rob and his missus turned up, hiding from the kids, keen for a bit of fun themselves, and ruined the party. Maggie had not been impressed with the sight of his pale-moon arse in the air and a spectacularly naked French tourist in her bed. Rob had told him to keep his use of the boat discreet and decent from then on. Or that had been the official line, anyway.

He closed his eyes and ordered himself not to spend another second of today on that waster over at Rose's place. What is she thinking? he wondered in spite of himself, and fell asleep, water lapping gently on the wood next to his head.

Rose brought a dusty bottle of red, a corkscrew and two glasses over to the low table between the sofas, and sat down. Kane was peering out into the night over by the glass doors, hands deep in his jeans pockets, fiddling with something in one of them.

'I've got a joint, if you want some?' he said. He turned and looked at her belly for a moment. 'Maybe not, hey.'

'That's all right. We'll sit on the verandah. You have one. I'm going to have a drink. Haven't had one for months. Figure the baby's about done now.'

She brought the things outside and she opened the bottle while he rolled his joint, quickly, expertly. 'Been a long time since I had one of those,' she said. 'Oh well, nearly there. How's it going on the Durham house?'

'You know. OK. Boss is a bit of a slavedriver. Might not do it for much longer.' He was fiddling with matches, lighting them, stubbing them out on a saucer, rolling his joint back and forth between finger and thumb.

'Can you manage, without the work?' The wine was good; it was James's and it was expensive. She hadn't tasted wine for a long, long time.

'I've got a bit tucked away.' He was quiet for a few moments while he smoked. He seemed to be breathing in peace, ridding himself of the jitters. It was hard to tell in the dark; maybe he'd really got hurt in the fight. 'What about you?' he said eventually. 'You're always at that computer. What are you doing?' he asked. 'Making a fortune on eBay?'

She laughed. The wine was going straight to her head. She took another sip. 'I write, kind of.'

'Really? What? Books?'

'Yes, books.'

'What? I won't laugh. Writing anything is cool.'

She looked at him. She was tired of shutting people out. 'Well, it's erotic fiction. You know, sort of rude novels for women.'

He laughed. 'Those pink things with women in black knickers on the front?'

'That kind of thing, yeah.'

'So how does somebody start doing that?' He took a drag on his joint, blew the smoke out over the river.

'Well, I used to be a subeditor for a men's magazine. You know them. They're not porn exactly, they're just about beer, tits and earning a lot of money. I interviewed this publisher once, for an article. Well, she's my publisher now. She said I should give it a go. And once you get the hang of it, it's easy, and kind of fun. Well, sometimes it's boring, but I can do it from home. And maybe it's practice, you know, for writing properly.' He was looking at her, his usual shyness gone. 'You think I'm an idiot, don't you.' She laughed. God, laughter. She'd forgotten what it felt like. She finished her wine. I could drink a bottle of that, she thought.

'I think you're really cool, actually.'

She reached over and took his hand without thinking. 'You're a sweet guy, Kane.'

'That's what my mum always says,' he laughed quietly. 'You probably want to get to bed.'

'No. I'm going to have another glass, actually. Keep me company.' He hadn't let go of her hand. Her knees were bare. She was wearing a cotton maternity skirt and a stretchy T-shirt. She felt deeply unsexy all of a sudden. He touched the skin below the hem of her skirt with his free hand.

He started to stand. 'I'm sorry, Rose. You just looked so pretty, sitting there.'

'It's all right, Kane. Really, stay for a while. I'd love the company.'

She took his hand, dangling by his side, and kissed his long fingers, her eyes closed. He pulled her up, out of her chair. She laughed. 'I need a crane.'

He shook his head. 'You're lovely, Rose,' he whispered, and laid his head on her shoulder. 'I can't believe someone left you all alone. He's mad, whoever he is.'

Early next morning Danny was woken by the sound of someone shuffling about on deck. A boat motor had briefly registered in his dreams, but you learned to ignore those; they were simply a subconscious reminder that you were where you belonged—somewhere on the river and reachable only by boat. Not a form of transport his old man would be big on these days. Then Rob's voice: 'You decent? Got company?'

'Come down,' Danny called back.

'No thanks, mate. Not till you've aired it out down there. I've got a flask of coffee if you're interested.'

Danny emerged a few moments later in his shorts.

'Something happen to your clothes, Dan?' Rob was leaning on the balustrade. He looked him up and down.

'I didn't bring her back. Promise is a promise.'

'Don't make me laugh. So what you doing here? Not that my home isn't your home, etcetera . . .'

'It was low tide. Didn't want to deal with the swamp at the beach.'

Rob nodded warily. 'If you say so.'

Behind Rob, Danny saw a small movement from Rose's house, a reflection glancing suddenly off sliding glass. Rob noticed him looking at something and turned towards the shore. 'Keep still for a tick,' Danny said softly. Rob gave him a quizzical look but didn't move. First the lanky, ambling figure of Kane appeared on her verandah, then came Rose, slower, more contained.

'Tell me he slept on the couch,' Rob whispered. But as they continued to watch, Rose wrapped her arms around his neck and kissed him. She seemed to be going for his cheek, but he caught her elbows, held her still, and gave her a long kiss on the mouth before hopping off the deck and next door to the boatshed. Rose peered out over the water for a few seconds before disappearing inside.

'She must like it rough,' Rob said.

'Mate—'

'Did you see him at the pub last night?'

'Yeah, I pulled him off that bloke. There's someone who owes me a beer.'

'You think she likes that?'

'She didn't see it. She was already home.'

Rob gave him a searching look. 'Right. Think someone should tell her?'

'Tell her what? That the bloke likes a fight? Everyone in the pub liked a fight last night. It was nuts.'

'She's gonna have a kiddie any minute. He's bad news all round, I reckon.'

'Yeah, maybe.' He gave Rob a quick look.

'What?'

'Jesse knows him, from up the river.'

'Yeah?'

'Drug dealer, she reckons.'

'Well everyone knew about the pot.'

'Looks like he goes after the kids, gets them onto it. One of their dads was ready to see him off, but he skipped.' He paused. 'Sounds like maybe he bashed his girlfriend, too.'

'Shit, Dan. We've got to sort him out. We don't want that round here.'

'What's it got to do with us?'

'I'd say it's got plenty to do with you, the way you're sleeping on my boat and spying on him.'

'He heard us, the other night. He was down there in his tinny when we were talking about Dad.'

'I say we sort this out before it gets anywhere. I know plenty of blokes who'd be happy to help.' He nodded at Mancini's. 'Would have thought you'd want to help her out, with your history.'

'What's that meant to mean?' he snapped. Slow down, he told himself. 'It's her lookout,' he said quietly. 'She chose him.'

'Maybe.' Rob studied him for a second. 'Guess it's none

of my business. Want me to tow you home before my shift starts?'

'Thanks. Feeling a bit tender.'

Danny sat in the morning sun, streaming sleekly through the glassy water on his towed dory, patting the water occasionally with a paddle to keep himself upright and straight. Rose—she was on the brink of a new life, in a new place. A pretty girl about to have her first child. Danny let himself imagine how his mother might have looked and felt, waiting to have him. He'd seen photos. She looked happy, sunlit. What would she have said if someone had tried to warn her? Could anything have made any difference? Or would she have plunged straight in regardless? Tied her fate and her baby's to a drunken thug, become so frightened and small that she wasn't even up to protecting her kids.

He was one to talk about duty to your kids. Here he was, no better than any of them, hiding on the river. He tried to imagine the girl, his girl. She'd been tiny when he left; she hadn't seemed his. She'd be seven now. A proper girl. At school, in a uniform and those cloth sunhats they wore. He wondered if they still lived in the next street, if his mum saw her. Did she need protecting? Was that his job? He paid what he should—more than any judge would ask for. The mum, Jackie, he'd heard she had a new bloke now. How could he know what sort of a bloke? But they were a family. No one would welcome his interference. The brothers. They'd made it quite clear he should keep his distance.

Bugger all of this, he thought. He had made his life simple; it had been a relentless, pure act of will to do it, one that he had to keep repeating every morning when he woke up. Rose was not his problem. From the look of it, she was a magnet for trouble. What could you do about people like that? His child—well, the girl's family had shut him out from the beginning and now there was this bloke. Jackie was all right. Jackie was always all right. You had to make choices. He'd made his. But this Kane character, he was Danny's problem. The choice had been made for him.

# Chapter 9

Tom was hung-over, bruised and shaking at his girls' graves, in a secret corner between the village and the old highway. A hundred tourists drove past it every day in the summer without noticing. He parked his ute in the shade so Dog wouldn't get too hot in the cabin and made his way to their corner. There they were, side by side—Edith Cathleen Shepherd, Molly Elizabeth Shepherd. Spot for him, too, grass overgrown. He regretted doing their headstones in granite. Never seemed to get old. Like it happened just the other day. Not like the sandstone ones, wearing away, peacefully crumbling back into the earth.

He wasn't alone. Iris Jensen was spending her Christmas Eve over at the old man's grave, kneeling, praying. How she could stay on her knees at her age, wrong side of eighty, he couldn't imagine. After a few moments she left. Nodded at Tom as she passed. 'Sorry for your loss,' she murmured.

'And you, Iris.' Both their losses decades old.

A red ute, big engine, growled at the edge of the cemetery. A young dark bloke jumped down from the cab and trotted over to her. Bred a different race of young people now, Tom thought. All huge. Make us look like midgets. Iris, next to the young man, was papery brittle—a dry leaf alongside the tallest, broadest tree in the forest, one that had survived fire after fire and only grown stronger, when they were the ones, really, who'd done the surviving. These young people were still wet from their mothers. The young fellow made as though to help her into the cab, but actually lifted her into the air a good couple of feet like she was nothing.

Grandkids, Tom thought. One would have been something.

The years on their graves were different but they were gone within six months of each other. What was he doing still here? Proved what he'd always reckoned. Wily old buggers would inherit the earth. The meek would go to God before it was time and you'd spend the rest of your days missing them.

It was twenty-five years ago; he'd been a young man then, not that you think you are, when you turn forty. Remembered through all the fog of thousands of nights of drink, his Molly stumbling into the pub. First thought: what's she doing this side of the water this time of night?

Then he saw. Blouse ripped. Mini-skirt muddy. One shoe. Lipstick across her cheek. His second thought: Mancini. The way he watched her from his verandah next door; he'd seen him. Looking at her legs like they took the wind out of him, even with his boy on his lap. Talking to her over at the public wharf when he thought Tom wasn't around. He'd stand over her, lean against the boatshed, looking down at her, looking down her blouse. Behind the bar Marian was tutting. 'Shut up, Maz,' he said. Molly was there in front of him. Panda eyes with wrecked make-up. Curly hair limp and wet. Looked like she'd crawled out of the river, a swamp thing. She pushed herself into his arms; he had to tell himself to hug her. He didn't want to touch her. He didn't want this to be his daughter. He could feel the skin at her chest, her ripped blouse covering next to nothing. She was sopping, and she smelled of low tide. 'I washed in the river, Daddy,' she said. 'I got myself clean.'

The pub was silent as they crossed the floor. It was awkward to move; she wouldn't let go of him until they got down to the boat. Even then, he had to peel her off. He held her away from him. 'Who was it, love?' She wouldn't look at him. She climbed into the boat, took his blanket from under the dash and huddled in it on the floor at the back. Wouldn't sit up front with him.

Edie was asleep when he got home. He had to wake her up, to bathe the girl. Molly was sitting in the lounge room with a cup of tea, her hair in her face. They whispered in the corridor. When the colour had come back to Edie's face, she said, 'We can't wash her. The police, she has to go to the police.'

'She's already washed herself in the river,' he said.

'Did she say who it was?'

He shook his head. 'I've got a fair idea.'

Edie nodded. 'What are you going to do?'

'Go round there. Put him in the river.'

'Don't go there now,' she said. 'Don't go upsetting her.'

'Talk to Alf then, I reckon. In the morning. We'll sort something out.'

He wished now he'd gone, straightaway, just got him while the rage was hot, while you didn't have to think. In the end, they'd done everything short of it. They wrote things on the wall of his fish and chip shop; they cut his tyres; Alf stole his petrol so he ran out in the middle of the river, but a pleasure cruiser, someone who didn't know the river business, picked him up.

Molly never said a thing about all that, because she didn't know. She just sat in her room, playing with the tag on her teddy. She let her mum tidy her hair, and cuddle her, but she didn't come out, and she never talked. Hadn't talked much in the first place, but used to laugh. Had a laugh so low and dirty no one could resist it; you had to laugh, too. That was gone now, like the part of her she needed to do it had been cut out that night on the river.

Then Mancini went back to Italy, and the wife and the boy went to live in the city with relatives. And the day after they left, Molly walked into the river, and never came out again.

\* \* \*

He knelt by Molly's stone, knees creaking, his hip making a sharp pop. He touched the cool granite. 'Little mate,' he said. 'Little Molly.'

He stayed there until an insistent barking broke into his thoughts and the sun started to blister on his neck. Dog was going nutso in the ute. 'Coming, Dog,' he muttered, raising himself stiffly to his feet. His knees were sore and his neck was slick with tears he hadn't noticed shedding. He looked around him, but the cemetery was empty.

Rowing back, he turned it over again in his head, what Alf had said. He supposed this was what he'd be spending his time doing, going over it all to the point of bloody exhaustion, if his days were almost up. That was what you did, it seemed—poked yourself endlessly with the sharp stick of regret till you were worn out with frustration and couldn't remember how anything had happened in the first place.

If he'd sorted old man Mancini out, lit a little fire under his house and locked him in, say, how would he have been sure to get him and not the wife and little boy? Not that he lost any sleep over that pointless yuppie these days, but back then he was just a mite. Molly used to push him on his swing on the Mancinis' verandah, let him help her with her crab pots.

He could have done something to the boat; something a bit more decisive than Alf's little stunt. God knows, he'd thought about it, at the time. But again, how not to get the missus and the kiddie? She took the little fella everywhere on the river in their dinghy—no way to know who'd be in it next. Couldn't have that on his conscience. And the other ways there were to kill a man ... well, he couldn't even look them in the eye. When it came down to it, he'd been scared. Wasn't scared of anyone now, too pissed usually, but in those days he'd been different. Mancini was a bloody big fellow; and he couldn't prove anything. Didn't do the DNA stuff then, and anyway, Molly had washed herself in the river, afterwards. So he did things the Shepherd way— made a pest of himself until the bloke got the message and shot through.

If I'd done it, Molly, when I had the chance, he thought, his bones creaking as he rowed his tiny boat across the wide river, I would have spent the rest of my days inside. Wouldn't have made it out again, that's for sure. A pelican dived into the water right in front of him and came up with a gleaming mullet, scarfing it into its big bill sack in a convulsing movement before soaring low over his head. It made him ashamed, to think he couldn't have given up the river for his girl, but there it was, and now it was done. He knew he wouldn't be joining her, one way or another, old goat like him. There was just the river for him, too old and sauced to even get out past the heads on the rumour of a school of salmon these days. There was just the river, and the bottle, and the few old-timers he'd managed not to piss off beyond repair. And after the river, there'd be a bloody great fire, or more likely, nothing at all, a black hole like sinking down beneath the water, beneath the mud, it closing over your head so you were hidden, and then forgotten, the last of your kind all gone.

# Chapter 10

K ane felt the warmth of the morning sun on his neck as he made his way down Rose's steps and back to his shed. The pub, the fight, his blindness while he hit that bloke, it had all gone, though he felt the tenderness of his bruised ribs and temples like there were hot fingers pressing his flesh. His whole body felt awake, energetic, alive. The bruises simply reminded him of his skin, of the touch of hers.

He let himself into his shed and lay down on the unmade bed, closed his eyes. Naked, she'd been creamy, gorgeous. Huge breasts, tight round tummy, long limbs, and her hair when it was out was amazing. So much of it.

And they'd talked afterwards. Well, he'd talked, she'd listened. Nothing much, shooting the shit, about the river, about where he was before. But she was interested, didn't use all those little tricks they do to put you in your place. Maybe, someone like her—that was what he'd been missing, why he'd never made much of himself.

He had this feeling now, in his belly. The world was looking out for him for once; that was what it was. This was what it was like for all those people who had everything handed to them on a plate. It was pure warmth he felt, a gorgeous heat. A feeling that everything was for a reason, that anything was possible.

Rose lay back in bed, strangely restless. She needed to get off this little strip of land between the cliff and the water. She wondered whether she wanted breakfast. The queasiness of the first trimester had returned, and yet she was beginning to spend large parts of each day thinking about food. It was hard to tell what time it was just from the light in the room, there was so little in the morning. She guessed it was between eight and nine. She had work to do; she'd gotten behind and would spend Christmas catching up, but she knew if she tried to work in the morning she'd just end up making too many cups of tea and finding pressing little tasks to do that weren't work.

A tall shadow passed by the blind at her bedroom window. She recognised the walk and burrowed deeper under the covers. Bloody hell, Rose, she thought. She would have to talk to him, though. He'd said she could borrow the boat whenever she wanted, and she wanted it now. Better to get things back to normal straightaway, in any case.

She got out of bed and dressed, and knocked on his door. The glass slid back instantly. She'd never actually seen inside the shed since he'd come. She caught a glimpse behind him of a dark, squalid space: coffee cups, strewn clothes, the smell of socks and ashtrays and his body. He stepped outside and closer to her, wearing only shorts. She knew the shape and colour of him already, the scar on his chest. She wondered, as she did last night, what it was from. 'War wound,' he smiled.

'Sorry,' she said. 'I didn't mean to stare.'

'That's all right. Seeing as it's you.'

'Listen,' she said quickly. 'You know you said I could borrow your boat? Do you mind if I take it now for a couple of hours? I've got a few things I want to do. Just if you're not using it.'

'Help yourself.'

'Thanks.' She turned and began to head back to her place for her things.

'Need any help with it?'

She turned back. 'No, I'll be fine. Thanks.'

He watched her until she was on her verandah; she could feel it. She waited inside, though her bag was packed and she was itching to leave, wondering if he was still out there. She gave it a minute, then heard his door slide shut, and bolted without bothering to lock the door.

Fortunately, he'd left his little boat tied to the ladder at the end of the jetty. She would have had no chance getting down to it alone if he'd tied it to the wall; it was low tide. The motor started with the first pull, and she settled into a balanced spot in the middle of the bench and headed out onto the river. This was a good boat, slow and small. She'd found James's big and twitchy, too powerful for a novice, too liable to flip. There'd be no flipping this one—she weighed too much.

There was a place the locals talked about that she'd never got round to seeing. It was called the Tanks, a series of waterholes at the northern end of the ridge behind her house. The man in the post office had told her there was an easy path up there, though the Tanks were quite high up. That sounded good: somewhere quiet and alone where she could see the river and have a dip. She took the boat past the houses to where the rocky cliff was so steep there could be no building, and into a fold in the rock that opened out to a tiny beach and a shallow area between oyster beds. It was cool here and dark, a little rainforest gully. The fire had been further south and behind the ridge; here everything was green and cool, the leaves glossy as they shifted in the morning sun. There was a large boat here already, tied to a mangrove root, but she knew the path continued past the Tanks; perhaps they were bushwalkers, off along the track somewhere, and she'd still have the place to herself.

She saw the opening of the path in the bush beyond the shoreline. She edged her way around it in the shallow water with the motor up, pulling Kane's dinghy by placing her hands on the surface of the larger boat. The baby was wriggling and kicking, but as she hit the path and began to stride up into the dense growth the movement subsided. It was still and quiet here. There were bell-miners, like knives tapping on glass, the rustling of the breeze in the leaves, her breath. The sky was deep blue above the crowding gum leaves. 'Sleep, baby,' she said, and patted her stomach. The little creature filled her now; you could make out hands, feet, the curve of the head, sometimes even through her T-shirt. She didn't know, before now, how her parents must have felt, waiting for her. Of all the things people told you when you were pregnant, there was only one that had stuck: this is when you realise how your parents loved you, a midwife had told her. Maybe it's when you begin to worry, that's when you know. She'd been sick as a kid. Her dad had stayed up at night watching her for a month while she had whooping cough. How did you become a person that could manage that? How could the act of childbirth suddenly turn you into a person that had such reserves of strength, of patience? Maybe it didn't happen for everyone; it hadn't for her mother. She just never got strong enough. She'd gone, after all.

As she climbed the path she grew warmer. She hadn't showered since she'd been with Kane, and felt a little sticky, and dirty. She'd been too keen to get out of the house. The cool water of the Tanks was appealing: to be clean and cold and fresh, for one day to wash her skin and leave everything behind her, down below, in the world of other people.

She stopped for a moment. Had she heard voices? It sounded like singing. How could that be? She was approaching the end of the bushy path; she could see light up ahead, a golden sandstone ledge. She moved towards the opening quietly, keeping her breath low and quiet. She could hear more clearly now; it was singing—it was a group of people, singing what sounded like a religious song. Exclamatory, joyous, more exuberant than the hymns she knew but with that same quality of rapture. How strange, to hear such a song in a place like this. There was a male voice, stronger than the rest, and when the song had finished he began to speak, but she couldn't make out all of what he was saying. Just words, separated from each other by mumble, with the group breaking in every so often to affirm his words. 'Yes, brother!' it sounded like they were saying, and laughter. What had she stumbled upon?

As she reached the end of the path she saw them, ten or so metres out into the clearing—a little group of men and women, maybe seven of them, in ordinary clothes. Jeans, shorts, T-shirts. Strangely, a man's head and shoulders seemed to hover above the ground in front of them, and then she saw that he was in one of the pools. He beamed into the sun, and held out his arms to a young woman in jeans at the front of the little crowd. She hesitated; another of the group placed a hand on her shoulder and nudged her gently forward. She sat down at the lip of the pool, plunging her jeans into the water, heedless, and the man took her in his arms and cradled her like a child. He spoke over her and the group called again: 'Yes, brother!' He submerged her in the water, her hair spreading on the surface, and Rose put a hand to her mouth, took an involuntary step towards them. After a moment he lifted her up again, and she beamed into the sunlight, blinking, before throwing her arms around him. The group cheered and clapped. Then he sat her down at the edge of the pool and raised his arms for the next one. Rose saw that he had already done half the group—they were dripping puddles on the rock—and there were only a couple left to go.

She watched the next, a teenage boy who solemnly handed his glasses to another of the group before stepping forward. It was the same process: the submersion, the blinking bafflement followed by pure joy. Rose was transfixed.

But then, as the last dry one stepped forward, it suddenly seemed important not to be seen; she was sure she shouldn't be watching. She edged backwards into the bush. She would have her dip somewhere else, in the river itself. She made her way quickly back down the path, not knowing how long it would be before they followed. Down at the river she punted the boat with her oar around the corner, away from the shallows, before she started the motor, out of breath now from the walk up to the cliff and back with only a brief pause.

She opened up the motor and headed out into the broad channel between the cliff and the island, out towards a little beach she'd heard about around the next bend towards the ocean. Still sheltered by the river, it had a view out to sea where you could watch the sails and share the beach with no one. Did she dare head so far away from the houses on her own? She couldn't swim here in the open river; she'd never get back into the boat, and you had to watch the current, when you were out of your depth. It was a beautiful day, the river flat and blue with the reflection of the sky, and she felt the urge to let the water close over her, to float and dream. She would find the little beach. She would be fine; if she got into trouble, she could swim. You were never too far from one bank or another, or a sandbar. She'd have to watch out for those—she was sitting low in the water in this little boat with her weight and the motor's.

Those people, surrendering themselves to submersion, emerging new. She'd never believed in all that stuff; her dad had told her religion was like the tooth fairy, or Santa, and she swallowed greedily everything he ever taught her. His funeral was one of the few visits to church she'd made in her life. She wished for a moment that she could believe. But she didn't, not since she'd prayed to Jesus as a child. Still she imagined the walk back down for them, climbing into their boat and heading back out into the open water, refreshed, joyful, the future different from the past, and the moment it changed a clean slicing, never to be forgotten.

She pulled the tiller and pointed the dinghy's nose away from the island, motoring slowly towards the bend in the river. As she drew level with her house, and the boatshed, Kane's body returned to mind. She didn't regret what they'd done, in itself. She felt much better for it, relieved, less aching and needy. She was nervous, though, of the look in his eye now, the sudden ease of his body. He was happy, she knew. She'd made him happy.

Once around the bend there was more swell, and she could see the ocean beyond the rocky uninhabited island between the heads. She saw, too, to her right the beach she'd heard about. Misjudging the swell she swung the boat around a little too fast and a surge came over the side and drenched her. 'Bugger,' she said, and laughed, but then the motor was spluttering, and cut out. 'Damn.' She looked around her. She saw the yachts way out to sea. Behind her, a good couple of hundred metres distant now, was the bend. There were no boats anywhere near her. She stared at the silent motor. She knew nothing about mechanics. What could be wrong with it? The bend was moving further away by the second as the tide took her towards the ocean. She placed a hand on her belly and told herself to be calm, gave the motor a couple of pulls: nothing. There was a life jacket lying in the boat. She put it on, feeling overcautious and panicky at the same time. She pulled the starter several more times, then gave up and started buckling the life jacket. Maybe she should jump over and swim for the beach. It couldn't be more than fifty metres, and if she didn't decide now it would be too late; she'd be in open water before she knew it. She heard a motor behind her. Rounding the bend was a large runabout. 'Oh thank God,' she murmured. She saw the beach slip by as the boat approached and was glad she hadn't jumped. Her record of hanging onto people's boats had not been looking good. What would she have done at the beach anyway? It was in the middle of the national park; it could be a day's walk out of there, if you knew the way and had water and food. She had neither. And she was eight months pregnant.

The boat was soon close enough to reveal itself in more detail. She watched it approach from under her hand. It was the water taxi. What was he doing out here? She put a hand in the air so he wouldn't just think she was out fishing, but he was coming right for her in any case. He brought the boat alongside her and she threw a rope up to him clumsily. He caught it and pulled her in. 'Are you OK?' he called down.

'The motor cut out. I'm glad you're here. I didn't know what to do.'

'My friend Rob saw you headed out this way from the island. This boat's not big enough to come out here. Your mate should have told you that.'

'You followed me?'

'Thought I'd better check on you. Where were you going, anyway?'

She pointed to the beach. 'Just for a swim, and a quiet morning.' She felt incompetent before this man. He was such a river rat. She wondered if he was one of those who had always been here, whose parents had always been here.

'I can still take you there, if you want. Shame not to have your swim after all this.'

'Don't you have to be anywhere?'

'They can wait.'

He helped her up onto the bigger boat and then jumped down onto the dinghy. He lifted the petrol tank and shook it: empty. 'I'm an idiot,' she said.

'It's not you.' He looked pissed off nevertheless. 'It's that idiot. Shouldn't have let you go off without petrol.' She felt the urge to stick up for Kane, but kept silent. He just wasn't the sort to worry about things like keeping his tank topped up, that was all. There was something a bit—childlike— about him. Irresponsible, like a kid, not in a way you could hold against him.

At the beach, when Danny had anchored and helped her onto the sand, he peeled off his T-shirt and chucked it into the boat before striking out into the river, spearing the water with his hands until he was just a little black spot. She sat in the shallows and let the water swish around her belly. There was a sort of creaking inside her, nothing so definite as a kick, or a headbutt. It was as though soft discs were rotating against each other in liquid. She didn't know whether she heard it or felt it, whether it was sound or movement, a distant surge on an inner sea. Are you growing? she wondered. Are you changing? The tide began to push more forcefully against her, and the feeling was lost in the rushing of water.

When Danny returned twenty minutes later he found her floating off the running board at the stern of his boat. He joined her, and they drifted silently, heads on hands in the sleepy sun as the boat bobbed on its anchor. He watched the water drying on her tanned forearm. She was so close that he could see the droplets, little hexagonal prisms, glinting and disappearing. There was a force around her, a whirling chaos of disaster and mishap. Her eyes were closed. She seemed to be stealing a moment of peace. He felt an urge to reach through, beyond the noise of all that trouble, and touch the still centre of her. 'Rose?'

'Hmm.'

'Are you OK? You seem—sad. Whenever I see you.'

She lifted her head drowsily and opened her eyes. Her eyelashes were wet. Her eyes, rimmed with brown, had a wide sparkling circle of green around her pupils. 'I didn't used to be like this. My dad died. I can't stop missing him. And it just seems to dredge up a whole load of other stuff. It's been a while now. It doesn't seem to get better. I just want to do something, you know, to move on. But I'm scared, of forgetting him.'

'Are you close to your sister? Who's helping you?'

She shook her head. 'She's all right, really. We just don't seem to get on. It's probably me.'

'When is the baby coming?'

'Another four weeks, but I feel like it's going to come early. I don't know why. It just feels—ready.'

'Must be hard, doing all this on your own.' He put a hand on her forearm. It was cool and damp.

'I had to keep the baby,' she said. 'I couldn't do anything else. Say it—looks like Dad. Say it has his eyes, or smile, or something. I want to meet her, I want to see who she looks like.'

Danny smiled. 'It's a girl?'

She nodded and smiled herself for a moment.

'I went up to the Tanks, before,' she said. 'I saw some people. I think they were being baptised, or something.'

'Oh, you saw them? They're the River Baptists. I've never seen them.'

'Do they come a lot?'

'Just religious holidays, I think. They've always been here. Since the river was settled. The church is back up past the bridge somewhere.'

'They seemed happy,' she said.

'Maybe,' he said. 'Will you baptise yours?'

'No,' she laughed. 'I don't believe in anything like that. Wish I did, sometimes. Be nice to believe there was a purpose for you. But all the things that happen to you, they just seem random, messy.'

'You're about to have a baby. That's purpose, isn't it? But I know what you mean.' The sun was hot on his neck. It must be close to midday. 'Listen,' he said. 'We'd better be making a move. Alf'll be wondering.'

They motored back slowly so the dinghy, jumping and skittering along behind, wouldn't flip. He dropped her and the little boat back at the house. The day was bright, the river flat and glassy, and his skin tingled with salt from the brackish water. He felt a tugging sadness as she disappeared along her wharf into the shadows. He had been so sure of himself, here. He'd wanted to believe it was his place, his time at last, but it seemed for a moment he was starting from scratch, knowing nothing, lurching about in a little boat on a big sea.

# Chapter 11

Tom was picking about the scrap in his yard. A bloke at the pub wanted a drive shaft for his old Camry. He was sure he had one somewhere, stashed at the bottom of a pile of lumber to keep the rain off. Buggered if he could find it, though. He sat down on an old sofa he'd left out for so long it had weeds growing from it and rolled himself a ciggie. Finished the mug of tea he'd started earlier as he watched young Danny tearing off in his taxi. Fellow from the boatshed up on her verandah while the wake was still spreading beneath her jetty. He was in front of her, on the steps, before she'd seen him coming. She was a pretty lass, he had to admit, hair like hay in the sun. The bloke said something to her, touched her arm. From where Tom was sitting she didn't seem keen; flinched a bit, stepped backwards onto the verandah. Gave her a bit of a fright, from the looks of it. She said something back, and went inside.

Then Kane was picking his way through Tom's rubbish to where he sat, an idiot grin plastered across his chops. Plonking himself down on the arm of the sofa he pulled a small bottle of whiskey from his pocket, poured a slug in Tom's mug and took a swig from the bottle for himself. Gazed out across the river with a look in his eye like he was planning how to spend his lottery winnings.

'See you're making inroads with your landlady, there. Looking for classier digs, are you?'

Kane smiled at Tom, and shrugged.

'Like 'em on the large side, hey?'

'She won't be big for long. She's gorgeous, anyway.'

'Whose d'you reckon that baby is, then? Not worried about him coming back?'

'I dunno. Figure he'd be here already if he had any interest.'

'I'm betting it's Mancini's. So you're probably safe there. They're all worthless. But maybe he's sending her money. She doesn't seem to go to work.'

'She works from home—she told me.'

'Oh yeah. One of them web designers or something.'

'She's a writer. She writes books.'

'No. She famous, your bird?'

Kane was quiet for a second. 'Don't reckon. Don't reckon she writes the kind of books that make you famous.'

'Spill your guts, then, before you do yourself some damage.'

'Nah. Maybe I shouldn't say.'

'Oh for Pete's sake.'

'Promise you won't go blabbing?' He looked back at Rosie's place. He was bursting with something. Seemed young all of a sudden. Tom felt a stab of envy. It was about a bazillion lifetimes since he'd felt anything like this bloke did.

'She does those, you know, those erotic novels for women.'

'Christ almighty.'

'Don't tell anyone. I probably shouldn't have said anything.'

'Well, young fella, you're welcome to her. That is definitely not a woman's work in my book.'

Kane's brow creased. He pulled a packet of tobacco from his pocket, containing his rolling papers and weed. 'Smoke, Tom?'

'No, mate. Not after last time. Nasty stuff.'

'Mind if I do?'

'Help yourself.'

Tom leaned back in his chair and watched the ferry idle into the wharf while Kane rolled his funny tobacco, for once not even thinking to swear at Steve under his breath. He was truly stunned. What a generation. In the space of twenty-odd years you could go from his Edie, a quiet, tough woman who looked after her family and never complained, to this bloody strumpet at Mancini's, writing filth for a living. And that other blonde bit, he'd seen her here before with Mancini. Something weird was going on. They all swapped around these days. Probably had bloody orgies all over the place, and now one of them was pregnant. What chance did the little kid have, born to those people? It made his skin crawl to think about it. And this young fella. Messing around with a woman carrying another bloke's baby. Who dragged these kids up anyway?

Kane was standing, lighting his joint. 'See you round, mate,' he said. Tom watched him mooch back over to his place, leering at that woman's house, dragging his heels in case she came out. Tom shook his head and called for Dog. Couldn't sit here and watch this; it made him sick to the stomach. Better off over at the marina. Have a chat with the boys and take his mind off things. What would they say about a woman writing filth? 'Carn Dog,' he said. 'Let's get out of this bloody place for an hour or two.'

Danny dropped his last customers at the petrol bowsers at seven-thirty, just as the red of the cliffs was fading, filled up and dropped the boat back at Alf's. At the café, Jesse was just emerging from behind the counter with her bag over her shoulder. 'Hey, stranger,' she smiled.

'Hey, yourself. Fancy a Chrissie drink?'

'Why not? Pub or marina?'

'See who's down the marina, shall we, seeing as we're already here.'

'No worries.' She linked an arm through his and smiled up at him.

So she was giving him another chance, then. He'd been living the life of a monk lately. Tonight, he thought, I'm buggered if I'm sleeping on my own.

It was the usual suspects hanging around outside the shop, bit more pissed than usual, in honour of the season. Couple of blokes from the island and the beach, old Tom already on his very unsteady high horse about something, poking Gareth from the shop in the chest, making a loud and drunken point. But Rob was there, so he left Jesse with him while he bought a six-pack in the shop. When he emerged, Jesse beamed at him. Rob was telling her a story about how in Danny's first week on the water taxi job, he'd gone straight into an old jetty without slowing down and had taken out one of the piers. 'Oh, great,' Danny said as they laughed. 'She really needed to know that.'

'I thought so, mate.'

'How'd you keep your job?' Jesse asked, laughing.

'Alf had buggered his back. He was desperate.'

Behind him, Tom was getting louder and starting to sway about. 'Easy there, Tom,' Rob said as he bumped into Jesse.

'It's OK,' she said.

'These bloody birds today,' Tom shouted in Rob's face, gesturing vaguely at Jesse. 'They're a bloody disgrace.'

'Easy, Tom,' Danny said. 'What's the problem?'

'That bird, for example, pregnant sheila.'

Everyone was silent. Even Jesse's smile had disappeared. 'What are you on about?' Danny said quietly.

'Bird at Mancini's. Guess what she does for a living?'

'What's that got to do with the price of eggs?' said Rob.

'She only writes bloody porn. Women these days. Christ.'

'Come on, Jess,' Danny said to her. 'We'll go to the pub. Bit feral here tonight.'

'And she's letting that wastrel in her boatshed into her bed,' Tom slurred while a little circle of space opened up around him and people tried to start up other conversations. 'What is wrong with these people?' Danny heard him say as they slipped through the shop and out to the car park.

'That's that pregnant girl you took home, isn't it?' Jesse said as she, Danny and Rob walked up to the pub. 'That's who he's on about, isn't it? D'you reckon she's really with that Kane? Someone should tell her what he's like.'

Rob gave Danny a look over the top of Jesse's head.

'She couldn't really write porn though, could she? Don't look the type,' she continued.

'Hell of a way to make a living, though,' Rob said. 'Beat driving a rig, I reckon.'

'He's just a pissed old fart,' Danny said. 'About ten per cent of what he says makes any sense, and how you'd know which ten per cent is anyone's guess.'

'You mates, you and her?' Jesse asked. 'Bit weird, isn't it? Pregnant chick, writing porn.'

'I've just given her the odd lift. Look, it doesn't matter whether any of it's true. Point is you listen to too much of old Tom's ranting and you'll fill your head with a lot of garbage. But that's up to you.'

'Point taken,' she said, and winked at Rob.

Danny took a deep breath. She was just kidding. He put his arm around her shoulder. 'You giving me a hard time?' She laughed, and moved in closer.

At the marina, the little crowd had quickly thinned out to just Tom. The shop had closed quarter of an hour earlier, and the men had all made excuses about getting home for their dinner, wrapping the kiddies' presents for the morning. Tom took his last swig from the flask in his pocket and went through the empty café area to the car park to pee, Dog in tow. He noticed Alf's van parked outside the toilets and, not having made up with him yet, decided to piss on the bonnet. He was shaking himself off when he heard breaking glass and voices, a couple of lads. Over near the closed fish and chip shop, two figures were letting themselves into a car. He fumbled for his fly and staggered towards them, pulling out his fishing knife from his jacket pocket.

The boys emerged from the car with a stereo and a pile of CDs, one almost fell over Tom as he turned around. 'I'm gonna fucken kill you, you little arsehole,' Tom said, and flashed the blade in the small space he'd left between their noses. Dog took hold of the leg of the boy's pants in his teeth and gave a low growl.

'Jesus!' the boy said. He was only about fourteen, his voice high with shock. All the more reason to teach him how to behave now, Tom decided, before it's too late. 'He's got a knife, Lachie!' But his mate was gone, running for the train pulling into the station.

'Lachie don't give a shit about you, boy, and neither do I. I'm gonna chop you up and feed you to my dog here.'

'Please—let me go. I'm sorry. It was just a dare.'

'No, fuck it. I think I'm gonna kill you. My dog's hungry.'

'What you got there, Tom?' came a voice behind him. It was Alf.

'No cops about tonight, Alf. Up to the likes of us to deal with the criminals.'

'You gonna chop his fingers off?'

'I thought I'd just put bricks in his backpack and drop him in the river. I've had enough of these little shits.'

'Want to chop his fingers off first?'

'Hadn't thought of that. Why not?'

The boy began to keen. 'Please. I'm really sorry. Please let me go.'

'Put the CDs back in the car,' Alf barked at the boy, who backed away from Tom slowly, threw the CDs through the broken window and bolted after his mate, who'd already reached the footbridge.

'Wait up, Lachie,' he shouted, and ran up the stairs two at a time.

'Merry Christmas,' Tom called after him. He chuckled to himself. 'I think he pissed himself,' he said.

'Shouldn't go round pointing your knife at kids,' Alf mumbled. 'Draw attention to yourself.' But he was laughing quietly; Tom could see his big chest wobbling in the dim yellow glow of the streetlights.

'Well they shouldn't go round breaking into cars.

Come and have a beer, Alf. I haven't had so much fun in years.'

Alf shuffled for a moment. On the water, some kid belched and laughed.

'Allergic to beer now?'

'Listen, Tom. Sorry about before.'

'Ah, be quiet.'

'It was stupid.'

'Well, no one's ever threatened to award you a Nobel Prize, Alf. Come on. You can get the first one in and I'll tell you what those bloody dopey docs have been telling me.'

# Chapter 12

Jesse was awake before him. He opened his eyes and she was watching his face. 'Not some freaky-arse stalker, are you?' Danny smiled.

'Maybe I am, maybe I'm not,' she said, and pushed the covers off to get out of bed. A pretty light fell on her, the water outside reflecting from the ceiling so that moving shadows fell on her skin. She was naked, and surprisingly curvaceous and graceful. She was quite boyish clothed, for all her flirtatiousness. He hadn't seen much last night. Too pissed for a start. He grabbed her arm and pulled her back into bed.

'Come here and do some stalking then,' he said, into her neck.

\* \* \*

Danny watched the boats putter in and out of the channel from Jesse's balcony while she cooked him breakfast. The view from up here was one of the best he'd seen of the river. A bit of elevation, no trees, though he liked the dappled views from the island. You could see up to the freeway bridge, past the village in the west and way down to the last bend before the ocean to the east. It was a gift of a view on a sparkling morning.

Jesse served breakfast with a Christmas cracker, and they wore paper hats while they ate their bacon and eggs. The silly season was in full swing, and there was the odd tourist doing something daft in a dinghy. The sandbar over near the island had claimed its latest scalp; a houseboat was stranded on it, wouldn't be moving for several hours. A family was wandering about on the sand, maybe ten metres from the rocky shore of the island, poking about in the mud and gazing over at the mainland hopefully. Danny shook his head.

'You look like you're somewhere else,' Jesse smiled into the high morning sun.

'Nowhere else I'd rather be, Jess. Colour me happy.'

But he'd made an excuse when he helped her with the dishes, and left her with a kiss on the cheek and a long stroke of her bare arm with his forefinger. He sent Alf a text and let himself into the chandlery, borrowed the keys to the boat and backed her out into the river.

It was quiet now on the water as he chugged slowly up the channel past the swimming enclosure and the oyster leases. Just the stranded houseboat and a couple of tinnies between here and the island, maybe five white sails near the bend in the river that took you out to the heads. Coming out of the channel, he passed the ferry.

'Shout you a beer, Dan?' Steve called through the open window, on his last run of the holiday shift.

'No thanks, mate. Errands to run.'

He felt the pull of home and sleep, the island so close. But it was a dream of a day—the smell of the nearby sea, shining blue water, soft breeze, not too many tourists away from the village and the island—shame to waste it in bed. And he'd been waiting for a day off to do this. He raised an arm to Steve, made a sharp turn at the end of the channel and stood, opening up the engine, headed for the broad shining water beyond the railway bridge. The dory was his boat of choice, his oars stroking cleanly through the water, but he enjoyed the power and speed of the Quintrex occasionally, tearing down the river at full tilt, charging towards his destination without effort or attention.

The wind on his face woke him up as he headed towards the dark ridges, spread out in folds either side of the twisting river. He felt he could keep on going right into the centre of the land, on an endless voyage away from people and towards some welcoming source meant just for him.

Travelling upriver, he was putting water and land between himself and the past. How much was enough, though? He should end all this; go round there, get Mum. Give the old man something to chew on while he was there. But what would he do with her? He'd gone through all this before. She wouldn't come, anyway. He'd pop his dad one and she'd stay there, and get a black eye herself for her loyalty. And then the old bloke'd hunt him down and make his life a misery.

Since that night at the pub, with the bar stools flying and that reject spitting in his face, he'd indulged his little fantasies of violence, and not just towards his dad. When customers got shitty with him about the fare or if he turned up five minutes late, he saw himself smashing their arrogant heads against the hull. It didn't take much. A bloke the other day had whistled when he'd asked for fifty bucks, and Danny had glared at him, feeling his eyeballs fill with blood.

He ploughed on, the boat skimming onwards without faltering. Danny tried to imagine the land, told himself this was just a little outing, no point in getting carried away. He might not even like it, and where would he find the cash in any case? But as he sped further and further away from the ocean, he plotted and schemed. Dollars and cents; hundreds and thousands. After a while he saw nothing of the wide, shining river, the steep banks of bush tumbling down towards the water. His mind was a blur of calculations: running costs for the boat, profit margins, mortgage payments. Everything was always slowed down by the money he sent back for the girl, but that was the price of sleeping at night—he couldn't stop that now.

He limited his fantasy to a builder's cabin. He'd earned enough favours around the river to be sure of a concrete floor, timber for the frame and tin for the roof. He even knew someone with a spare dunny and septic tank.

Working the river at all hours in a big reliable boat—you ended up doing favours for all sorts, keeping secrets, saving marriages. It put him ahead. He was grateful for it; it might be what made the difference.

He saw windscreens glaring on the freeway in gaps in the dark ridges of the wooded hills, a man in a dream. He continued with his sums. Save much faster when the boat was his. No wages—he'd do it all himself, every fare, take his business up the river and get well and truly lost. Build when he got an hour or two to himself. Sustain himself with his work in all weathers and in all the river's temperaments. Take any fare that would pay. There were days it might as well be the ocean and those were the busiest. Ferry not running, people not daring to go out in small, fickle-minded boats. But who'd find him, up here? That was the main thing, starting afresh, beholden to no one. There'd be the instalments to Alf, but that was all right. He wasn't a man to hold something over you, so long as he was on your side.

He realised he was passing the town, could see the petrol bowsers, people eating fish and chips at benches outside the general store. Almost there. He followed the instructions he'd been given, took the taxi up a little creek on the right about a mile past town, kept going till he saw a jetty with an aqua pontoon. He tied up and made his way past the stand of trees at the jetty to the track beyond. Walked maybe fifty metres along the track, overgrown with gums and tea-trees, to a gate. Beyond the gate the land spread into a sloping paddock that swept up towards the wooded ridge above. He could see there was a nice level building spot towards the top of the property. Once he'd walked partway up he turned and saw the creek below, the water green and glossy, moving quietly over rocks upstream in eddies and whirls.

He carried on up the hill to the spot where he'd build, if it were his. He'd see what the view would be like from the verandah. It was turning into a warm day; the cicadas were loud as he climbed and it seemed a mob of flies had recently hatched. They clung to his damp skin as he climbed. Hot wind blew across his neck. Wouldn't let himself turn again until he reached the top.

He was soon at the plateau. The bush began about twenty metres beyond the front of it. Dense knots of eucalypt marched away into the endless hills. He turned around. Below, a surprising way down, was his boat, then the wending creek, wide and steady, off to the river around a few more bends. Couldn't see the river from here, just the ridges that surrounded it. Further upstream he could see wide patches of the creek that were almost sand. Only take the dory up there if you wanted to get out again before high tide. This was a good place, hidden from the world, and you could see visitors long before they saw you, if you built the place right.

He sat on the grass under the hot sun. Sometimes at night, slipping into dreams beneath an old grey blanket grown soft and worn, a picture came: a wooden house, a deep verandah, an orchard, a swing with a tyre hanging from a gum tree. He let the picture come now, dared himself to hope for a moment. Evening after a day's work, gardening, building sheds. Cold beer in his hand. At last a life that he had chosen, that had not been forced upon him. Could he ask if his girl could come sometimes? He used to be mates with her mum, good mates. They'd known each other since they were kids, though she was a few years younger. Then he'd ruined everything and slept with her after the pub one night. Stupid enough to assume she was on the pill without asking. Never done that again. She was a funny bugger, though; if the kid had her sense of humour, she'd be a riot. He hoped her mum still laughed. He hoped he hadn't stuffed that up, too. They had a new family now. That was all decided. It had nothing to do with him. He'd just keep paying what he owed, as long as she needed it, and that was his part in it done.

He stood quickly and began to make his way down the hill. Better not spend too long imagining before he'd heard a price. He was warm and filmed with sweat after his hike, so he slipped down into the creek from his running board, floated on his back beneath the trees, listened to the birds. Naked, cool, light. Let himself dream just a little longer. He could see himself here. It was like a place in his imagination that already existed in his life, somewhere in his past, that he'd rediscovered. If he could keep his head down, save the money, organise things right, he could do it. It's time to let yourself want something of your own, Danny boy, he told himself. Time to want something and just keep going till you get it. Bugger everything else. Christmastime next year, he decided. I'll have it all sorted out by then.

\* \* \*

The blue of the sky was deepening as Rose stepped from the bathroom wrapped in a towel, hair wet. She'd almost finished a chapter, but despite her shower she was groggy from the warm afternoon spent staring at the computer, the strange, hot barrenness of a Christmas alone, her first not in her father's house with the three of them quietly pretending to be happy. They'd followed the ritual for so long, she thought now, that they actually had been happy in the end, to be back, to be doing this thing every year that never changed no matter what else did. The girlfriends never came. No one ever talked about it. It was just a rule that didn't need to be spoken.

She sat down to work at the dining table. Her study was now the baby's room. She had it all ready. If she kept working she could just ignore Christmas until it was over. Maybe she could churn out a chapter or two tonight and take the next few days off, get some rest, buy some things for the baby in the sales. After staring at the screen for ten minutes while her blood rushed in her ears, she tried to focus on the story, such as it was. She was fed basic plot-lines, which she liked; it freed her from the burden of trying to make things credible. Still, a reality survival show that turned into an on-camera orgy? Please. She decided she'd leave it for now, see if she could get some old *Survivor* series on tape. That's it, she thought. Can't work. Must research first.

She closed down the file and looked out at the river. It was quiet out there now and black, moonless. She kept the blinds up and the lights off, the only light the glow from the laptop, so she could see out but not be seen. Good house for that, set well back from the jetty, behind the wide low branches of the jacaranda. She heard the low insect noise of a tinny. Emerging from the lights of the island was a single beam growing steadily clearer and larger. It seemed after a moment as though it was headed right for her jetty. James, she couldn't help thinking. Then the light turned south towards the other end of the strip. She shook her head. She couldn't even imagine his face; he was just a body to want, to keep her warm, to carry her baby when it grew bigger. He wasn't hers, never had been. She didn't even like him. She wondered if Billie really did.

She took the coffee pot and her mug out to the kitchen to do the dishes. Through the tiny window above the sink she could see nothing at first. Then as she plunged coffee mugs and the small plates she used for her endless snacks of toast, fruit, nuts, in the hot soapy water she could make out the scrub on the bank moving in a slight breeze. She thought about the River Baptists. She'd never seen people so blissful, except perhaps in nightclubs when their pills were coming on. It was strange to her, and she couldn't get it out of her head. She had no experience of such things. She wandered back out to the living room to check for stray plates and cups. She thought she heard a noise, had to stand still to be sure, to stop the creaking of the boards beneath her feet. There it was—a faint tapping at the other end of the house. A twig on glass? A blind next to an open window? Was it the baby's room? She didn't want to go, but it was her job now, to check noises, to secure her home, to always be ready for what was required of her. No Dad, no James. No Billie.

The crib was made up with crisp cotton sheets. Rose held her breath, glanced only briefly at it, not wanting to jinx anything by hoping too hard. In a world of sudden, random catastrophe: be safe.

The tree encroached across the verandah at this end of the house. She should cut it before it broke a window in a storm. But there was so little breeze tonight. She couldn't see far beyond the window in the dull glow of the lamp on the drawers, but she could see enough to know it was not the tree tapping the window. And now she was in here, she knew it was not in this room. She stood still, forced herself to look out the window, beyond the verandah. Nothing, the lights of the island, a houseboat, the blinking green marker.

Now it was at the other end of the house. She padded slowly along the dark corridor towards the living room. At the corner she stopped, peered around the wall at the glass sliding doors that ran all the way along the front of the room. She stood there for a full minute in the dark. Water buffeting the boat gently against the jetty. A train crossing the bridge. She waited, heart thudding, for its noise to disappear inside the tunnel. Walked softly across the room and checked the doors were locked. Though how you could protect yourself with all this glass, she didn't know.

There it was at the kitchen window. A little scratch and then two light taps. She span around sharply. Ran into the little alcove. Leaned over the bench and pressed her nose to the glass. Ferns, the rotting shed. Then two big round eyes peering from the trunk of the angophora. A possum. She breathed again, but slowly picked up the bread knife from the bench.

There was a loud rap at the door. 'Bloody hell!' she gasped and turned back to face the front of the house. She could make out Danny—scruffy blue T-shirt, hair beginning to curl in spite of his haircut—from the computer's light. She was at the door in four long strides.

'What the hell do you think you're doing?' she snapped as she slid back the door.

He stepped backwards towards the far edge of the verandah, eyes on the knife.

She looked at him for a second, her heart pounding. 'Were you tapping on the windows?'

'No. Except for just then, when I knocked. What's with the weapon?'

She stared at the knife in her hand. 'Oh God, I don't know.' She stood back to let him in. He hesitated. 'Come in. Quickly.' She locked the door behind him.

'Is there someone outside? Do you want me to have a look around?'

She put the knife on the dining table. 'I don't know. Yes. Have a look. It feels like someone's taking the piss. There's just this tapping.'

They stood silently for a moment in the dark, listening. He was carrying a boat torch, a bright yellow brick. He turned it on. 'Lock the door behind me. I'll have a quick look.'

While he was gone she closed down the computer and turned on the reading lamp beside the sofa. His torch flashed through the windows like a police helicopter as he moved around the house. It swept across the verandah, over the black water beyond the path.

She met him at the front door. 'Can't see anything. He must have gone when I came.'

'He?'

'Whoever it was. Do you want me to stick around for a while? Sit out on the deck or something?' He glanced in the direction of the shed.

'What?'

'Nothing. Just looking around.'

'It's not him.' Danny said nothing. 'Look, it's not him. I know he smokes a bit, but he's OK, really. Anyway, his boat isn't here. Couldn't speak for that one, though,' she said quietly. Her eyes flicked in the direction of Tom's place.

'Don't worry about him,' Danny said. 'He wouldn't hurt a fly.'

'Right. Sorry I shouted at you. Freaking out over nothing. You don't need to stay.'

'If you're sure.'

She nodded. 'Thanks,' she said again, and began to close the door.

'Merry Christmas,' he said, and walked slowly down her steps to the jetty, where his dory was tied. She watched him untie and row into the night, his torch resting on the passenger bench. He merged into the blackness, becoming a faint dot of light, jerking faintly with each stroke as he rowed towards the island.

Later, in bed, wide awake with coffee and adrenalin and fantasies of Tom falling off his jetty pissed, she finally got around to asking herself why Danny had come. She hadn't given him a chance to tell her what it was. She couldn't imagine. She picked up her book, a guide to natural childbirth techniques that a midwife at the hospital had recommended, read twenty pages, took in nothing, and fell asleep with it resting on her belly.

Tom saw it all, the waster from his shed hiding his boat a few jetties along, then creeping around her place with a stick, water taxi bloke waving his flashlight around like it was something else. Didn't take 'em long to come sniffing. He'd been sitting on the barge with his mug and flask. He loved a still, dark night. What was that Kane up to? Funny way to woo a bird, but what would he know?

At the bottom of the bottle, he sat with his empty mug lolling, wondering whether he could be bothered to get up to go to bed or if he'd just rest his head on Dog here and watch the stars for a while. Wouldn't be the first time he'd woken up damp at dawn on the river, but Dog had developed some shocking digestive troubles of late—too much fish, that was the trouble. Even Tom had standards.

Still, next thing he knew, a baby's sharp wail woke him. He felt a lurch in his stomach, like it was his own baby, like there was something wrong. Had he imagined the sound? Like when Molly had that year of on and off sickness, and they'd had to watch her at all hours because of the fevers. Edie couldn't do it all. Sometimes she was so exhausted with worry she slept straight through. Perhaps that was when she'd gone odd, Molly. He'd never known. Never would now.

It took him a moment to realise it wasn't his baby, that he didn't have one, that he'd fallen asleep on his barge on the river. The baby filled its lungs again and again and cried wildly for help. Where was its bloody mother? He sat up, sweating in the cool night. Beneath him ran the deep unknown waters where Molly had drowned. Had Alf been right? If he'd done something, said he'd do something even, would that have stopped her?

But what could he have done? he asked himself for the millionth time. Edie was the boss of anything to do with that child, especially when it became clear she was touched. Soon as they'd known, nothing he said counted. Edie cosseted and spoiled and lavished. And he took himself off to the pub of an evening with the boys.

He'd told Alf now, made his feelings clear on the subject. Maybe things'd be quiet again. The odd fishing trip. Bit of foraging for scrap. Keep him in whiskey money till it killed him, or the river got him. Wouldn't complain about either. Better than the other, at any rate.

'Shut that bloody child up, would you?' he bellowed at the row of houses in the dawn. There was sudden silence. A brief pause before the baby began again. 'Fuck me drunk,' he muttered. He nudged Dog forcefully with his toe and they shambled inside. He slammed the bedroom window shut and picked up a half-empty longneck from the floor beside his bed. Dog began to howl. He took a long swig from the bottle, shoved a pillow over his head and immediately began to snore.

The row home always sent the blood rushing around, filling Danny's brain with thoughts and plans. He usually used the shot of energy to propel him up the hill, mind ablaze with dreams of land or memories of a girl. As his thighs pumped him up the hill tonight, though, through the lush corridor of eucalypts, oleanders and palms, thoughts tussled in his head. It's Kane, trying to stir her up. I should have told her; that's what I was there for. Rob's right. We can deal with him. But he could feel their troubles tangling, him and this girl; he needed to get himself free— stay well clear of that fool in her shed. Maybe it was just as well he hadn't told her. If it had been Kane, she'd find out for herself what a loser he was, soon enough.

He was up the hill and on the rocky track up to his shed before he knew it. A lone gum towered above him, grey in the night, bone-white by day. He only wanted one thing, and it depended on him keeping his nose out of other people's worries. He needed goodwill, a quiet life, no trouble. The bloke wouldn't last. He'd be gone soon, and life could go on as before, without his involvement. Like his dad used to say: Don't stick your neck out, son. You'll get your head cut off.

He climbed up into his loft bed, fully clothed, watched the stars through the trees beyond the window. Let his

breathing slow. She's alone in the world. And the baby—
no dad. Another one. Maybe they didn't need fathers.
Maybe you were just good for helping to make them in the
first place, and you should just get out of the way after that,
for all the good you did. Eventually, he began to slip
beneath his life, the stars blurring, into a place where he
dreamed of rowing, endlessly on a flat ocean, hopeful
always of a glimpse of a gentle green land.

A boat passing close to her window woke Rose from a
dream. She'd written about sex of one type or another for
years, with barely a second thought once she'd submitted
it. Tonight, though, her dreams were filled with her own
subjection and humiliation at the hands of endless leering
men. She couldn't find it in her to fight, couldn't find it in
her to want to. She had woken from a dream in which
Kane stood above her, at the front of a queue of them,
saying, 'You asked for this, you hot little bitch.' She sat up
in bed. I like Kane, she thought. She felt shamed somehow,
embarrassed at having dreamed this about him, for
allowing Danny's suspicions to infiltrate her sleeping self,
and lay awake until dawn while her baby rolled and kicked
inside her.

Kane sat on the branch of a gum up on the steep incline
behind his shed. He watched Danny wave the torch
around, watched him row home, saw her lights go out.
You're awake though, aren't you. I can feel it, he thought.
His book said you had to make your own opportunities,

and here he was. The trouble with Rose, with all these girls now, was that they thought they could do everything on their own. So you had to be clever, show them they needed you without ever saying anything.

Hadn't counted on Dan the Man stepping in every time she broke a fingernail, but he'd sorted that, too. He was learning from the past, creating his own future. Last week, at the marina, he'd seen a red-nosed, watery-eyed old bloke stepping out of a Fast Freeze truck. He looked just like Danny, when you realised who he was, only kicked in the teeth by life for an extra thirty years. He knew, the second he saw him, what he should do.

The old man hadn't wanted to believe him at first, he could tell. His face had turned red; he'd grabbed the front of Kane's shirt. Then Kane showed him a picture he'd taken with his phone. It was blurry—Danny had been shooting past in his taxi—but there was no mistaking who it was, the old bloke's face told him that much. The man left without speaking, hopped up into his truck out the back of the shop and was away.

Kane swung his legs beneath the branch, listening to the rustlings from the bush, from within the house. He was making things happen. Never got any help from anyone. He didn't need it. He was changing his life all by himself.

# Chapter 13

Down at the island shop, Danny drummed his fingers on the formica counter as he waited for his mail. He didn't like coming here; the daughter of the people who owned the shop was on his list of girls best avoided. Today, though, he wanted a coffee; he'd seen Jesse the night before, and there'd been little sleep to speak of and a late row home—her dad had been due in the morning.

It was the girl's mother behind the counter today; she gave him his post—a single letter—with a glare thrown in for good measure.

'Something eating you, Joan?'

'There's no need to rap your knuckles on the counter. I was being as quick as I could.'

He stared at her for a moment. Christ, he thought.

I just want to kill everyone. 'Sorry, sorry, sorry,' he said and threw his hands in the air. She was already moving on to the next customer with a sour look on her face.

He sat at one of the tables out on the waterfront, took a sip of his coffee and studied the envelope. It was his brother's handwriting—barely legible—the postmark was Broken Hill. That was the idea. Get away, way away. He tried to imagine the orange dirt, a country town, but there was too much water around him. Inside the envelope was a flimsy Christmas card with a note scrawled in tiny handwriting. 'Someone's dropped you in it with Dad. He's got the shits bad. Giving Mum a hard time. Watch yourself. Trev.'

He read the message again a few times before crumpling the card up and throwing it in a nearby bin. He stood from the table. I'm going to kill that guy, he thought. He saw he'd left the envelope on the table and picked it up to trash that, too, but it was stiff—there was still something inside. He pulled it out: a photo of a little girl. It looked like her birthday. She was grinning from ear to ear and wearing ribbons in her hair. Her skin and hair were different shades of brown. Her eyes were blue, like his. So big now. This must be her eighth. He sat down again. He turned the photo over, though he knew what he would see. There was a word on the back: Abby.

He vaguely noticed a little crowd emerging from the boatshed, having just come off the ferry. Among them, moving slowly, was Rose. She saw him, hesitated for a moment and then began to walk towards him, holding her back with one hand, a bottle of water with the other.

'Hey,' she said, before sitting down opposite him.

He stared at her.

She was looking at the photo, still in his hand. He put it in his pocket. 'I didn't ask you what you wanted, when you came round.'

'What?'

'When you came round the other night.'

'Oh.' He paused for a moment. 'Don't worry. It doesn't matter.'

'Run out of sugar?'

He sighed. 'That bloke Kane, he's bad news.'

'I told you, it wasn't him. He's all right.'

'OK,' he said. 'I did my best. It's your life.'

She studied him for a moment, getting to her feet awkwardly. 'I know it is.' He looked out past her to the blinding sheen of the river, shook his head. She paused for a moment, seemed to think better of saying anything and extricated herself from the bench. He watched her walk away up the hill, more purposefully than she'd walked towards him but still far more slowly than anyone around her. She was huge: tall, slow, stately. He finished his coffee. He'd done it now. He could stop bothering himself.

Up the river a pleasure cruiser was taking the oldies out on a coffee cruise. He watched it pass beneath the rail bridge, and then a few minutes later the highway bridge, then the freeway bridge, bound for the settlements further inland. That bit of land up there, it had to be the answer for him. He had some savings now. If he could talk that woman who owned it down a bit, make some arrangement about paying it off, he could go, right now. Do a deal with Alf about delaying payment for the boat. He'd make it an absolute rule never to tell anyone where he lived, and that'd be the end of it. Then his dad could have the shits all he liked. He'd go over to Alf's now, see if any extra jobs needed doing. Sometimes when the taxi was quiet he'd pick up some parts or clean out his shed, up along the Gut, alongside the village. A terrible bloody job—you smelled of grease and tackle for days—but money was money. And his own place, where no one knew how to find him. He'd clean out a hundred dirty boatsheds for that.

He thought about his brother as he rowed across to Alf's. He'd heard his voice when he read the note: He's got the shits bad. Watch yourself. He was not a man of many words. They both got that from the old man. But with his dad it was belt first and ask questions later, if he remembered to get round to it when he sobered up. With Trev and Danny it had always been safer to keep quiet, just in case, and then you were in the habit of it.

Trev had been the one to go first. The last time Danny saw him he'd still been a boy himself—twenty-one, his brother twenty-two. They were both doing odd jobs for the old man, working on the rig, making deliveries of knocked-off gear from the depot: trainers, women's underwear, crappy Chinese toys. That last day, Trev had made a delivery and let the bloke talk the price down. Trev wasn't worried, Danny could see when he came back. He knew his dad would sort it out. Probably just made a mistake, pissed as usual. Danny and his dad were checking the tyres. His dad was on a run that night. It was his longest run—down to Adelaide then back up to Brisbane before he came home. Danny and Trev and his mum reined in their excitement, but there was always something in the air just before he left. The promise of relief, a quiet day or two when she'd cook the boys' favourite meals, and get the baby albums out, maybe even have her neighbour over for a Bacardi and Coke. She wasn't allowed to drink when he was around; he didn't like it in a woman. Said she got maudlin. And anyway, they couldn't afford it.

Trev appeared from around the back of the truck on his pushbike, whistling, and let the bike clatter to the drive while their dad stood from checking the front wheel and waited. Trev gave him the money and punched Danny gently on the shoulder, grinning, letting a little of his excitement leak out. The old man counted it, twice, his face turning red, little white flecks of spittle forming at the corners of his mouth. Danny's stomach sank. 'What the fuck is this?' his dad said, thrusting the wad of notes in Trev's face.

'Oh, he said it was only two hundred you'd agreed. Said you'd buggered it up.'

Oh, Trev, Danny thought. Trevor was older than him, but he had a death wish. He'd let his natural cheeriness get the better of him and it just seemed to obliterate any sense of caution. His dad had cuffed Trev's ear before there was time to know what was happening. First Danny knew about it was Trev standing there holding the side of his head, his face screwed up in pain. Then he did something

Danny had never seen him do before. He punched his dad in the face with a gristly crack, looking surprised himself for a moment, then scrambled onto his bike while his dad held his bleeding nose, and wobbled off down the driveway. Danny looked back at the house instinctively. At the kitchen window, he saw the net curtain fall back into place. That was the last Danny had seen of Trev, and it had taken him another year to bugger off himself. It was always her—couldn't bring himself to leave her behind. And they reckoned Danny was the smart one.

Now he got Christmas cards, which he read hurriedly and binned. They always mentioned his mum, how she was doing. Apparently she always asked after him. He'd told Trev to tell her, early on, that he was all right. Trev and his mum had some arrangement where he made sure she had his number if he moved and she went to a phonebox when their dad was on a run, and then Trev'd call her back at home so there was no record of it on the phone bill. Sometimes it seemed to Danny it would be less complicated for all concerned if they just killed the old bastard. He wondered what sort of a hard time he'd given his mum, when he found out he was alive. He'd know she knew— always did know that stuff. Came of believing the worst of everyone.

He liked to hear about Trev's kids, though—two small boys. He had a little fantasy going that these two kids were living a replacement childhood for him and his brother. He'd seen photos; they looked like them as boys. Freckles, wild hair, cheeky grins. Trev would bring them up right, with a good, strong woman who loved them, and these boys would have a childhood so happy and carefree it would somehow balance things; it would fill the hole in the world his and Trev's childhood had left.

Over at the marina the first person he saw was Kane, up on the boardwalk with Tom. Standing in the sunlight, laughing, he just looked like a young bloke who didn't take anything too seriously. As he walked past them, Kane looked up. 'Howdy,' he said, and nodded.

Danny stared at him. Kane had done his worst; he had nothing on him now. 'Watch your back, fella,' Danny said under his breath, and carried on up to the chandlery to find Alf.

Rose had walked a few circuits of the track that led in a figure eight around the island, her irritation slowly dissipating as she pushed herself up the hills and trudged her heavy feet along the short sandy beach. High up on the shady track she saw no one. Through the trees were yachts, the railway bridge, the pale, flat water. She thought about Kane, his hesitation, the way he seemed to lift his head above the parapet before he moved forward, like a soldier in enemy territory, or a meerkat. He'd really stirred Danny up, one way or another. Maybe it was the pot. Some people were funny about it. And how did Danny know what she'd been doing, anyway? But everybody knew everything here, except for her. What did it matter? She knew no one. No one knew her. Nothing she did made any difference to anyone else.

An angophora, its knobbled fork shaped like a rhino's head, surprised her, leading her away for a moment from her thoughts. She saw the odd-shaped tree and stood still, catching her breath. Danny had seemed agitated—about something else, not her, not necessarily Kane. Usually, he was different. There was something warm and sunlit about his skin. Something in him was attuned to women, not any particular woman, just femaleness in general. He had a tenderness towards it. It was in the way he'd spoken to her when he picked her up, drifting out to sea. It was in the way he spoke to that girl from the café, Jesse. A sort of focus. Ben was like that; her dad was, too—but with him it was about beauty. She missed Ben suddenly. She'd been so busy with herself, isolating herself from judgement, always looking inward and back. She spent her days surrounded by wide expanses of flat water, acres of gleaming space, and yet she had spent most of a year burrowing down the dark tunnels of the past. What she wouldn't give for a long boozy lunch listening to Ben crap on about the bar, imitating his dotty old mum, making her laugh.

She heard the ferry coming around the point. She looked at her watch; it was due to leave in five minutes. She hurried, as much as she was able, down the hill towards the water. When she arrived at the wharf the ferry was just about to go. Steve was unlooping the rope. He grabbed her hand and pulled her across the gap, and she panted onto the bench, fumbling with her purse, trying to catch her breath. There were no other passengers on this weekday morning, and he dropped her off at her wharf rather than leaving her at the public jetty to pick her way between the houses and sheds to get home.

She was on the verandah before she realised there was someone sitting in her chair, a man who had watched her approach. She saw with a jolt that it was James. He was like a creature from another world, another life. She said nothing while she waited for her heart to slow.

'Rose,' he said, trying not to stare at her belly.

'Well there it is,' she said. 'Pretty much ready to blow.'

He shook his head. 'Can I come in?'

'Sure,' she said. 'I'll make a cup of tea.'

'So,' he said, staring around him at the changes she had made to his parents' house, his childhood home. 'You still haven't told Billie. Planning to?'

'I don't know. I don't want to land you in it.'

'Reckon you can keep it up?'

She looked up from the bench where she was organising the tea things. 'I guess I could. But this is the sort of secret you have to keep your whole life. The baby's going to want to know who her dad is. I can't ask her to keep it secret.'

'I know, I know. Look . . .' He fiddled with change in his pocket. 'If I'm honest, I don't really understand why you kept it.'

'Her, James.'

'Her, OK, good.'

'I wanted her. It never really occurred to me not to. I mean, I asked myself the question, obviously, but you know. I'm on my own. Maybe I'll always be on my own.

Maybe I won't get another chance. And she's part of my family. I thought my family was over with my dad. But it's not. It's still going. It's her.'

'What about Billie?'

'What about her?'

'She's your family.'

She put down a mug of tea in front of him at the dining table, chewed her thumbnail. 'Well, where is she? She hasn't even called since that day you guys came over.'

'She's under the impression you can't bear her.'

Rose rubbed her eyes and sat down at the dining table. Fuck, she thought. In her head, it was a long, drawn-out syllable.

He sighed, took a seat next to her. 'This isn't why I came round, anyway.' She watched his hand approach her face. He laid it on her neck, beneath her hair. She glared at it until he removed it.

'You need the house back?' She thought about moving again, about packing boxes when she was so tired, so cumbersome.

'No. Really, stay as long as you want. Forever if you like. No one else needs it. I was only going to sell it.'

'Well, surely you'll need the money, then.'

'It's not a great time to sell. Think of it as my contribution, for as long as you need it. There's Kane's rent now as well. Just worry about it later. Honestly, I've got no plans for the place.' She looked at him. 'I'll deal with Billie. Don't worry about it.'

She nodded into her tea.

'No, I just wanted to check in. How have the neighbours been treating you?'

'You mean Tom?'

'Yeah.'

'There's always something. He's nuts. He shouted at me at the doctor's. And someone took a dump on the deck. The police said it was an animal, or kids. They wouldn't even come over. And the other night, there was tapping on the windows. I haven't done a thing to him. Why are you asking now?'

'I was just picking up Kane's rent from the PO box—I saw the doctor's receptionist over there. She told me what he said to you. There's a bit of history with my family and him. I never thought he'd bring you into it. There was an old feud. I can't believe he's still going on about it.'

'He wouldn't actually do anything, would he? I mean, anything I should worry about? I'm having a baby any second.'

'No. I don't think so. This house was empty for years, since I was a kid. Dad was back in Italy, and Mum wouldn't come back, or sell it, or anything. When I started using it he was mostly fine, just kept out of my way. But every now and then he made a nuisance of himself. Left his garbage on my wharf, hassled visitors. You know, no big deal. If he's giving you trouble, though, you might be able to get an AVO out on him.' He laid a hand on her belly, studied her face. 'I could sort it for you. I feel like you need protecting.'

'James. Please—don't touch me.' If this was his idea of a deal, she'd rather be homeless. He took his hand away.

'I don't want to get an AVO out on some old bloke who's lived here forever. I'm not Miss Popularity around here as it is. Anyway, Danny reckons no one worries about him.'

'Danny?'

'The water-taxi guy.'

'Right.' He gave her a look.

She felt a little match-flare of anger. 'What was the feud about?'

'I'd rather not say. But I can talk to him.'

'You're worried enough to come and check up on me but you won't tell me what it's about? I'm not supposed to get stressed, you know. God knows what you're doing to my blood pressure.'

'Rose, it's all right. It's family stuff. It's personal. It's about my dad, and he's dead now, so it's not really up to me to talk about it. And no one ever believed what Tom said about what happened, anyway, according to Mum.'

She felt water prickle behind her eyes. Why cry now? she thought. She ordered herself to stop.

'But I thought I'd check in on you, anyway,' he said. 'Maybe go and have a word with him, now I'm here.'

Ben had told her once that men couldn't be blamed when it came to sex. They were universally crippled with a biologically inescapable stupidity. If that was true, then what they'd done had been all her fault, because she was the only one with any brains. She caught the look on his face: sheepish, in damage control—and could he really still be hoping for some action? Or was he just checking her responses, that he could pull her strings? She should hate him. He was an arrogant, reckless boy, trying to emerge from this mess smelling of roses. But what did any of it have to do with him? Who messes around with their sister's ex? Who? Thank God her dad would never know; thank God she wouldn't have to see his face.

'I don't care what you do, James. Go and see him, if you think it'll make any difference.'

Tom, for once in his life, had set the old radio alarm clock before he'd gone to bed. Some goose was talking in his ear now, it sounded like a traffic update—out there in the world there were lane closures on the freeway, trucks spilling their loads—but then suddenly the bloke was spouting the wonders of a surf shop up the coast. Was he even awake? What was going on with the world?

He slowly came to himself and got his head a little straighter. He had a doctor's appointment at ten, and had to catch the 9.30 ferry because he'd run out of petrol on the way home from the pub. He'd got himself a tow from an oysterman but he'd been drifting around on the river for a good hour first. There was a scratchy tiredness there behind his eyes now. He shuffled into the kitchen and poured some biscuits into Dog's bowl. Dog devoured them in slavering seconds. 'Steady, Dog. Don't hurt yourself.'

Tom made himself a cup of tea and began to talk himself out of going to his appointment. If he was doomed he was doomed. Might as well get on with his life in the meantime. Who wanted to know if you had six weeks? Or two?

There was a knock at the door at the other end of the house. He thought at first he was hearing things, but there it was again. Dog, bowl empty, went very still and alert for a second, then began barking for all he was worth. A knock at the door was more excitement than he'd seen for months.

He opened the door, realising as he did so that he was stark naked. Ha, he thought. If it's that pregnant sheila, she can write me into one of her stories. But it wasn't her; it was a man. It took him a moment to realise who it was standing in the shade of the bit of iron roofing over the door, stepping back at the sight of Tom without a stitch on.

'I can come back later,' said James.

'Bugger me backwards. What the fuck are you doing here?'

'I wanted to talk to you about Rose, and the baby.'

'So it is yours, you mongrel. I see you Mancini blokes are still taking your responsibilities seriously then.'

James let out some air. Nervous, are you, young fella? thought Tom. You should be. Dog growled at his ankle.

'Dad's been dead a long time now. Rosie just wants things nice and calm so she can look after her baby.'

'What do you think I'm gonna do to it?'

'I'm sure you'd never do anything to a child. I just don't want her to have to worry.'

'Look, sunshine. I don't know what she's been telling you. I don't go round interfering with people's kids, unlike some I could mention. Now fuck off before I throw you in the river.'

James put his hands in the air, a piss-weak gesture of surrender in Tom's opinion, and scuttled off his verandah back in the direction of his old man's place. He couldn't keep up with that woman and her gentleman callers.

So, Mancini was dead. No one had told him, but then he didn't suppose anyone round here knew. Not like they'd be keeping in touch with the old crowd. Maybe he would keep his appointment. He was out in front already now, by a long way it seemed. He hoped it had been something nasty and slow and demeaning. It made Tom feel positively cheerful, for a man who was quite possibly off to hear his own death sentence.

After dressing, he came out of the house and saw Kane starting up his little fibreglass dinghy down the end of Mancini's wharf. It gave him great pleasure to stride along the jetty, in full view of the little scumbag's lounge room, and ask Kane for a lift. 'No worries,' Kane said. 'Hop in.'

'So,' Tom ventured as the small boat with its load of two men and a dog made its slow journey across the wide river. 'Not worried about the return of the old man, then?'

Kane appeared to have settled into a comfortable little post-pot haze as he steered the boat in the vague direction of the opposite shore. He stared out over the water, didn't seem to have heard. 'What?' he muttered after a moment.

'The bloke that knocked your bird up. He's back in the house. Thought you'd have seen him, way you mope around that place.'

Kane turned his watery gaze on Tom. 'I thought he was out of the picture.'

'She's certainly an enigma, that young lady of yours. That's for sure.'

'She's not like that,' Kane said, turning the handle to full throttle. The boat sputtered along marginally faster.

Dear oh dear, thought Tom. What have I started now? He reflected on what an eventful morning it had been so far. With all these promising signs, maybe the news at the doctor's wouldn't be so bad after all.

It had taken Danny the best part of the afternoon to clean out Alf's shed. It was a job Alf only seemed to remember at New Year, so it had been a while, and Alf was not an orderly man. He seemed to use the boatshed not only as a place to clean and fix boats and keep parts but, judging by the porn mags, TV and rotting sofa and blankets in one corner, as a little hovel away from home as well. There was also a bar fridge full of little surprises: the usual mouldy cheese and soft carrots, but also a layer of gristly grease along the racks inside that made Danny gag. And that was before he'd got to the horrors of the toilet.

Walking through the village along the road that ran behind the row of waterfronts—dilapidated fibros squeezed in among the shadows of three-storey glass palaces—he felt filthy and reeking. One of the single mums he'd broken his rule about single mums with was approaching, walking her toddler back from child care in a stroller. There was nowhere to go, she would see him coming a mile off. He kept as much distance between them as he could when he stopped for the inevitable chat, feeling even grubbier next to her fat, clean little boy and her own washed hair and bright, smiling teeth.

By the time he drew level with the pub he would have killed for a nice big schooner of ice-cold beer, but he couldn't go in there—even among the afternoon oystermen, drunks and junkies—smelling like this. Who knew who you might see? And anyway, he couldn't stand the stench of himself for much longer. He'd just look in at Alf's, give him back his keys and get home for a shower. Then he'd ring that woman about the land, see what he could arrange. Maybe he could work his charm, you never knew.

He reached the junction where the pub sat in the glaring afternoon sun, a hulking grey slab of concrete steadfastly refusing to pretty itself up even as the river filled with yuppies. He was just about to cross the road down towards the water when he heard shouts coming from the terrace. He turned to see one man punching another in the head, down on the street beneath the terrace where the other men were drinking. It was Kane, and a dark bloke who seemed vaguely familiar. He wasn't putting up much of a fight. He was motionless—stunned, it seemed. And then he was down and Kane was standing over him, trembling with anger. 'Don't fucken go near her again. She doesn't want you, you fucken ape!' He walked away from him, towards Danny, glaring at him as he stormed past.

Danny walked over to the man who was picking himself up from the pavement, looking dazedly after Kane's disappearing back. It was the guy who'd been with that blonde girl; the ones he'd taken to Rose's place. 'What happened, mate?' Danny asked him as he found his feet and picked his bag up off the ground.

'I have no idea. He just came from nowhere. Who the hell was that?'

'Reckon it was your tenant. He lives in Rose's shed. Complete psycho.'

'That was Kane? He was talking about Rose?'

'Say anything before he hit you?'

'He said I'd better keep my dick in my pants, or something. Lunatic.'

It was you, then, Danny thought, looking him up and down. Her sister's bloke. He couldn't help but think: everything, everything that girl touches seems to turn to shit.

'I'm about to head home. You want a lift?' Danny said.

'I could do with a beer. Then I'm going back to the city.' He shook his head. 'This place.'

'Suit yourself. Thought you might want to check in on her.'

'He wouldn't do anything to Rose.'

'Didn't worry about doing something to you.'

'No, no, I guess not. OK, thanks. I'll go and see her.' He began walking towards the marina with Danny, nursing his face. 'He's full of it, though,' he said after a few moments. 'I mean, what would Rose see in him?'

Danny shrugged. Could say the same about you, he thought. 'You'd have to ask her,' he said eventually.

# Chapter 14

Rose chopped onions and cried in her tiny kitchen. She was a completely average cook—if only there was a food pill—but she was almost enjoying this moment. Onions always gave you an excuse to have a sob. Then you washed your face and you were fine. After the preparation was done, the bolognaise simmering, the pot full of pasta boiling away, she sat down in the living room, still teary. She was due in less than a month. She'd been cleaning all morning—a frenzied scrubbing of skirting boards and windows that was compulsive and terrifying. She had stopped taking commissions, asked for an extension on the one she'd started. It made her anxious, stopping work now, with nothing to do but wait. It seemed a waste of time off, but she was so tired and in such a remote, dreamy mood for so much of the time, she couldn't apply herself. The material had begun to turn her stomach for the first time. It seemed too connected to her own body, and her own body was so full of the baby, the link made her queasy. She wanted to lie down, but she couldn't. She'd fall asleep, she knew, and there was the food on the stove. Be just her luck if she burned James's house down.

The phone rang, and she pulled herself to her feet, made her way over to the table to answer it. 'Hello, stranger.' She felt her heart pound, as though she'd had to run to reach the phone. It was Ben. She couldn't speak. 'You there, Rose?'

'I'm here,' she said quietly, after a moment.

'It's been a while, Rosie.'

'I know.'

'I ran into Billie on Pitt Street. She told me your news.'

'OK.'

'Congratulations, right?'

'Thanks.'

'Come on, Rosie. Talk to me. How are you doing?'

'I don't know, Ben. OK, I suppose. The baby's nearly due.'

'Why didn't you tell me?'

'I knew you wouldn't approve.'

'What's there to approve? I bet you haven't been in touch with anyone, have you?'

'Not really.'

'Oh, Rosie. You've been all alone in that house. You must have been going batshit.'

'Well—' she laughed.

'You haven't told Billie—about James. Have you?'

'No,' she sighed.

'Look, here's what I think. I think you have to. I'll come with you.'

'It'll split her and James up.'

'Well, like you said, he is a tosser. And you can't keep this up once the baby's born. Please Rosie, just tell her yourself, before she finds out some other way. I'll be there.'

'She'll never forgive me. It's unforgivable. I honestly never meant to hurt her. But how's she going to believe that? I wouldn't.' Don't cry, Rose told herself. Grow up. Face it.

'I think—I think you underestimate her. I know it's a pain in the arse. Her looks, the attention she gets. But who cares, Rosie? You're a beautiful girl, for all it matters. I don't know why you don't know that. Didn't anyone ever tell you?'

She was quiet for a moment. 'You haven't seen me since I put on fifteen kilos.'

'Oh Rose.'

'I've got food on the stove, Ben.'

'OK. Please, just ring me, will you? This is stupid.'

'All right. I will.'

She went into the kitchen. The pasta was boiling over. She took it off the stove and stared at it for a moment. She tried to grab hold of something, some solid case against Billie, an example of her vanity, her selfishness that she could hold up, say, look, Ben. This is how it was. All she could find was her own fear of her sister's beauty, not just her: the girlfriends, photos of her mother—all of them, anyone who bewitched her father, if only briefly, if only from a distance.

She left the food and went back out to the sofa, lay down, watched the water glinting through the verandah posts. As soon as she allowed her body to relax in the cool dark room, with its old mismatched furniture from another life, she lost all control; the past was there with her, a presence in the room. But her memories were not complete. They talked about pregnancy vagueness—maybe it was that—but she couldn't follow the stories through anymore. She tried again to tap her store of childhood slights, Billie's petty crimes of adolescence, her dad's benign acquiescence. The memories she'd kept at hand, taken out, refreshed, kept new, were slipping from her now. Part of her panicked; once she'd forgotten all that, her dad would be gone, forever, no retrieving him. But the details were being replaced by a feeling, a warmth, a smell, and in spite of her, Billie was part of it.

She laid a hand on her belly and let herself imagine, for the first time, how Billie would feel when she knew the truth, and she was filled with shame, not as an emotion or a thought, but as a physical sensation. Her skin was suddenly hot, her cheeks raging. The muscles in her legs ached, and she curled them up beneath her.

She woke like that sometime later and went out onto the deck for some air. There she watched the last of the light sink behind the island, its pinnacle glowing red—the sandstone flaming beneath the bush, then almost black. She saw a boat, small in the distance, bypass the island and head towards her. It grew larger without changing its course. Soon she recognised it as Danny's water taxi, two men at the helm. In another couple of minutes Danny and James were climbing the ladder onto her wharf. But as they grew closer she saw there was something wrong with James. He wouldn't look up as he walked towards her, and he moved stiffly. Something about his approaching shape seemed ashamed.

Danny let him reach the verandah first. In the last light on the stairs she saw that he'd been beaten. His cheek was swollen and there was blood drying around his nose. His usually immaculately groomed hair was dishevelled. She looked at Danny; he shrugged and looked away.

She moved towards James. 'What the hell happened?'

'Rose, I think you should get out of here,' he said, finally looking at her.

'Why? What's going on?'

'That guy that's renting the shed. Did you—what did you do? You're not—together . . .'

The baby kicked her, hard. It felt as though her heart and stomach were being pushed up into her throat. 'What's that got to do with you?' Her voice was weak.

'He just went me at the pub. I didn't even know who he was. He seemed to think I was a threat to him—and you.'

'Look. One thing happened. That was it.' Somewhere on her skin, she thought, in her hair perhaps, some secret place not touched by the river or her showers, you could probably find some part of him still on her, some scraping of DNA to prove what they'd done. She studied his face. 'You're a mess,' she said quietly.

He dropped his bags on the timber boards. 'In the morning, I'm going to arrange for someone at work to write him an eviction notice. Maybe you should come to Billie's place tonight.'

She stepped back. Danny had edged down the stairs and back onto the jetty. He was watching the hills across the river turn black. 'I'm not going anywhere. I'm about to have a baby. I've just got this place clean. I mean, really clean!' She felt close to tears again, but she couldn't cry, not in front of him, not in front of Danny.

'Rose, he's a complete wacko. He's got the idea you two are an item.'

'Well, I'll sort that out. But I'm not moving. Ask him to leave or something. I'll do it if you don't want to.'

'How about we just follow the legal channels? Please, keep out of his way if you're not going to leave. I'm going to go with the water taxi now.'

'You're what?'

'Look, me being around is just going to antagonise him. I'm going to steer clear.'

She shook her head and picked up his bag. She pushed past James to hand it to Danny. 'Your fare's ready.'

He turned to look at her. 'I'll come back, when I've taken him over,' he said quietly.

The space around her felt close and distorted. 'You don't have to do that. I can make things clear with Kane. I'm sure it can be sorted out. He's just a bit—intense.'

'I'll come back,' he said again, and walked down the jetty with the bag towards his boat and the darkening water. James paused for a moment, before hobbling after him.

She didn't stay outside to watch them go. James, she thought. You bring disaster in your wake. I wish I'd never met you. She placed a hand on her belly. Then she drained and ate her cold, overcooked pasta, even though she wasn't hungry, and went back for seconds. She sat in the darkening room, waiting. Her mobile rang. 'What now?' she said to the dark room and shuffled over to where it glowed and vibrated on the coffee table. Billie's name flashed on the screen. 'Hi,' she said, her stomach turning over. 'How are you?'

'Me? James just called. What's happening? Get out of there.'

'It's OK, Billie,' but she felt a little of her sister's panic seeping through the phone, across her skin. 'He's just a bit of a pothead, Bill. I'll ask him to leave in the morning.'

'And you think he'll just go, do you?'

'Why not? When it's clear he's crossed the line?'

'Rosie! Why didn't you let James stay?'

'He doesn't need to.'

'Did he sort out the washing machine?'

What? she thought. 'Oh, it's fine now,' she said after a moment.

'Listen, I'll call James right now and tell him to get back there if you want me to.'

'Danny's coming back in a minute, don't worry.'

'Who?'

'The water-taxi guy. He brought you across last time.'

'Oh—cute! No wonder you packed James off.'

'Don't, Billie.'

'OK, Rosie. All right. Listen, you be careful. And we'll come and visit soon, I promise. I'm sorry I haven't been back. Work's been a nightmare.'

'OK. Thanks, Billie,' she made herself say. 'Danny's here. I've got to go.' She ended the call and turned off her phone.

When she reached the door, Danny was shifting quietly from one foot to another, a bottle in a paper bag in one hand. 'Hey,' he said. 'I don't know if you're allowed to drink, and I don't know what you drink, but anyway . . .'

He handed it to her. She looked inside the bag— champagne. 'Thanks. What are we celebrating?'

'Oh, nothing. Sorry. I don't know what you drink.'

'It's OK. A glass of champagne would be really nice. Come in.' She turned on a lamp by the sofa and he sat down.

When she returned with glasses he said, 'It might be easier to lay low tonight. To stay somewhere else.'

'Where am I going to go?' she shrugged, and began to open the bottle. 'Did you see the fight?'

He nodded. 'Wouldn't call it a fight so much, though.'

'What do you mean?'

'Well, Kane was all over him. Moved so fast there wasn't much room for fighting back.'

'Oh God.'

'Listen, Rose,' he said, gulping his drink like he was downing a beer with the boys. 'The yacht, just off your jetty out there, it belongs to some friends. They wouldn't mind if you stayed there for a night or two.' She wondered where Kane was. He could be below the kitchen window, or outside one of the bedrooms, listening.

'I know he's being a bit nuts, but I'll talk to him. There's been a misunderstanding. He doesn't worry me,' she insisted.

'He worries me, mate.'

'Why?'

'Didn't you see what he did to your boyfriend out there?'

Blood and champagne bubbles rushed to her head. 'He's not my boyfriend. He never was, really.'

Danny was silent. He drained his glass with his second gulp. The glow of the table lamp illuminated one side of his face. It seemed older than it was. Deep creases from a life on the water fanned from the corners of his eyes. His brow was furrowed, careworn. He had said that she seemed sad, whenever he saw her. Perhaps he just knew how to recognise it.

'Why does he bother you so much?' she asked quietly.

'He's just trouble. There's no missing it. Maybe it's the drugs. Maybe he had a bloody awful childhood. I don't care. He's just bad news.'

'Has he done something to you?'

He studied her for a moment.

'What?' she said.

'Yes, he's done something to me.'

'Well, what?'

He paused for another moment. 'When I came here, no one knew who I was. Except Rob. That's my mate with the yacht. Rob used to work with my old man. We were on a fishing trip, me and my dad, and I went overboard. The papers reported me missing, and when I didn't turn up, my dad decided I was dead.' She waited for him to go on. He seemed relaxed, leaning back in his chair, but his forefingers were pressed so firmly against his glass they had turned white. 'Anyway, until now, Rob, and his wife Maggie, they've been the only ones who knew that was me. Now Kane knows, and I'm pretty sure he's found my old man and told him.'

So, it had been true, what Kane had told her. 'How did he manage that?' She didn't ask why he didn't want to be found. That he didn't seemed enough of an admission.

'He's a cunning little toe rag. Look, don't worry about that. I don't think you're safe. I've got a feeling.'

'It really seems like there's been a big misunderstanding. I honestly can't believe he'd do anything to me.'

'But Rose,' he said, exasperated. 'Who's looking out for you? That joke I just put on the train?'

She laughed without humour. 'Well,' she said, pouring some more champagne, unable to hold his gaze. 'I'm a big girl. I've always looked out for myself.'

'You don't have eyes in the back of your head. Sleep on the yacht tonight while his dander's up.'

'I've never slept on a yacht before. Might be fun, I suppose. But I'm still going to talk to him, tomorrow. This is stupid.'

'It's the best place to sleep. You can hear the water. No one can sneak up on you without you hearing them first. It's a peaceful night. You can keep an eye on your place, too, from there.'

'So that's how everyone knows what I'm doing every minute of the day.'

'No,' he said. 'It's not. Well, I saw him leave. But he told Tom, I'd say. And Tom's not known for his discretion.'

'And he doesn't like me for some reason.'

'It's not you.'

'That's what James said. What the hell is it, then?'

'There's history between him and the Mancinis, that's all. But for the most part, he's just a pissed old fart. Really, no one worries about him.'

'It's like a secret club on this river. You know what Tom said to me? He said I should drown my baby! And I'm supposed to be satisfied that it's not me he hates. Well, he worries me more than Kane. He's insane.'

'Look, I'll tell you when I've got you over to the boat. Everyone else knows anyway. Mostly he's just drunk and mad. Harmless.'

'OK, done.'

'Get your stuff now, before Kane pops up. I'm surprised he hasn't already.'

'I won't be a tick. Thanks, Danny.' He smiled, and for a moment she felt happy in a simple way: still and oddly calm, despite the eddies of disquiet whirling up around her.

* * *

It didn't take her long to pack, but when she came back into the room Danny was asleep on the sofa, his empty glass on the rug. She turned off the lamp above his head and sat in the chair next to him. She heard a big boat on the water, maybe Tom's barge, someone swearing with frustration, dropping something, drunk perhaps. There was the train on the bridge, then its roar was muffled by the tunnel. She could see Danny's outline in the shadowy room, a dark man-shape asleep in the chair, legs apart, head back, arms flopping over the sides. His bare feet were a few inches from her hand, hanging over the side of the sofa. If she touched him, would he stir?

She closed her eyes. She knew she should wake him so he could get home to his own bed. But the bulk of him lying there was peaceful, comforting. She wanted to stop things for a moment with him there, before life hurried on in its usual lonely vein. For a few seconds she would do nothing and not force herself to make any decisions, large or small.

But then, moments later it seemed, she was woken by a weight falling against the sliding glass door. She opened her eyes instantly. There was a weak light in the room—morning—and she saw a dark figure at the glass, a man etched against the pale dawn sky. He was leaning on the door, hands over his eyes, peering into the room. It was Kane. He was smiling—but his smile looked off balance, excited.

She glanced quickly at Danny. He was still asleep. Kane planted a palm heavily on the glass and Danny blinked, sitting up quickly. She found herself struggling to her feet from the long low sofa, supporting herself on the coffee table with one hand, smoothing her wild hair with the other. She approached the figure leaning full-weight against the other side of the glass. 'What is it, Kane? Do you need something?'

He ignored her, and smacked the glass again, eyes never leaving Danny, who was now on his feet and walking away from them towards the front door. Out on the verandah, he doubled back towards Kane, who pushed himself back off the glass to face Danny.

'Problem, mate?' Danny asked quietly.

Kane's shoulders were clenched, stringy beneath his singlet. He was hunched, ready for something. 'Yeah, there's a problem. Me and Rose have got an understanding. Looks like she hasn't explained that to you.' He was still smiling. Rose felt a wired alertness surge through her body.

'She wants you to leave,' Danny said quietly. 'You should take your stuff and go today.'

Kane moved quickly, so quickly Rose couldn't be certain she'd seen what she had seen. Could Kane really have slapped him? All she could be sure of was that Danny was holding his hand to his cheek, a look of still violence on his face, in his tensed body. The look was shocking to see in a gentle man. Kane stepped closer to Danny and jabbed towards Rose with his finger. 'I'm not going anywhere. Rose?' He was smiling at her. 'I'll talk to you later, Rose, all right?'

She stared at him, nodded. Oh, God, she thought. I should have talked to him before now. She could still make it OK; she just needed Danny to go. Her skin was hot and she was suddenly thirsty. She stepped towards the verandah. Kane put his face close to Danny's. 'This is your only warning.' He banged down the stairs and disappeared around the side of the house.

She began walking towards the open front door, but then Danny, too, was leaving, walking quickly away from her along the jetty, the usual grace of his movements marred by a stiff-limbed anger. Without a glance backwards he was down the ladder, untying his dory, and rowing across the channel towards the island. Though he faced her, not once did he look up at her house until he was a long way off, too far away for her to see his expression. When he was most of the way across he rested his oars and gazed at her house for several seconds, right at where she stood behind the glass, before finishing his row home.

# Chapter 15

Rose sat on the deck of the yacht in the moonless night, watching her house. A woman called Maggie had arrived in the morning, not long after Danny had left. She was a practical-looking woman wearing gumboots, a navy blue fishing sweater and jeans, and holding a flask and a greasy brown paper bag. 'Bacon sandwich?' she offered, holding it aloft. She appeared to be in her early forties; wavy, dyed red hair, lived-in skin, friendly, handsome face. Rose recognised her from the ferry. She always got off at the island with some constantly rotating combination of her brood of kids. 'I'm Maggie—Danny's friend. Rob's wife. That's our yacht out there. Danny said you needed a place to stay for a few nights.'

Before she took her over to the yacht on her dinghy,

Maggie crept behind Rose's house to the back of the boatshed where there was a small, high window. Rose leaned out the kitchen window, heart hammering, while Maggie climbed up on a milk crate and peered inside. She came back, shaking her head, wrinkling her nose, presumably at the state in which he kept the shed. 'Asleep,' she whispered.

On the curved shelf of Rose's belly lay her mobile. Danny's number was on the display. Maggie had made sure it was in there before she left, as well as her own, and Rob's, and the fire chief's in case she went into labour and needed the fire barge to come across from the island. If she pressed the green button it would dial Danny now. 'I don't think he'd want me to call him,' she'd said to Maggie. 'I think I'm bad luck for him.'

'Don't be daft,' Maggie said. 'He was just angry this morning. Not every day you wake up to a slap.'

'I'm sorry about all this,' Rose said. She glanced through the porthole over to her place and the boatshed. All was quiet.

'No worries. Come up on the deck, but sit down. We'll try not to advertise the fact you're here, I think. I can move the yacht, if you want, while I'm here.'

'No, that's OK. But I think I should go over there, and sort things out with him. This is going to make it worse.'

'Gone a bit far for that. He's taking a swing at anything that moves. We'll get some of the fellas to have a quiet word with your mate over there. Sort it all out for you.'

'I should have explained things to him. It's my own fault. Stupid.'

'We all make mistakes, kid. Doesn't give him the right to go round punching people. The boys'll sort it. The last place he should be is next door to a woman with a baby on the way.'

Rose felt close to tears, suddenly, at this description of herself. It made her sound like someone honoured and precious, a member of the village that everyone had known since she was born. She couldn't trust herself anymore. Her hormones seemed to betray her every five minutes. She nodded, waiting for the feeling to pass. Maggie poured her a coffee and handed her the sandwich.

'It's OK, mate. I remember what it felt like, with my first. You want the whole world to be safe around you. You want to control everything. We'll keep an eye on you, love. Don't worry.'

Rose turned away and blinked. There he was. She gestured silently towards her jetty with her head. Maggie followed her gaze and nodded. He was leaning on her door again, no knocking this time, just peering inside for several seconds. He stayed there for perhaps a minute, then hopped over the balcony and onto Tom's property, disappearing around the back of the little fibro house. Rose stared at Maggie. She wanted to put a hand on this woman's arm and tell her: what had happened to her dad, what she'd done, why she was alone. After a few minutes, he was out at the wall, untying his boat. He passed close by the yacht and she stared into her lap, making herself and the boat small, insignificant.

When she eventually looked up again, she saw a dark

blur among the junk in Tom's yard—Dog, chasing his tail. 'Why does Tom hate me?' she asked, after a moment. 'Danny was going to tell me. Then he came,' she nodded towards the boatshed.

Maggie had grown up on the river, knew James, knew his father. Had heard all the stories that ran between the people here. Knew which parts of them were true, and what had been added over the years as the stories were passed on.

She told her—about Tom's daughter, never right in the head, always in trouble with the boys once she was a young woman. About how she staggered into the pub one night and something had happened to her. No one knew where the rumour started that it was Mancini—no one even knew if Molly had said it herself. Tom had never been keen on him, and he seemed to believe it all right. But after they'd chased the Mancinis off, Molly drowned herself. It was recorded as an accident because Tom's wife had been Catholic, but no one believed that. Now Tom blamed Mancini for her death as well as the other thing. Then Tom's wife went, too. A bit later, a bloke from up at the ridge was put away for attacking young girls. He never gave any details, so no one knew for sure, but it made people wonder, and Tom just went on his fishing trips, picked up his scrap, drank a little, stayed quiet. But the last few years he'd been hitting it harder, and then when James came back he started going a bit loopy every now and then. Still, everyone knew what he'd been through. No one worried about what he did. It was just old Tom. He was one of those old fellas that was just part of the river, like the smell at low tide or the days when the septic tanks were on the nose. No point complaining about it.

Rose slept all afternoon, a fitful sleep in which she threw off the covers, found them again, needed to be wrapped up, hidden, but then felt suffocated and anxious. She woke at sunset and sat facing the shore, trying to let the strange currents within her settle. She could see Tom now, his podgy, bent old shape etched in the light of the rooms of his house, feeding his dog, fetching beers. Then he came out on his jetty, eased himself into his low fishing chair, raised his bottle to his lips. Sad, sad old man, she thought. She watched him for a moment while her hand rubbed her belly in wide circles. From the corner of her eye she saw, or felt, something move at her place. He was at the door again, Kane. She could just make out his boat at the jetty. He must have rowed it, or paddled quietly, drifted to her door, right by her. So it wasn't true what Danny said, that you'd hear anyone coming. He'd been within a few metres of her, who knew how many times, and she'd had no idea. In the light spilling from Tom's place she saw him press his head against the sliding glass door, looking into the dark room. His body moved and there was a sharp rap on the glass. Tom's head turned to see what was happening. When there was no answer Kane knocked louder, with the side of his fist it sounded like. 'Rose,' he shouted. Then more softly: 'Rosie, mate. Come on. We need to talk.'

Was he as mad as everyone was making out? The idea, the possibility of violence and pain, was suddenly in her world, where it never had been before, or at least not before the death of her father. It was as though, once it had arrived, you passed through a membrane into another world—one that looked the same but where ordinary objects vibrated with threat—and couldn't return.

She dropped out of her chair and onto her knees, edged forward to the balustrade to get a better look, her mobile gripped tightly in one hand. Her belly stopped her getting right up to the edge, but she was close enough to hold onto the rail and peer through the gap between it and the fibreglass hull. He banged on the glass again, flat-palmed, then made his way unsteadily down the small flight of stairs off the balcony. 'Come on, Rosie,' he said quietly, and disappeared inside the boatshed. She felt a pull towards him, towards the gentleness she'd seen in him. Her father had taught her—for all the good it had done her—about the power of words, and courtesy, and directness. She had been brought up to apologise to other children, to behave graciously, to set an example. She would go over there, and talk to him face to face, and stop creeping around behind other people. Perhaps, though, it was a job for morning. Daylight would make everything normal. She'd take him breakfast, and she'd sort this thing out, once and for all. She'd treated him like one of those city boys; made an assumption about what he wanted. She would clear it all up tomorrow. For now, though, she would keep things quiet and go to sleep without further upset to anyone.

She crept over to the stairs on her knees, slipped her legs out from under her and climbed down into the dark galley. She didn't turn on the lights or use her torch. Fully clothed, she inched her way under the covers on the bed. The pillow smelled of Danny—soap, beer, cigarette smoke from the pub, laundry detergent. Her breathing seemed loud to her; she deliberately let it slow. Much later, as the light began to creep through the porthole, she closed her eyes, thinking not about Kane, nor her father, nor even James, but about Billie, sitting at the other end of a kayak from her, on the bay, at the age of eleven, laughing. She couldn't remember why Billie had been laughing but she remembered what she'd said. 'Oh my God, I'm going to wet myself, Rosie.' Suddenly she'd jumped over the side, disappearing beneath the dark blue swell. When she emerged, her hair plastered to her head like a water rat, she was still laughing, snorting water from her nose. 'You did it, didn't you,' laughed Rose. Billie nodded and grabbed hold of the side of the kayak. She rested her blonde head on the side of the boat, smiling, bleached in the sun.

Rose carried the image into sleep. She'd loved her so much when she was younger, she'd wanted to be her. She remembered the feeling now, of adoring her sister, her hair, her skin; let it flood through her and take her down.

Kane sat in his tree and watched her house. It was dark now and she hadn't turned the lights on. He'd looked in every window but still he had this feeling she was there. She was close; he felt as though he could smell her in the warm night air above the smell of the salty river and Tom's flowering frangipani.

He had his fishing knife out, and without realising he was doing it he carved slim strips of bark from the tree trunk next to him and laid them out carefully in a row on his branch. When he put his hand down and felt them there, hanging over the branch like skins, he didn't remember making them. But the action had calmed him, like cleaning a fish. Brought order to his thoughts after the blindness he'd felt all day.

'Bugger it, Rosie,' he murmured into the leaves. It wasn't like he'd given her a reason to worry, to bring him into line. She'd had him from the day he'd set foot on her wharf. He hadn't pushed her, he'd been a mate, giving her lifts, checking she was all right, taking care of her. Not like Flash Dan and even flasher dick with the blonde. How many did those blokes need? He'd just asked for one. Hadn't ever pushed her. She'd asked him, when it came down to it.

She'd see, when she had the baby. She'd see how much use those others were then. And he'd be there. He'd do anything she needed him to do. His mum, last time she'd seen him, she'd known. 'There's something different about you,' she said. 'Something's happened to you, I can see it.'

He slithered down the tree, touched the wall of her house, the weatherboard slats still warm from the day's sun, and slipped inside his shed where he could sleep, dream of her, of the night she lay right next to him, sleeping against his body until the sun woke them. He knew she hadn't forgotten. It was the others, getting between them, putting ideas in her head about him. If he could get through the bloody bodyguard and talk to her, she could be here again. I am the one who decides my future, he whispered. He would have her again: her heat, her skin, right here beneath his hand.

# Chapter 16

Tom sat in the cool sliver of shadow between the house and the shed, surrounded by the detritus of a quarter of a century of not giving a shit about personal and domestic cleanliness, facing a hangover of proportions that even for him were discouraging. On his lap lay a gleaming glass bottle, a bright new yellow duster and a bottle of metho. Alf had made him promise not to think about fires anymore. The police had been through town after the last ones. Alf had connections, heard things. There was a whisper they suspected there was a local arsonist. There'd been patterns over the years that they'd started to notice. He didn't want Tom put away, especially now he knew he was ill. Done time himself when he was younger. It'd kill old Tom. If the locals found out it'd be worse. You'd get skinned alive around here if they had you down for a firebug—if it was even a rumour on someone's lips. And they'd sorted out this thing about Molly. Alf said now he had his doubts about Mancini—everyone had since that bloke had been put away. It was just Mancini turning up again, stirring the pot, and now another one of them in the same house. Alf said he'd been nasty with booze that night—stewing. He knew how that was. But they'd been off their heads on tequila down in Alf's boatshed and high on having freshly patched up their quarrel—nothing they said counted. And it didn't make sense what Alf said about Mancini. Everyone knew it was him. That bloke they arrested never admitted anything. He had nothing to do with it. And Tom had believed it for so long now; he'd let Edie go, believing it. It had to be true.

Now it looked like he was going out early. They'd been vague at the doc's—the way they are. Maybe a year, if he looked after himself. They offered him chemo, but he couldn't do that alone. He'd helped Edie through it, and he often wondered whether he'd done the right thing. Not much point in the operation, they'd said; he'd left it too late. No use in putting himself through it. You'd think they could let him anyway, just something to give him hope. People got up and walked all the time, didn't they, when they'd been written off by the medical profession? Who knew what hope could do, if they left him with a scrap? But those people that got up and walked, they were burning with something—either God, or love, or some fuck-you sense of destiny. The only thing that burned in

Tom was a nagging bitterness and a love of whiskey, and a decent fire, of course.

He didn't have it in him to decide today. He'd just make sure everything was ready, that it was all where he needed it, just in case. He knew Alf would come and find Dog; that was one less thing to worry about. Tom closed his eyes, breathed in the cool moss growing on the pile of wood next to his feet, swore silently at the pain that was expanding inside his head and dozed off.

He woke to the sound of Dog barking, and a woman saying, 'Bloody hell! OK, easy there!' His eyes opened a crack. It was the pregnant one—that bush of straw hair, her face red—holding a hand out between her belly and Dog, other hand clutching the wall, ready to duck behind it.

'C'm 'ere, Dog,' Tom growled. She was sweating, flustered. 'Just a dog, mate. Won't hurt ya.'

'No, that's OK. It is his house. I didn't mean to sneak up on you.' She stared at his lap for a moment. He looked down. Still had his gear sitting there, fallen asleep with everything left out. That'd be choice, if the dopey bird sent the police round to make his last weeks a complete pain in the arse. She looked behind her, and then back at him. 'Have you seen Kane today?' she said quietly.

'Not his keeper, love. Thought you two were thick as thieves.'

'Thanks anyway. See you.'

And she was gone. Tom took the empty bottle and rag from his lap, put them back in his locker and went inside to fetch a glass of water. He had a raging thirst, and a pain in his gut that had come from nowhere.

Rose moved through the shadows into the dank space between her house and Tom's. She could see the rear end of Kane's boatshed beyond her place, the small, high window Maggie had used to check whether he was there. The milk crate she'd stood on was still by her back door. Before she could talk herself out of it, she'd scooped it up and was placing it amid the long scratchy grass next to the shed. There was a metre gap between the shed and the house through which she could see a slice of the river and the island but not much else. She listened for a moment before stepping onto the crate and edging her eyes slowly above the bottom frame of the window. It took a moment to adjust to the gloom, but the curtains across the front sliding doors were a few centimetres too short and enough light spilled inside to see that he wasn't there, and that the place was in its usual chaotic state. She leaned her head against the glass for a second, exhausted. On the unmade bed, she noticed, were a couple of books. As her eyes grew accustomed to the dark she could make out the cover images, then the titles, but she already recognised them. They were the ones she had written.

She stepped down quickly from the crate. Too quickly; she almost fell, landing hard on her ankle. Stumbling along the back of the house she threw herself inside the back door and locked it. Safely inside, she let her breathing slow, trying to listen for other sounds above her own.

There were too many other noises: she heard a tinny on the river, a bird calling, a train emerging from the tunnel and rushing across the bridge. Even in the moments between those sounds there was the constant rhythmic whoosh of her blood, like the river against the seawall, a noise that had come with later pregnancy and was always there. She made herself move around the house to check all the rooms. Once she had covered every corner, she sat down on the bed and forced herself to think about what to pack.

Danny boarded the ferry, repelling conversation with the set of his shoulders, a fixed stare out the window, at nothing. 'How's it going, Dan?' the young deckhand grinned at him. Danny handed him his fare, gave him the shadow of a nod and looked away.

The boy—it was Steve's boy, with the same wild red hair—took his money with a shrug and moved on to the next person. Danny studied his grimy fingernails, giving them a bit of a clean with a toothpick. This Kane thing, he knew in his gut it was going to turn into a bloody awful mess before it got sorted out. He should have told her exactly what Jesse had told him. Maybe he could have saved her all this trouble. Rob was all for getting up a posse and teaching him a lesson. Seemed to relish the prospect. 'I don't need a bloody lynch mob to sort out my problems for me,' Danny had said, and Rob had shut up. But he knew what he should do. He should cut this thing off at the source; go and see the old man. End this.

And there was Alf, being difficult. He'd struggled to

keep his temper, surprised himself with the rush of heat he'd felt when Alf had told him he wanted to hold off the sale for another season. Alf's partner had some tax problem; couldn't sell his half of the chandlery right away, couldn't be flush with cash until he'd sorted out this stoush with the ATO. Danny had built a persona—his whole life—out of rolling with the punches, but he'd had to walk out of the shop, walk off his shift for the first time in his life, so as not to say something that would stuff things once and for all. Then someone had pinched his oars and he'd had to wait the best part of an hour for the next ferry because his spares were at the shed.

He heard the engines shift, their rumble intensify under his feet, and they were away. Thank Christ. He needed to go bush for a couple of hours, get himself up to the high platform of rock in the reserve behind his house and watch the river from a good way up until things had straightened themselves out in his head. Looked like it might rain, but that wouldn't kill him. Help clear out the cobwebs, if anything.

Then Steve's boy was laughing and shouting out the window of his cabin: 'We're not coming back for you, you dag!' But the boat was reversing, and the lad was standing at the door, holding his hand out to help the latecomer jump on. He heard her voice before he saw her and something flipped in his stomach. 'Thanks, Bill. Train was late.' Then, 'Hey, stranger!' and she was on her way over to him.

He forced a smile onto his face, tried to keep the flatness out of his voice. 'Hey, Jess. How's it going?'

She had that gleam to her lips and eyes. His stomach sank. It had been several days. She'd sent him a few texts, which he'd ignored. That was the trouble with being the water-taxi driver, your mobile number was printed on posters and cards all over the river.

'What you been up to?' he asked. She was sitting so close that her leg vibrated against his as the engines opened up again and they pulled off for a second time.

'This and that. Breaking hearts, mostly,' she laughed.

He nodded.

'It was a joke, cowboy.'

He nodded again. 'Listen, Jess.'

'What am I doing tonight?'

'Listen, you're an awesome girl. I've had a great time with you.'

Something in her face closed. The gleam in her eye dulled in an instant. She sighed, a deep breath that lifted and released her shoulders. There was an impatient little shake of her head.

'I'm not looking for—'

'Right, right, right,' she cut in. 'Spare me the details. Man, who do you think you are?'

'I don't think I'm anyone,' he said quietly. There were only a few people on the ferry at this hour—a mother with a stroller, the elderly lady who ran the island bowling club—and they weren't doing a very good job of pretending not to listen. 'I never meant to hurt your feelings.'

'Too late, Danny boy. Jeez, you sure took me for an idiot, didn't you?'

'It was just a night or two, Jess.'

'Whatever. See you round.' And she made a production out of gathering up her things—a plastic bag, her handbag and a brown paper bag that clinked—and shuffling the four or five steps to the back of the ferry, where she sat down sharply on one of the plastic seats and stared out the opposite window. There was a good ten minutes to go until they got to the island. He put his feet up on the bench opposite, stretched out his legs, leaned his head against the cool window and closed his eyes. Could this morning get any better?

He opened his eyes a crack as the ferry made its sweeping U-turn for the island wharf. She was sitting with her arms crossed, still staring blindly out the window, not making a move for her bags. Didn't look like she was going anywhere. At least he wouldn't have to walk up the hill pretending she wasn't walking right behind him, or in front.

There was only one pair of legs coming down the stairs at the wharf. The boy didn't even bother tying up for Danny to jump off. He realised only as he passed the new passenger that it was Kane, smelling of tobacco smoke, pot and petrol. His front foot hit the stairs and they were away. He watched the old wooden ferry for a moment as it made for the sandstone cliffs. Kane was standing in the doorway, growing smaller, watching him. 'Damn,' Danny muttered. He wondered where Rose was. He tried Maggie's mobile and got her on the third ring. 'Hey, did you put Rose on the boat?'

'Yeah. I settled her in. Left her the dinghy so she could go and get some more stuff. She seemed OK.'

'So you reckon she's over there now?'

'I guess. I haven't spoken to her today.'

'Do you have time to go and check on her? Kane just got on the ferry at the island. He's going over there now.'

'I'm on the freeway, Dan. Call me if you can't get hold of her. I'll go straight there when I get back.'

'Thanks, Maggie.'

He tried Rose herself and got her on the first ring. She was whispering. 'Hello?'

'It's me, Danny. Are you all right?'

'I'm fine. I just don't know where he is and I want to get my stuff and get out of here without him noticing. I was going to have a talk with him but I changed my mind.'

'Look, he just got on the ferry. I reckon he'll be there in five.'

She was silent for a moment. 'OK. All right. Looks like I will be having that chat after all.'

'Listen, Maggie'll be back soon. Don't talk to him on your own. You've got her dinghy, right? Just hop over to the yacht now. Don't try and get across the river in that little boat. I couldn't get over there before him now. I'd be rowing.'

'I still think it's better to talk. This is just going to stir him up.'

'Wait for Maggie, would you? Please.'

'It's starting to rain. I'll get back now and have a think.'

'I'm going out for a while. But I'll take my phone.'

He felt the first spots of rain. It was warm and soft. Perfect, he thought, and headed up the hill to dump his bag at the shed, grab a beer from his bar fridge and go bush for a while.

On her verandah, Rose scoured the water for the ferry. She heard it before she saw it, and there it was, chugging past the north-eastern point of the island. She was glad Danny had rung; she'd been keeping a vague eye out for his dinghy because it wasn't here. She wouldn't have expected him on the ferry. He must have broken down somewhere, or run out of petrol.

She locked the house and walked quickly down the jetty to Maggie's little dinghy. It was a tiny boat, just for getting from shore to a yacht mooring. It was starting to rain, and she hurried as much as she could on the slick wood, with her unwieldy belly and her overnight bag.

The tide was lowish, and she didn't fancy trying to get down the ladder to the boat with the bag, particularly as the longer she took, the more likely it was the ferry would cross her path as she tried to get over to the yacht unseen. She held the bag outstretched over the boat and dropped it, hoping there were no breakable toiletries near the bottom. There was a little chop, and the boat shifted, but it landed safely, if a little nearer the edge than she'd intended. She checked on the ferry, it was substantially closer, but still small with distance. You would have had to have been looking for her to spot her from that far away.

She climbed down, worrying about her footing on the

wet metal rungs. She slipped once, but caught herself and continued down. She had stupid shoes on, slippery flat pumps that were comfortable but had no grip. What had she been thinking? 'Why are you nervous?' she asked herself. 'What do you think he's going to do?' I should face this, she thought. I've got to start facing things. I'm about to be a mother.

She took a breath and stepped unsteadily into the little boat, trying to retain her balance in spite of her belly and the increasing movement of the water. The ferry was perhaps twenty metres away now. The driver would see her, and so would anyone else with their gaze cast in this direction. She hoped there were others on the ferry. OK, she thought. Squeeze the fuel line bubble. Hook up the lanyard to the kill switch. And pull. Nothing. Not even a little cough. OK, that's all right. Maggie had said it sometimes took a few goes. Don't panic and flood the motor. She squeezed the bubble again. Gave the string another yank. This time there was a faint splutter. Come on! she said, but then it gave out. She pulled it again, twice. The first time it gave a little cough, the second a weird grinding noise. She was sweating and wet from the rain. She wondered whether it was possible to rupture anything with these sudden tugs, unmoor anything important inside her, between her and the baby. I'll give it two more goes then I'll just go back to the house, she told herself. What happens happens. The two pulls gave up nothing at all. She gave it two more, just in case, then hauled herself up the ladder. Her foot slipped on the top rung and she landed on her knee, but again caught herself. The ferry was right behind her. She made herself walk at a normal pace. Nothing's wrong, nothing's wrong, she said to herself. But once inside, she locked the door and moved quickly through the rooms of the house—kitchen first, then the two bedrooms and the little bathroom at the back—to check all the windows were closed and locked. Her hair was wet; it was dripping on the floor. She entered her bedroom last, drew the curtains closed and sat on the bed, drying her hair with a towel she'd left on the chair days ago.

The ferry would drop him at the public wharf, about eight houses south. Would he go home first? Would he come here at all? Just talk to him, Rose, she told herself. Don't turn him into something he's not. She checked her pocket for her mobile. No, it was in her bag. On the boat. Getting soaked in the now-heavy rain. There was a knock on the glass door of the lounge. It sounded normal, a run-of-the-mill rap. She fought the urge to hop off the bed, let him in, make him a cup of tea. Wait, she thought. Just wait. After a short period, ten seconds maybe, there came another knock. Still normal, nothing threatening about it. Again, she had to tell herself to stay where she was. She stood for a moment, then thought of the books on his bed, sat down again. She couldn't tell anymore what was the right thing to do. Just ride it out, she told herself. He went away last night, he'll go away now. Unless he'd seen her, trying to start the boat, then locking herself in the house as the ferry approached, so jittery she'd left her bag out in the rain and not gone back for it.

Outside the window the rain was so heavy she could see it through the curtains. It drummed on the tin roof, gushed from the eaves. Heavy creaks moved along the verandah in her direction. Then there was a shadow at the curtains, leaning forward, trying to peer into the room. She held her breath, frozen on the bed. The fabric he was trying to see through was thick, and if she didn't move, perhaps he wouldn't see her. She just needed to stay still. It would be too strange now, to admit she was here. Then he was gone, his creaks moving back towards the front door, then down the steps. She sat in silence, listening to the rain, letting her breathing slow. A heat spread through her lower back. She lay back carefully on the pillows, closed her eyes.

There was a creaking on the verandah again; had she slept? And there was that heat, suffusing through her back to her belly. This time there was a dull echo of pain, like when she knew her period would begin in the next few hours. Once more, she heard him move down the steps and away. She stood slowly, made her way down the dim corridor, supporting her lower back with her hand.

From the end of the corridor she could see the bank of glass doors that ran along the front of the living room. He wasn't there, but on the doormat outside was a piece of paper. She'd have to open the door to get it. He could be anywhere. 'This is ridiculous,' she said and strode across the room to the door. She couldn't bring herself to slide back the door noisily, though, and instead opened it a couple of inches, carefully, retrieved the note and slid it back into place, locking it. The phone rang as she flipped the latch and her heart leapt into her throat. She ran to it to stop the noise, picked it up, said nothing.

'Rosie—' It was Billie. In the silence that came after her name she knew that she knew. She was crying; Rose caught a snagged breath, then more silence. 'How could you not tell me?' A bolt of pain shot through her lower back. 'Rosie, are you there?'

'I'm here. I just don't know what to say,' she said quietly, a hand on her back and an eye on the glass doors. She sat down at the dining table.

'He came home, covered in bruises. He told me. Well, he tried not to, but he was being so weird. What's wrong with you, Rose?'

'Oh God, I don't know, Billie.'

'Why did you do it? Do you hate me so much?'

'No, Billie, I don't. I'm so sorry. I am so sorry. You had split up. It was really nothing. I never intended for any of this to happen.'

'He's gone now. He's yours if you want him.'

'No. Please, Billie. I don't want anything from him. Maybe you can make a go of it, if you want to. Really, I don't want anything from him. I'll never ask for anything.'

'You should have been the one that told me, Rosie.'

She had to wait for a contraction to subside before she could speak. 'I thought this would be the end—of my family.'

'What is there left, anyway? You can't stand the sight of me.'

'That isn't it, Billie. I'm sorry. I'm so sorry. I'm having the baby, I think. I've got to go.'

She placed the phone gently in front of the cradle and, still gripping the note, retreated to the dark corridor. There was just enough light spilling from the front of the house to read it, its ink bleeding from the rain outside. As she opened up the folded piece of paper, that heat returned, except this time a searing pain shot through her lower back and abdomen, doubling her over. She moaned, and with a hand on the wall, got herself down onto her knees. It was difficult to tell how long the pain lasted, but it seemed to squeeze her, intensifying as it went on, and then roll away again. She looked at her watch. It was 3.37. OK, she thought. OK. When is the ferry? She needed to work it out in the gap between the spikes of pain. She peered out the front windows from the corridor; there it was, halfway between her house and the island, growing smaller as she watched. That was the 3.30; there wouldn't be another until five. Maybe that was OK. They told you to make sure the contractions were regular and quite close before you went in. She'd just keep everything locked until then, and make sure she was on that ferry. She could call a cab to meet her on the other side in the meantime. She needed to pack. She stood and saw the note in her hand. 'Rosie, Please come out and talk. I know all these others don't mean anything to you. Why are you hiding in there? Come out and talk.' The pain hit her again with no warning. She curled up, lying on her side on the floor. At first she repeated to herself, I've got to call Danny. Her eyes were very close to the floorboards. She focused on the particles of grit. Were they sand? Then they blurred. There was no space in her head for anything but the pain, and all she could do was remember to breathe, eyes screwed tight. There was nothing, and she was in another place, away from herself. Just patterns of light, moving in the shape of her pain, as the world fell away.

Danny opened his eyes. A stone slab lay a couple of centimetres beneath his face, his skin and hair were wet. He shifted a little, looked around. A low sky hung over his shelf of rock, high above the river. He saw the railway bridge; a train emerged from the tunnel and roared across it. Trucks bumped across the freeway and the rain grew heavier, soft, fat drops of rain, soaking his skin, his shirt. He sat up, though he didn't mind the rain. It was good and warm and kept everyone else away. Up here in the reserve, above the highest ring of houses on the island, behind his own shed, you never saw anyone. The odd snake. That was it. He felt for his phone. He should check in on Rose. His pocket was empty; he'd left it in his bag in the shed on the way up. He lay back on the rock and let the rain fall on his face. Five more minutes.

When she came to, another contraction was beginning. She wondered if she'd slept through any. Was that even possible? Now she couldn't tell how far apart they were. It was almost four. She must have slept through at least one. She would sit this one out and then she had to get outside, flag someone down. Kane could give her a lift if no one else did. The talking could wait now. Rain was lashing against the windows, but she could see a couple of tinnies out there. She'd have to flag someone down. She leaned her head against the cool wall and felt the heat spreading through her. She groaned, but tried to time it—about a minute long. When it finished she headed outside, wondering if her bag, still sitting on Maggie's little boat, would have kept the stuff inside dry. Some of it would be useful for hospital; there was her toothbrush, her phone, pyjamas. As soon as she was on the verandah, a man's figure appeared at the corner of her vision. She tried to move a little faster but he was on the steps, in front of her, in a couple of strides, so close she could smell the pot on his clothes, his dirty hair. 'Where you going, Rosie?'

'Hospital. The baby's coming.'

'When are you going to talk to me, Rosie? Are you trying to mess with my head?'

She looked into his face. His eyes were red, unrested, his skin pale and wet. She did not know what to make of the expression he wore. She lifted a hand, forced herself to look him in the eyes. 'I'm having my baby. I need to get help. This is going to have to wait. I didn't mean to upset you, Kane. I will talk to you, but I need to get to hospital now.' When she'd finished speaking she was exhausted.

For a moment he said nothing, and it seemed he was thinking this over, perhaps contemplating giving her a lift across the river. But then he slapped her, hard across the face. No one had ever hit her in her life. A contraction began, the pain in her abdomen raging against the blow. She grabbed hold of the verandah railing. She could do nothing while this pain gripped her. She couldn't even feel the stinging in her cheek. He was standing back a little; his hands were in the air. 'Look what you made me do,' he said. 'Fuck.'

As the contraction subsided, she straightened. There was another figure in front of her, staring at her in silence. It was Tom. He turned to Kane, who was backing away from her. Tom's dog was growling softly at him. 'Better help me get her down to the barge, fella,' Tom said. 'I'll bring it over.'

She sat down on the stairs, in the rain, and put her head in her hands. She would not look at him. 'Rose,' he began.

'Leave me alone,' she said through her hands. 'Don't speak to me.'

He whispered, with urgency. 'You can't just be with someone and then mess around like this.'

She heard the barge grumble into life and a few moments later it was pulling in at her jetty. He put his hand on her elbow. 'Get your hands off me,' she said.

'You need me to help you onto the boat.'

'If you touch me again I'll push you in the river.'

'You're upset,' he said, retreating, hands shoved in his pockets—wet, dejected. 'The baby and that. We'll talk when you get back.'

She began to walk down the jetty, hoping she could make it onto the boat before the next one hit. The ladder was slippery, but Tom took her arm to steady her, and the tide was high, so there were only a few rungs to negotiate now. She had just managed to ease herself down into a seat when the next one began. The boat roared and they sped towards the point of the island. It was a green blur through the pain, and yet she felt still, and silent. Nothing would happen as long as this journey lasted. While she was crossing the river she was safe from the future. She thought about nothing, let the pain wash over her like the surf, felt the engine reverberate through the metal, through her body, as she gripped the rail.

But then they were slowing. She looked ahead. It was Danny, rowing towards them from the island's little beach, bringing himself around. 'You OK?' he called up to her.

'Time for her to get to the hospital,' Tom said.

'How you getting there?'

'I'll drive her,' said Tom. 'Better get moving.'

Danny nodded, watching her, watching them speed away. Help me, she thought, but couldn't speak.

'Listen,' Tom said, as they slowed for the marina. 'You still getting a decent break between 'em?' She nodded. 'OK. Well, I reckon we'll be there in twenty minutes. You'll be right. Wait here. I'll get the ute.' The dog rested his chin on her thigh. He looked flea-bitten, but he was warm.

In the cab of the ute, hurtling up the freeway, she felt as though she had come to the end of something, reached a place where there was nothing left to hide behind. In a moment of calm, one of the four- or five-minute intervals between contractions, she said, 'I know why you hate me.'

'Reckon you do, do you love?'

'I've heard the story, anyway. It doesn't matter. You're allowed to hate me. It makes no difference. If it helps you.'

'Am I acting like I hate you?' He turned to face her briefly. 'Christ al-fucken-mighty!' She turned to see a truck swerving into their lane and then out of it again, a metre or so from impact on her side. She screamed and the pain began again, no build-up this time, just maximum intensity until suddenly it was gone.

'OK,' he said. 'Maybe I've been a bit of a prick, but you don't understand everything that's happened.'

'No, I don't. I'm sorry about your daughter.'

He nodded. They were exiting the freeway, climbing the hill towards the suburbs and the hospital. They covered the last five minutes in silence. When they reached the maternity building he leaned on his horn and a pissed-off looking midwife emerged. 'Don't you worry about that Kane character,' he said. She climbed down from the cab, he honked the horn a couple of times and was gone.

'Friend of yours?' asked the midwife.

Rose shook her head and let herself be walked inside. As she did, she saw her phone in her mind's eye, in her bag, in the dinghy. She was really going to do this alone. Who would she have called? There was a moat around her, wide and unswimmable. She knew—she'd dug every inch of it with her own hands.

# Chapter 17

Danny paddled after them in the flat part of the wake. He'd kill a few hours and then go up there himself on the train and wait for her to come out. No rush, though. The first one always took forever, everyone said. First he had to sort things out with Alf, see if he could stash his oars in the chandlery this time, too. Alf was OK about everything. Stubborn bugger, but didn't take offence. They'd work it out. No fares in this weather, not until the commuters got home at least, so he said he'd wait the shift out at the pub. If no one needed him by seven, he'd go to the hospital then and see how she was doing.

He sat outside under an umbrella and watched the rain drip from its edges. The trains snaked through the station, steam blurring their wet silver hides. He was on his second beer when there he was, facing him at the edge of the terrace. His father. He'd aged, lost weight dramatically, become haggard with it, but the familiarity of him returned in an instant. The wariness in his stance, the cold focus of his gaze. Danny was the only one out here, and his old man's milky blue eyes landed on him straightaway. He paused for a moment before limping over. That was new, the limp. Or it might be years old, now, he'd been away so long. Danny's heart pounded in his chest. The physical presence of him was strangely disappointing. He'd built him up over all this time, and this was the reality of him? All the violence Danny had been carrying slipped from his body. He felt—filleted. A soft, clear creature stranded on the beach at low tide. This wasn't even a man you could fight. It wasn't that he was too mean, too big, too strong. He wasn't worthy. You'd be scorned for even touching him. Not that Danny would ever have the guts to touch anyone, anyway. This Kane business had made that obvious to him, once and for all.

He sat down. 'I didn't believe it,' his father said. 'That young fella told me you were here. I've looked a few times. Thought you were dead. Thought your mother did, too, for a long time.'

She'll have payed for that, Danny thought, the old guilt twisting his guts. 'Here I am.'

'So I see. Alive and well.' He coughed, for longer than you could ignore.

'Want me to get you a glass of water?'

He shook his head, still coughing, and pointed at Danny's beer. Danny went into the bar. The landlord gave him a look, with his change, but said nothing. Danny smelled the pub. It always seemed stronger in the day. It was the smell of his father. When he came back with the beer and placed it in front of his dad, he saw he was red-faced, but over his fit, gazing out now at the hills beyond the train tracks. 'I could kill you, what you put me and your mother through.'

'At least you'd know for sure I was dead then.'

His father's face darkened, but he seemed to stop himself saying something, and let out a sigh. 'It was not knowing. It nearly finished me.' He coughed again, but recovered more quickly this time and took a gulp of his beer. 'And the kiddie. Thought I'd brought you up to take your responsibilities seriously. Why'd you do it?'

Danny looked at the old bloke in front of him, spluttering into his beer. He considered thinking up some lie that took the edge off things. Did you let people off the hook because they were getting on? Wasn't this the same man who punched the living daylights out of his mum, his brother and himself on a regular basis until he and Trev had taken off, leaving his mum to it? Danny would beg her to leave, to take them away. He would get her so she looked on the brink of something—he always thought he had her if she started crying—but he knew now he'd never got close to persuading her. 'It'll just make it worse,' she'd say. 'He knows everyone, all over the country. When he finds us it'll be much worse.'

He looked at his father, the broken skin, the swollen nose. If he had no clear memory of his own acts, because he drank them out of his heart, did it mean they weren't his anymore? 'I didn't want to risk ever seeing you again, Dad.' He made himself look into his father's eyes. 'Even to see Abby.' His father's nostrils flared for a moment, then he blinked and looked away, back at the hills, the rain, a gleaming black four-wheel drive screeching round the corner, windows open, music blaring. He nodded and finished his drink.

'Anything you want me to tell your mother?'

Danny took a moment before shaking his head. He watched his father drain his glass and creak slowly to his feet. Eventually he said, 'You might think about helping to support your family.'

'Does Mum need money?'

'Some'd say it's your duty, after us bringing you up. Then all the worry.'

'If Mum needs something, tell her to ask me.'

The old man looked as though he wanted to say something more, shout even, but he swallowed it down and limped away. Danny watched him, not knowing what he felt, not recognising who he was seeing. His father climbed into the cab of a small refrigerator truck parked outside the doctor's surgery opposite, and drove away, exhaust belching. Now the feeling prickled through his chest. It was like having dreamed of an intruder. In the dream, you can do nothing. You watch the dark shape enter your house and you're unable to shout, or pick up a chair, or call the police. It's only when you wake that it floods through you, now you have time to feel it, now you know it's over. He watched the truck labour up the hill towards the bridge across the tracks and sat, immobile, the aftershock of fear flooding his system. After a few minutes he stood, leaving his beer unfinished, and began to walk slowly towards the train station.

# Chapter 18

'You've still got a way to go. Is there anyone you want to call?' The midwife who'd shown Rose to her room seemed kind enough, but very, very busy. Her face was lined and sunken with exhaustion. Rose shook her head. She was kneeling on the floor, face pressed into a hospital bed.

'Maybe that's for the best,' she said, regarding Rose's bruised cheek. 'Well, I can't stay with you; you've chosen a busy afternoon to have a baby. There's a buzzer there. Press it if they get any closer together.'

Oh God, she's actually going, Rose thought. She's really going to leave me on my own. Is this why you're supposed to have a birth partner? Because no one actually helps you until the head's coming out? A contraction began and she reminded herself to breathe. Panicking seemed to bring them on without any sort of build-up. The midwife had set up a gas inhaler for her. She decided she'd left it too late for this one as she'd have to stand to unhook the mask. Suddenly, a searing pain between her legs cut through the dull ache of her contraction. She wouldn't have believed there could be more pain. At what point did your body just give up? Her underwear was wet, and then her pants. As the pain died down she pulled herself to her feet, gripping the edge of the bed, and pushed the buzzer at its head. Exhaustion overwhelmed her and she fell onto the bed, curled on her side. The pillow grazed her bruise. Two more contractions came through before the midwife arrived. 'I think my waters have broken,' Rose said. 'Unless I've just wet myself.' She had a strong feeling that she was taking up too much of this woman's time with ordinary concerns. Perhaps there was an emergency caesarean happening down the hall. Perhaps your waters breaking was not a good enough reason to press the buzzer.

The midwife helped her take her pants and underwear off. 'There's meconium,' the midwife said. 'We'd better keep an eye on you.'

She had no idea what that meant, but was glad of it if it meant this woman would stay. 'What's that?' she whispered as another contraction began.

'It's waste, from the foetus. It may be distressed. Did you try the gas?'

Rose shook her head. The midwife handed her the

mask. 'Wait till the next one begins and take a suck from it as it comes. You don't have to use it. But you do seem a bit edgy.'

Rose nodded again, though inside she was protesting. I'm being so brave, she thought. You have no idea. 'I'll be right back,' the midwife said, and disappeared again. Rose didn't know how long she was away. She took the gas; it didn't stop the pain, just made it seem less important, less connected to her. She lay back on the bed and watched the rain drive against the window in the darkening sky. At the opposite end of the room, beyond her feet, was a Monet print of a field of poppies. There was a light in the air of the painting that seemed inexplicably nostalgic. She had never been to France and yet was filled with the sense of a late afternoon in a stone village, the air beautiful, life precious. Of people buying food, of children playing after school. An image of Kane's face in the rain, after he'd hit her, broke into her thoughts. She pushed it away. Eventually, the midwife came back with a doctor, an Indian man. 'I'll examine her,' he said to the nurse, and proceeded to her nether regions without ever addressing her face. She took more gas, and opened her legs. 'Two centimetre dilation,' the doctor said to the midwife.

Rose knew enough to know that was nothing. That it had to be ten centimetres before she could think about pushing. How long had she been here already? There was a feeling in her head, a smell, that reminded her of being fifteen, of having drunk too much, of sitting outside a pub in the city while a boy rubbed her back and she tried to hold his arm away as she threw up on the ground. 'Do you want to be on the bed or walk around?' the doctor asked her.

'Can't walk,' she said, removing her mask.

'Good,' he said. 'We'll monitor you on the bed.'

Suddenly there were more people in the room. A contraption was wheeled in and the midwife was fixing wide velcro straps around her belly. She heard a fast, regular beat coming from the machine. It began to speed up. Another contraction was coming but this time she didn't take the gas. 'Is that the baby?' she managed to ask before it reached its peak. Then a force hit her, seemed to separate every molecule in her body and leave her entirely rearranged.

'That's the baby,' said the midwife. The room was emptying again. Rose listened to the beat. It was so fast. She was filled with terror. It was coming. She wasn't ready. There was really a baby in there—a being that she was solely responsible for. She closed her eyes and let the pain wash through her.

Danny watched the curtain of rain pouring off the roof of the station a metre in front of his bench. Beyond the veil of water were the inlet and the hills, dark shapes, reflections in the wet evening. He'd been here for perhaps an hour, but it was only just occurring to him that there was something wrong. No trains had come through at all, in either direction. There was no one else on the platform. He had been sitting here, remembering his mother, as though she was dead. She used to try to protect them by teaching them to anticipate the old man's moods. She was so used to doing this herself, from the way he parked the rig, his footfall on the verandah; these signals were enough to make her stiffen on the sofa, her boys either side. 'Go to your room,' she'd say quietly. 'Put your pyjamas on and jump into bed. I'll be in soon.'

Danny remembered his mother as beautiful, not the way women now were beautiful, in their strength and confidence. She was the opposite; she didn't want anyone to look at her. Kept herself tidy and clean and nothing more, and yet she always smelled sweet and soft to Danny, and her blonde hair shone in waves, and her clothes moved like a dream when she walked. He didn't know if other people would have considered her out of the ordinary, and he had no photo to test her beauty with now. Perhaps he remembered her this way simply because she was something precious that he'd lost, or because his father guarded her like a soldier with a gun outside a palace.

When she had assessed his father's mood, sat him down with his steak and his beer, she'd creep quietly down the corridor to their room. They slept in bunks and swapped beds every night, neither able to give up a minute of their share of the spot on the top. You felt safer there. It was your ship, you were the captain. It made no difference, but you had to imagine what you could. There'd be a chink of light at the door and the smell of her perfume. You could feel her standing by the bed. If you were on the top bunk, she did not have to bend to kiss your forehead. You'd pretend to be asleep, and she'd lay her hand on the side of your face. Sometimes she'd whisper things to you. 'I'll take care of you, Dan. I'll keep you safe. You're my boy. He'll have to get through me to get near you.'

And he did. She was like the wall of water in front of him. He just walked straight through. What could she or anyone do in the face of the mad force he was, the raging, solid core of violence he carried around with him? He was the only one who could hold himself back. There was a time when he'd try, you could see the struggle in him, the hung-over shame at breakfast, but as the boys got older he seemed to stop caring enough to bother.

Danny stood and walked along the wet platform to the ticket office. He peered through the window. There was a man at the back of the office with a long blond mullet leaning back in a chair, laughing into the phone. He spotted Danny and turned his back, continued his conversation for another couple of minutes. Eventually, he approached Danny slowly, like he wouldn't want anyone to think he was going to too much trouble.

Danny sighed. 'Something wrong with the trains, is there?'

'Could say that.'

'What's the problem?'

'What isn't the problem?'

'I don't know. Maybe you could give me a hint.'

'All right, mate. No need for that. Lightning put the signals out. Now there's a tree on the line up on the ridge. Bastard of a spot to do much about it.'

'When do they think it will be sorted out?'

The man shrugged. 'Not tonight.'

'You couldn't have told me that before I sat on the platform for an hour?'

'Not my business what people are doing on the platform. You might like the view.'

Danny shook his head and left the window. It was dark outside. Hell of a row home. She'd be there for a few days, anyway. He'd ask Maggie to drive him up in the morning if the trains were still down. Rose had been bent over on Tom's boat. Her hair was in her face. There was something odd, though. Something apart from the contractions. She wouldn't look up. Wouldn't look at him. Like his mother; she never looked people in the eye, was always looking at her feet or her hands. She was like a little kid playing hide-and-seek, believing if she couldn't see other people they couldn't see her.

He rowed home in the rain. He thought about the baby, wondered if it was in the world yet. He remembered when Maggie's younger one was born. Standing by the bed, not knowing where to look while she fed it. Afterwards Rob handed her to him. She was light, and warm, and asleep, but her little fingers gripped his large one when he tapped her palm. The world was a wild place. The baby was so small. But you couldn't help but be excited for her, for everything her life might be. He looked at Rob, a meaty bloke, fat around the gut, muscled arms from driving the rig. Fond of a beer, fond of a meat pie. Tears were running down his face. 'You old sook,' Maggie said. 'Look at the state of you.'

He'd only ever seen Abby briefly, a glimpse of a pretty brown girl inside the pram as he passed her mother in the street. She would only stop for a moment, glancing nervously about her; there was always one of her brothers, somewhere, never far away. There was a feeling that hung around for days after he'd seen her. He would wake from dreams of kicking, blood, gouging, always so close to his assailant he didn't know who he was, just that if he stopped fighting he would die. Then he would lie awake and watch the patterns on the ceiling, wait for hours for the feeling to drain from his blood.

His loft bed in the shed on the island was close to the rain on the tin roof. He closed his eyes, imagined rowing Rose across the river on a sunny morning to their house. Her yellow hair, the baby bundled up in a wrap in her arms. The rain was so close it filled his head and his body. He fell asleep filled with it, trickling, pouring through him, his veins alive with falling water.

'You have to push, Rose,' the midwife said.

'I can't. I'm tired.' Her eyes were closed. She didn't feel like pushing. She wanted it to be over, but it couldn't be time yet. She just didn't feel it.

'Nearly there. You have to do it.'

There was so little between contractions now. Another one came, hot and fast. There were five staff in the room but she lost the sounds of all of them. She could no longer hear the midwife ordering her to push. She could see nothing. All she could hear was the beeping of her monitor.

She went to a place inside herself away from the pain, away from her memory. She knew she was dying for a moment. She knew she would come back. It filled her with a terrible stretching feeling. In this silent place, she could feel her father. She did not want to go back. A sudden, squeezing pressure returned her to the room. 'Push now!' the midwife was saying to her. She pushed. 'OK, stop for a second.' The midwife was watching her face. The doctor was watching the monitor. He said something quietly to the midwife. 'Now, Rose. Do it again.' Rose screamed, and pushed. She felt something, an emptiness in her stomach, a lightness, and then all the activity, all the people in the room moved their focus to what was happening between her legs. The doctor was holding something and then he pulled it clear. A bloody mass. A baby. The midwife cut the cord, and there were people everywhere. Rose caught glimpses of feet, an elbow, over on the counter. They were weighing it, checking it. There were two of them in her way. Then they brought it to her and there was a wet bundle of tiny limbs, a head on her empty belly. 'It's a girl, Rose,' the midwife said.

Rose nodded, her throat thick. 'Look at her ears,' she said.

'I know,' smiled the midwife. 'They're perfect. Like little shells.'

Rose nodded again. She was afraid the slippery little parcel would slide off her, that she'd be cold. She drew her closer. After all that time imagining, trying not to imagine, here she was. She was an alien creature thrust into a new world. Her chin, her mouth, were Rose's mother's—how they were in the photographs. She had a widow's peak just like her dad's. All she could do was stare, and try to get her grip right, try to make sure she didn't lose hold of her without clasping her so tight that she crushed her. She needed to sleep. She needed to watch the baby. She was starving. She looked at the clock. 'It's OK,' the midwife said. 'We've written down the time. Do you want some dinner?' Rose nodded. 'Well done, Rose,' she said. 'Good girl. Time to rest.'

# Chapter 19

The next morning the trains were running again, but the water taxi was busy. It was still squally, though the rain was intermittent now, and people weren't trusting their own boats. Just as he'd think he was close to the end of his shift he'd get another call from Alf for a pick up, and the cliffs were dulling with the last of the light before he could get away. He climbed out of the boat, thankfully, slipped the keys under Alf's door and walked across the car park to the station, briskly, head down. He'd seen glimpses of Jesse working at the marina café all day as he zipped back and forth out of the channel. No chance of her not seeing him on his big white boat. When he absentmindedly glanced in her direction he caught her wounded gaze.

On the train, he saw in the fading light where the tree

had come down. It was chopped up in massive chunks by the side of the tracks, glistening from the last shower an hour or so ago. The sky was clear now, the first of the stars appearing in the purple sky over the canopy of the national park. Why was he going to see her? Would she even want to see him? He didn't know. There didn't seem to be any choice about any of this. He was on rails, moving towards a destination without panic or decision.

His phone rang; it took him a moment to realise it was his. He answered it quietly, always self-conscious when it rang on the train. He didn't recognise the number, but as he said hello he realised why it seemed familiar. It was a number from where he'd grown up, but not his parents' number—he wouldn't forget that. 'Danny?' It was Jackie, Abby's mother. Her voice, as she spoke softly, tentatively, brought back a world he had forgotten. It was not just his house and everything that happened behind its walls, but who he was, where he'd grown up, in a suburb around faces that were familiar to him, that grew older at the same pace as his own. There was happiness in the feeling her voice carried. She'd been a good mate, before all this. 'Your mum gave me your number,' she said. 'She came round this morning. She was so happy to have it.' His dad must have got hold of it when he was down here. Danny looked out the window, at the people around him. His heart was full of who he used to be. Nothing around him was real.

'How are you, Jack?' he said softly. 'How's Abby?'

'We're all right. We're good. I've got a nice fella. Dan, Abby wants to see you. She's eight now. She's asking about you all the time. She makes up stuff, about who you are, to her mates.'

'What about your bloke? Doesn't he mind?'

'He's a nice man. He's all right.'

'That's good, Jackie,' he said, barely above a whisper. He didn't want these people around him to know, to even imagine, what was happening to him. It wasn't for them.

'Can she see you, Danny? Your mum says you're only down at the river. If you don't want to see me, maybe your mum could bring her down, on the train.'

'You could bring her. Mum, too.'

'That'd be nice, Dan. It's been a long time.'

'I'm sorry, Jack.' He dropped his voice again. 'I've been worthless to you. You never deserved it.'

'I knew you had to go, Danny. It was no secret, about your old man. And my brothers. It was sort of a relief. I thought they were gonna kill you. Honestly.'

He said goodbye as the train pulled into the station. He looked around him in wonder. The sickly green of the walls of the railway carriage; the long metal sheds beyond the window, spreading out from the station; the lanky bloke in front of him holding up his bike, ready to get out. Everything seemed different. There was something strange in the air, affecting sound, or light. He'd been forgiven. He hadn't known what he'd been missing, until she gave it to him. And his mum, she was the one who'd given her his number. She would come, too.

It was a good walk from the station to the hospital— ten minutes or so up a fairly steep hill. It was a cool evening, after the rain, but he felt sticky, unappealing, by the time he arrived. He noticed a florist's as he walked through the car park to the maternity ward. There was a woman closing up as he approached, flipping the sign on the door. When he peered through it, it was dark inside and she was slipping on a jacket, picking up her handbag and keys. He smiled through the glass. She smiled back and put down her things. 'I don't have much left,' she said as she opened the door a crack. 'I was going to throw this stuff out. We've got a fresh delivery coming in the morning.'

'Anything,' he said. He felt the need to have something in his hands when he went in there. 'Just something pretty. Whatever's left.'

She rummaged around in the darkness at the back of the shop and came back with a deep pink box filled with different coloured gerberas. 'How much is it?' he asked.

'Don't worry about it. I was going to throw it away.'

'But it's still OK, isn't it? I should give you something.'

'It'll be OK for a couple of days, if that's all she's staying. But she couldn't take it home.'

Danny looked at her. She was a little bit older than him, older than he usually took an interest in. Pretty, or carrying the memory of it, from what he could see in the dark shop. She was probing him. He knew the form. He smiled, out of habit. 'Thanks. It's nice of you.'

And he was walking away with the box clutched in his arm, trying to see the flowers in the poorly lit car park, wondering if they would look all right under the harsh lights of the ward. At the desk an incredibly tall, broad-shouldered woman was holding a sleeping baby while she spoke on the phone. The baby had a shock of black hair, and a white dummy seemed to take up most of the lower half of its face. Is that her baby? he wondered. To the left was a glass wall looking onto the nursery. There were five or six babies in clear perspex cribs under bright strip lighting. Who would know?

After an age, the woman came off the phone and showed him to Rose's room. It was the first door on the corridor; he'd been just a few metres from her. She was there, in the bed closest to the door. The other was empty. Between the beds was one of the clear cribs. It was small, but the bundle of baby in wraps took up only a tiny portion of it, tucked neatly into the lower part of the tilted cradle. The room smelled of fruit, and flowers about to spoil. Someone else had visited then. The baby was asleep, its face impossibly small and serene; Rose was reading a magazine, her mass of blonde hair falling over her face. When she looked up, it was with a jolt, until her face settled into recognition of Danny. She saw the flowers he brought and relaxed against her pillow again.

'Visitor for you,' the midwife said gently. She seemed to pause for a moment, gauging Rose's reaction, before leaving. As he drew closer to put the flowers on her bedside table he realised why. Across her cheek was a purple and yellow bruise. You could actually make out the shape of fingers in it. For a moment, he could see nothing, had to stand still for a moment, wait for the blood to stop pounding in his head. He held out the flowers, dumbly. She took them and put them on the bedside table.

'Thanks,' she said quietly. 'Do you want to see the baby?'

He nodded, unable to look away from her face.

'Would you pick her up? I did something to my back during the birth. I can't get her out of the crib myself yet.'

He continued to stare at her. He was having trouble reacting at a normal speed. Eventually he stood, and put his hands on the baby, the hot, living bundle. 'She's sleeping,' he said. 'I don't want to wake her.'

'It's OK. They said they wanted to feed her soon. She doesn't weigh much and my milk hasn't come in yet.'

He was afraid to handle her, but he lifted her gently. She was lighter than he'd imagined and it felt like he was raising her abruptly into the air. 'Do you want her?'

'No, it's OK. You can hold her. I'll take her if she wakes.'

He sat on the edge of the bed, cradling her. She was warm and smelled good, like fresh laundry and clean skin, but then something sweet, too. He looked at Rose. He couldn't say what was in his head. Something was erupting in him, surging. He fought it down, in case it touched the baby, disturbed her as she lay against his body.

She looked out of the window at the darkening sky. 'Someone's brought you flowers, and fruit,' he said.

She shook her head. 'They were the other woman's. She left them for me when she went home.'

'Has anyone been?'

She shook her head. Her face was still except for a softness in her chin, her lower lip, as she stared out the window into nothing.

'Hasn't your sister been in?'

'No. She's in a bit of a state. She's split up with James.'

He wondered about that, but let it go. 'Have you got your phone? Can I get it for you so you can call your mates? Is it at the house?'

'I left it out in the rain. It's on Maggie's dinghy. I'd say it's stuffed.'

'I'll check for you.'

'I don't want anyone. Not yet.' She looked him square in the eye.

The baby made noises against him. He tore his gaze away from Rose's face to the baby's. She did look like her mother, something about the mouth, though it was so tiny.

'When are you coming home?'

'They've said I should stay for another couple of nights because they can't send a midwife out to me on the river, and she was a bit early. They want us to get feeding before I go home. Thursday, I think.'

The baby whimpered and then let out a sharp wail. He instantly held her out to Rose. She looked quite nervous herself about the prospect of dealing with a crying baby. 'Shall I get the midwife?' he asked. She nodded. He was glad of a task, committing himself to it with more urgency than it required. There seemed to be no staff in the nursery. Anyone could take those babies. He went back out to the desk, where a new midwife he hadn't seen before had appeared and was leafing furiously through some papers. 'Excuse me,' he said. 'Rose, in that room over there. She needs help with the baby. I think it needs to be fed.'

The midwife continued to leaf through the papers. 'I don't believe this,' she muttered, 'Where is it?' before snapping her attention onto Danny. 'World's not going to end. You know, she could have a go at feeding it herself.'

'No, look, she says her milk hasn't come in.' He barely knew what he was saying, merely hoped that it made sense to this woman. That it would galvanise her in some way so he could leave and do what was required of him elsewhere.

The woman sighed. 'All right. Which room is it?'

'That one,' he pointed. 'And please—could you tell her—I had to go. I'll be back soon.'

She rolled her eyes and put down her papers. Danny crossed the corridor quickly, hoping Rose wouldn't see him through the open door. He couldn't speak to her now. He needed to think. As the double doors out of the ward slid open, he heard footsteps behind him. 'Excuse me,' said a woman's voice. It was the tall midwife, the one who had been at the desk when he arrived. She peered down into his face, thinking about what she was going to say. 'You're a friend of Rose's, right?' He nodded. 'Do you know anything about that bruise on her face?'

'I think I know who it was, if that's what you mean.'

'You can report him, you know. It's easier, when there's evidence. It'll be too late if you don't do it now.'

He held her gaze for a few seconds, before walking out of the building and into the rain.

# Chapter 20

Tom sat on his disintegrating pier in the dusk. The mozzies were out but it didn't bother him; he was two thirds of the way down a bottle of Jim Beam and wasn't intending to leave a piddling little bit in the bottom. There'd been no rain now for a couple of days and there was none on the horizon. Be dry enough for a fire tomorrow. Good the girl was away. Be a pity if he burned down her house when she'd just had a baby, but he wouldn't be sorry if he took the old place with him. It'd be a proper end to things. He'd leave nothing behind him. Burn it all to the ground and the world could start again.

The letter lay in his lap. He could just burn it, the thing itself, but everything else was falling to pieces around him anyway: the jetty, his body. Do it all at once, neat and clean.

He had read the letter once, yesterday morning, and would not read it again. But he couldn't help carrying it around with him, touching it. He didn't want to let it out of his sight. Didn't trust it. It carried the truth, a small, deep part of him knew that, and he feared unleashing it upon the world.

When a letter from the government arrived he'd assumed it was something to do with taxes. When he got letters like that he laughed. His disease was a joke on them. The only money they'd get from him they'd have to prise from his stiff fist. The more they wanted the better. 'Carn, Dog,' he'd said, 'let's give ourselves a laugh,' and opened it. But it wasn't about taxes. It was the police. What did they want with him? But he knew. He knew. Wished he'd stopped himself before he read it, but he couldn't help himself. Even when it was clear what the next page contained, he still looked. Read the whole thing. It was a transcript of a confession, from that man. That rapist from up on the ridge. 'Why now, you old fucker?' Tom said. In his transcript he called his Molly 'the slut'. She was 'the ugly slut down at the river. The last one before they got me. I didn't rape most of them,' he'd said. 'You can't call it rape, when they act like that. That one at the river fought like an alley cat, though.' That's my girl, Tom thought, the letter clenched in his lap.

Why hadn't Mancini ever defended himself? Why had he let him think this thing of him? Just disappeared, quietly gone away, back to Italy, never saying a word. The wife had had a few words to say, though, when she was left to pack up and take the boy to her relatives in the city.

She'd left the boy and the boxes on the garbageman's barge and presented herself on his verandah—a beautiful Italian woman, losing her figure perhaps, but not her fire. 'I want you to know that you've ruined our lives and I will never forgive you.'

'Your mongrel old man ruined your lives, love,' he'd said. 'I don't need your forgiveness.'

'How do you sleep at night?' she'd shouted.

'How do I sleep at night? Christ, I'm not the one to ask that. Why d'you think he ran off? Guilty as sin.'

'He couldn't stay here, after what you'd said about him. You ruined his business. No one would look him in the face.'

'If he'd done nothing, he might have mentioned it.'

'He didn't believe he should have to.' She swore at him in Italian, and marched down her jetty to the barge and the boy, who was watching everything.

Nothing had been right since the night it had happened. He'd been wrong then, wrong ever since.

Tom woke to the sound of a motor on the water beneath his jetty. The sun was full in his face and he'd been savaged by mosquitoes. His neck was sore from lolling over the back of his fishing chair. 'Tom!' some bloke was shouting from a boat. The sun was in his eyes. 'Tom!' Dog started barking at his side.

'Jesus. Hold on, fella.'

'Tom, it's Danny. I need a word.'

Tom creaked to his feet and shuffled the few steps to

the edge of the jetty, hand shielding his eyes. Danny was looking up at him from the water taxi. His eyes were bloodshot, his hair slept on, clothes crumpled.

'You look worse than I feel, mate. And that's saying something.'

'You seen Kane?'

'Not since the incident with your mate next door.'

'What incident would that be?'

'When he smacked her in the chops the other day as she was going into labour.'

Danny nodded. He handed up the water-taxi business card. 'Call me if you see him, will you.'

'Listen, fella. What you gonna do?'

'Don't worry about that.'

'Not worried. Like to help, that's all. Alf's always a good man in a sticky spot, too. You need my keys for anything, they're on a hook on the frangipani.' He nodded at the barge. Danny eyed him for a moment, squinting in the sun. He nodded, engaged the motor and headed for the island.

'You could get into a heap of trouble, Rob,' Maggie said quietly. She, Rob and Danny were sitting in the dark on the deck of the yacht, camping chairs in a semicircle faced towards the boatshed.

'You think he'd really say something to the cops?' Danny said.

'If he lives to say anything to the cops,' Rob laughed.

'Don't even joke about it, Rob,' she said. 'Listen, Danny.

He's a little shit. But you've got to be careful with this stuff. You could try the police.'

'They don't do anything. It's her word against his, and then there's endless legal fucking around that she won't want to go through with the baby. If she even reports him. Let's just sort him out now and be done with it.'

'Don't you think you should ask her about this?' Maggie said.

'She's got enough to think about with the baby. And she'll never do anything. She thinks she can have a friendly chat and he'll suddenly stop punching everyone in sight. He's our problem now.'

'You said it,' Rob agreed.

'He's not—predictable,' she said.

'There's two of us,' Danny said. 'And there's Tom, and Alf.'

'You're kidding me,' she said.

'The barge'll be handy, anyway,' Rob said.

'That's what I reckon,' Danny said.

'Do me a favour,' Maggie said, to both of them. 'Just let her get home. See what happens. See what she wants. He may be gone for good, anyway. No one's seen him in days. Danny, if you want, you can stay here to keep an eye on her. Then if he tries anything, you just have to call Rob, OK?'

Rob waited for Danny's response. Danny nodded, his gaze never leaving the boatshed. 'He won't touch her again, though,' he said, eventually. Maggie gave Rob a look, and went below to fetch more beer.

* * *

I've given birth, I can do anything, Rose said to herself as she stepped across the churning water between the wharf and the ferry, clutching the baby. Steve hopped back up the stairs and fetched the bag of nappies and food she'd bought at the marina when the taxi dropped her off. Who knew when she'd get out again?

She was home a day early, desperate to leave the hospital, the endless changing shifts of bossy midwives. She wondered now whether she'd been wrong to do it. What did she know about looking after a baby? This was the school ferry home, and the children seemed huge and insanely boisterous, their movements exaggerated and dangerous. And it was so hot. She held the baby close and watched her sleep, letting her hair fall forward over her fading bruise. The older girls in short summer uniforms wanted to touch her, but Rose tucked her further inside her blanket. 'She's sleeping. I don't want to wake her.' Though it seemed impossible that she would continue sleeping in this racket. Even as she thought this, the baby began to stir. Then the engines started up, and her tiny lids closed and she was still again. A woman from the island plonked herself down next to her. 'Oh, she makes me feel funny! Mine are all so big now. What's her name?' The question she dreaded.

'I don't know. I haven't decided. I'm not really getting anything from her yet.'

The woman nodded. 'That happens. Sometimes it takes a few days to know whether they're an Arthur or a Martha, if you know what I mean.'

Please go away, Rose thought. When the baby had

stirred, her breasts had leaked. She had to hold her close to cover them up. And now the ferry was moving, the wood beneath her bottom was vibrating. The effect on her stitches was making her eyes water. And always there was the thought, is he going to be there? How strong do I need to be? Haven't I already done more than should be asked of anyone? What am I paying for now?

The woman got off at the island, along with ninety per cent of the kids, and she let out a deep breath. Thank God the rain had stopped. She couldn't imagine how she'd manage an umbrella, even if she had one, which she didn't. She wondered about her gear in Maggie's boat. Perhaps Danny had salvaged it for her. But then he'd disappeared pretty quickly when he'd seen her face.

After the ferry dropped her at the wharf she picked her way past the houses towards her place. There was no one around. The baby was waking now; she'd have to feed her as soon as she got in. For once she was disappointed to see no sign of Tom as she made her way through the scrap in his front yard and onto her property. 'What is your name?' she whispered as she climbed her steps. 'Here you are, baby. You're home.'

Leaning against the glass doors was a guitar. She drew closer, studying the shape in the shadows. It was her father's guitar; there was the nick from when she'd dropped it when he was teaching her to play, when she was thirteen. He hadn't shouted. She'd burst into tears before he got the chance, but he wouldn't have anyway. There was a note hanging from a ribbon around the neck. She crouched awkwardly with the baby, putting the shopping down, and untied it. 'Rosie,' it said. 'Kane has gone. James served him an eviction notice. I'll come and see the baby when I've calmed down. Ben wants to come, too.'

Rosie brought the guitar to her nose briefly, breathed it in. She opened the door; it was unlocked. Had she not locked it in the chaos of leaving? She couldn't remember. Her heart thudded. Calm down, she told herself. You are a mother. He's gone. She laid the guitar on the dining table and carefully began to unstrap the baby's carry pouch, laying her on the sofa, but as soon as she began to feel the relief of separation the baby wailed, her face turning red, her mouth suddenly huge. 'Shhh, baby,' she said. She picked her up again. Tea would have to wait. She fed her. It took almost an hour. She watched the light on the trees, the water, the island. She had stepped into her future. What now? She felt dozy and closed her eyes for long moments, drifting in and out of the room, the baby warm on her lap, eyes closed, sucking, dozing, sucking.

Now what did she do? What did you do with your life, once they took away work, friends and family, and it was just you and this tiny person? She'd change her. Then she'd have a cup of tea. Then maybe she'd try and give the baby a bath, like they'd shown her in the hospital. She didn't have a baby bath, but they'd said the kitchen sink would do. Was the sink clean enough? Anyway, that was three things: changing, tea, bath. She'd worry about beyond that when she got to it.

After her feed, the baby was fast asleep, so she laid her

in her crib for the first time, then wheeled it out of the baby's room, into her own and placed it next to her bed. She had this whisper of a thought that they were supposed to feel closer somehow, that she should need her baby nearby, so she would act like that until it seemed normal, and real. Perhaps others would be convinced in the meantime. 'Who are you, little baby?' she said as she tucked her into the crib, and moved quietly through the house back to the sofa. She'd just sit down for a minute, then make a cup of tea. Who knew how long the baby would sleep for? She thought about finding a magazine or a book, but then she sank into the soft sofa, a hot breeze blowing in through the flyscreens, and was asleep instantly. When something woke her, the deepening of the light in the room or the breeze on her face, perhaps, she realised with a lurch of her stomach that there was a figure on the other sofa. In the moment before she recognised his tall, gangly frame, the angles of his face in the fading light, he was an unfamiliar demon, an apparition in her home. Billie had told her he'd gone. She couldn't speak.

'We need to talk, Rosie.' He sounded teary, shaken.

'How did you get in here?' she said, pulling herself up slowly to a sitting position.

He glanced at the door. Didn't I lock it? she thought. Where is my head? 'Can I see the baby?'

She stared at him. He looked calm, in spite of the tremor in his voice, but concentrated somehow, like a sniper lifting his gun.

'Where is it?'

'She.'

'Where is she?'

She paused. 'She stayed in hospital. She's sick.' She hoped she wouldn't cry. She'd need to get rid of him quickly now.

'She all right?'

Rose nodded.

'I want to show you my new place. We need to talk, Rosie. We need to be alone for five minutes.'

'We're talking, Kane.'

'No, no.' He stood quickly. 'You need to come with me. Bloody Danny or one of the others'll barge in on us. We need to go somewhere private. Got my own place now, up the river a bit. Nice and quiet. You got to come and see it.'

'I'll talk to you here, Kane. I can't go with you. I've just given birth.' Don't panic, she told herself. It's not time to panic yet. 'Do you want a drink or something? I'll see what there is. Let me get a light on.'

'No, Rosie. You gotta stop avoiding me now.' He leaned over and took her wrist.

'Don't touch me, please,' she said, staring at his hand.

He pulled her off the sofa so that she was standing, close to him. He put his arms around her waist, laid his head on her stomach, still holding onto her wrist. 'I can look after you, Rosie. You can't do this on your own. We can—we can make our lives how we want them. It don't matter about anybody else.' She looked out the window; the river was quiet, the lights were coming on over at the island. She couldn't see a single boat out there. The hot wind was gusting, rattling the flyscreens, rustling the leaves of the jacaranda and the gums behind the house. He stood and faced her, keeping hold of her wrist. 'Come on,' he said. 'We'll go now, before it gets too dark. Left my torch back at my place.'

She stood her ground. 'I can't come with you, Kane. Why don't you come back in the morning, when I've had some rest?' She thought she heard the beginnings of a whimper, from the back bedroom. 'Please, I need to go to bed now.'

'No, Rosie,' he said. 'I'm not gonna mess around. We've got to go now.' He began to pull her towards the sliding door, pulling it back.

'I'm not coming, Kane. Get off me!'

He yanked her back towards him, putting a hand over her mouth. It smelled of pot, the hydroponic stuff—earthy, overwhelming. 'Shhh!' he whispered. 'Stop fighting. You'll see.' She couldn't stop herself from pulling backwards, away from the meaty reality of him, his crackling, wired body. Then she saw—a knife glinted in his hand, finding the last of the light from outside. The baby let out a sharp wail and they both froze. 'You said she was still in the hospital. Why'd you lie to me?'

She said nothing, merely watched him, motionless, waiting to see what he would do.

'We can take the baby, too,' he said, his face inches from hers.

No, she thought. No, she's just been fed. She'll be OK for a little while. If he gets me out on the water, I'll get help, and get back. Or she'll keep crying and someone will find her. Tom, or someone. He can't be near her. 'No, leave her,' she said. 'I'll come and talk to you, and then I'll come back and feed her. How far is it?'

'Someone'll hear her,' he said. 'Go and give her a dummy or something.' She moved swiftly across the living room. 'I'm coming, too,' he said. He grabbed her wrist as she made her way down the dark corridor to her room.

'Please, stay here,' she whispered as they reached the door.

He leaned in the doorway, watching her. The baby was wailing rhythmically, her face crimson. Rose found a dummy on the dresser and gave it to her, stroking her cheek. She closed her eyes and sucked. Rose faced him from the opposite side of the crib. 'Kane,' she whispered. 'This is crazy. We can talk in the morning. You know where to find me.'

He nodded towards the door. She touched the baby's face again. Is this the right way to do it? she asked herself as she followed him. Should I keep her with me? But even his presence in the doorway of her room had made her throat tight, her heart pound in her chest. Get out of the house, get help, she thought. Get him away from her.

He walked her out of the living room, onto the verandah and down to the jetty, holding onto her elbow. Her back twinged as she jumped down into the boat. He jumped down after her. His back was to her as he pull-started the motor, but it kicked over first time and he was facing her again before she had time to think through the possibilities. Be ready next time, she thought. Shove him straight over.

She watched his face as they pulled away from the shore. He was concentrating on the shoreline, the trajectory of the boat. I've underestimated him, she thought. Simplified him.

At least he was putting space between himself and the baby. But he was putting it between her and the baby, too. She would be OK, for a little while. Then she would cry, and someone would hear her. Tom? Was he at the pub? She realised putting her faith in Tom was hopeless. And she remembered suddenly—him sitting there, the brown bottle, the metho, the yellow rags. Oh my God, she thought. Then: keep thinking, keep watching. Find your moment, get back to her.

Kane didn't look at her. His face was screwed up into the wind. He kept the boat close to the shore, beneath the dark canopy of the bush, and they hugged the point and made their way up the creek. She watched a train disappear into the tunnel on the opposite shore, twenty metres away. No one would know to look at them. She knew that moment of the train journey so well, had made it a thousand times travelling between the city and her father's house. Sat at the back of the carriage as the train drilled into the earth; the river, the boats on it, the tiny people down there part of the world you left behind. Could she make a signal? No one would see anything but a wave, if that, now it was almost dark, and it would just make him angry. She scoured the water, casting left and right, as far behind her as she dared, waiting for a sign, watching the water.

Tom's phone rang insistently in his kitchen. If you didn't know where it was, it would take you a while to find it among the dirty cups and plates, the crumpled tea towels, the old newspapers on the bench. Dog barked at the phone, and at Tom, who was within sight of the bit of bench where the phone hid, just outside the screen door, a quarter of a bottle of Jim Beam lolling in his slack hand. The other hand nursed another bottle in his lap. There was a smell of methylated spirits coming from it which had set Dog on edge even before the unanswered phone call. The matches lay neatly on the grey plastic arm of the camping chair—a fresh box of long barbecue sticks, bought especially from the general store at the marina the day before. 'Well, Dog,' he slurred. 'Don't do anything stupid. Just run like buggery, OK, and don't worry about your old man.'

He dropped the Jim Beam bottle on the stone beneath his feet. The smash set Dog off again. Tom picked up the matches. Beautiful things, those long ones. The pale wood, the perfect rounded red tip. He struck it, lit the rag in the bottle, chucked it over his shoulder into the kitchen. He heard the glass break. The river, the insects in the bush fell silent for a moment, then there was a whump as the house burst into flames. Despite the state of him, in spite of everything, he had to fight the urge to move, to run, to shout for help. 'Garn, Dog,' he shouted. 'Bugger off, would ya,' but Dog yapped incessantly in his face. 'All right, mate, your choice.'

He could feel the heat from the house. He would have to go in. Couldn't be sure he'd pass out from the smoke out here; certainly didn't want it to happen any other way. Except maybe another explosion when the fire reached the chemicals in the laundry. That might do it. But smoke, that was going to be best, stop him changing his mind. Pulling himself slowly to his feet, he had a strong urge to pee. He was broken, and nothing would fix him. Dog intensified his barking as Tom creaked to his feet. 'G'bye Dog,' Tom said. He took a deep breath, peering into the flames in the kitchen. The flue above the oven had caught and was billowing a wild blue fire.

He heard a cry. For a moment it seemed he was a huge being and the sound was a tiny wail from deep at the centre of him. And still he was torn between wanting to be left alone and wanting to be saved. He hesitated for a moment. It was there again, but it wasn't a cry that would rescue him; it was a baby. Oh Christ, the baby was home. Danny had said Thursday. That was tomorrow. Still, that was the mother's problem. Nothing to stop her getting away from the fire, getting out on the water, walking far enough along the shore to get the baby out of danger.

Now it was that constant waah waah that they did, stopping only to get a lungful. Say she wasn't there? Or she was asleep? No one seemed to be paying it any attention. 'Fuck,' he muttered, and picked through the crap in his yard around to the space between the houses,

Dog on his heels. The crying grew louder; no sign of the bird.

He turned to look at his own house; flames were escaping from the front bedroom window. Behind the house, a tree had caught alight. A thin column of black smoke reached high into the evening sky. Coming round the point of the island was the fire barge. 'Fuck,' he said again, and ducked onto her verandah, behind the sheltering trees. The sliding door was open; no sign of her in the lounge room. He went inside. Different to how it used to be. Hadn't been in here for over thirty years, since the Carmodys had sold Mancini their place and buggered off to grow bananas in Queensland. What a mess they'd left behind them. It was a pretty house now a girl lived there. The crying was coming from somewhere at the back. He walked into the corner of the wall where the corridor began. 'Bugger,' he said, holding his head. Dog scampered ahead of him towards Rose's room. 'All right, hold on.'

When he entered the room he saw no one. He stumbled past the double bed to the crib and peered inside. There she was, face red with screaming. He put a finger on her cheek. It looked dirty and old sitting there; you could see the contrast against her pale skin even in the half-light of dusk. 'Shhh . . .' he whispered, breathing in close, smelling his own fiery breath. 'Where's your mum?' He placed his hands on either side of the crocheted white blanket she was wrapped in. He couldn't get over his hands, almost black with dirt and a life outside, creases caked with grease. He could see smudges on the blanket already. He picked her up and cradled her to his chest. 'We'll have to worry about her later, mate. Come on.' She stopped crying as she reached his chest.

Outside, the barge was pulling up at his jetty. His place was already blackened beyond hope, consumed by reeking fire. He watched Steve unrolling the hose on top of the barge from the dark, hidden verandah, and gave the baby his blackened old finger to clutch. How come I'm still here? he thought, watching her face, her little tongue curling, ready for the next protest. The fire brigade scurried about on the barge in their yellow suits; water rained down on his house. He held the baby to him, felt Dog's warm dirty fur against his knee. He'd been so close.

# Chapter 21

As Kane steered the tinny into the creek, out of the open river, Rose tried not to let panic overwhelm her. She had seen no boats out there; the chances were much slimmer that she'd be able to get help on this dark inlet. Should she just throw herself in and swim for it? But she couldn't outpace a boat, and he was keeping well out from the shore. Even if she got away from him, she'd be stuck in the bush, with a cliff between her and home, or a wide expanse of tidal river to swim, not yet recovered from labour.

She watched him; he was peering into the darkening bush, looking for something. She saw it before he did, straight lines in the tangle of trees, the corner of a deck, the angle of a tin roof, pale, shining dully. He twitched on

the tiller and within seconds the prow hit sand beneath her.
Her pulse quickened. Was this the moment? She had to be
ready. Better if he provided the chance; less risky than trying
to create something. He's going to have to tie off, she thought.
He took hold of her hair. 'Tie it to a root. Be quick.'

She scrambled out of the boat. Her body felt light—she
was still adjusting to the absence of baby—but awkward:
cumbersome and alien. Her fingers fumbled with the rope
in the dark. Where was the root? A weak, unsteady torch
beam appeared on the sand in front of her. 'Come on, Rose,'
he said. She'd always been hopeless with knots, so she
wrapped it around the root a few times before tying it and
hoped that would satisfy him. No point in tying something
she couldn't undo herself. As soon as she pulled the rope
tight he was yanking her upright by her hair and leading
her into the trees, turning the torch off as he did so.

There was a little path; she walked quickly behind him
to loosen the tension on her scalp. She could only just make
out the forms of the eucalypts. The cicadas were close and
loud. She imagined them in her hair. Several times she
almost tripped over a root on the sandy path, but he pulled
her upright and kept her moving. She was close to him. He
smelled acrid, tangy, like he hadn't showered for days and
had been drinking cheap spirits and smoking pot. He
pulled her up a rotting staircase onto a gloomy deck. She
could make out places where the timber had simply rotted
away entirely and large black holes gaped. So this was 'his
place'. She saw a bong made from a fruit juice bottle.
Bundaberg and beer empties. A little heap of clothes.

A pair of rubber thongs. He let go of her hair and she hovered near the stairs.

'Listen, Kane. I need to know what you're going to do. The baby needs me. She'll need feeding very soon.' She felt the mozzies beginning to bite. The cicadas increased their volume. Her breasts were tingling; the flesh felt like someone was pricking her with tiny needles. He was standing at the balustrade next to her, his foot tapping the rotten floorboards, saying nothing, chewing a finger. Fall through, she thought. And then, where is the knife? Which pocket? 'You said you wanted to talk. I'm here now. Tell me what you need to tell me.'

'Give me a minute. We're gonna do this right. I'm gonna talk. You're gonna listen.'

'OK. We can talk. And then I need to get back to the baby. People will be looking for us soon, when she cries. You know, I won't say anything, if you take me back now. We'll just forget it happened. I'll make something up.'

He looked at her, almost absentmindedly, then looked away. He seemed to be having trouble concentrating. She let the thought enter her mind: if it's just sex he wants, I've done it before, would it make any difference to do it again? But her stomach turned over sharply at the thought. It would make all the difference in the world. 'Sit down,' he said. 'Don't move. I'm gonna work out how I want this to go.'

She backed against the unsteady railings and edged her way down to the floor, keeping as much distance between them as she could, checking beneath her for gaps in the decking. He sat down opposite her, maybe a metre and a half between them, reached for the bong and began to pack the cone from a pouch he pulled from his pocket. 'We need to relax,' he said. 'Can't think straight if you're not relaxed, can you.'

Danny tore across the river on the water taxi towards her house, churning up the water, bouncing over the chop. It was almost dark, but he could see smoke gusting in the high wind across the water from where her house should be. He'd smelled the smoke from the other side. The others had said it must be a burn-off, but he'd had this feeling.

Smoke obscured a stretch of perhaps five houses on the shore a hundred metres ahead. No way to tell which one it was coming from; perhaps it was all of them. As he approached he saw that the fire crew were still there, on the barge, moving about in the smoke. Above them on the hill the smoke had a red core. Now, this close, he could see which house it was in the fire barge's beams. Old Tom's—blackened, ruined, smoking quietly. He let out a long breath, then wondered about Tom. There was no ambulance or police here, just the fire barge. Was he over at the pub as his house floated across the river in a million cinders? Hope you're insured, mate, he thought, but what were the odds, a bloke like Tom?

There were no lights on at her place, but he motored towards it quietly. She wasn't due home yet, but he'd better check she'd cleared out if she was back, give her a lift if she needed one. There were little flares of red in the bush behind the houses. Firemen'd have to get onto it fast to stop it charging up the cliff, in this wind. Walking down the jetty towards the dark house, smoke in his eyes, in his lungs, he thought he saw movement in the shadows on her verandah.

'G'day, Dan,' Steve called from over on the barge.

'Tom all right?' Dan called back.

'Not here, so I guess so. His house is rooted, though. There's no one over there,' he gestured to the house. 'It's been quiet the whole time.'

'OK. I'll just double check.'

Steve lifted a hand in the air and began talking into his radio. Danny heard a strange sound that seemed to come from the verandah, a little snuffle, not quite human-sounding. He stepped onto the first stair quietly, slowly. Why would she still be here? What was she doing? His heart thudded. 'Rose?' he whispered, not knowing why he was whispering. There was a low growl, and then Dog had hold of the left leg of his pants, gripping the fabric quietly.

'Shhh, Dog,' whispered a voice in the shadows. 'Only Dan.' Dog continued to growl but dropped his grip.

'Tom?'

'Shhh,' he said again. 'Baby's asleep.'

'What?' He stepped onto the verandah and saw that Tom was sitting in the darkness on one of Rose's wicker chairs, cradling a little bundle. 'What are you doing?' he whispered. 'Where's Rose?'

'Don't know, mate. Gone. Bub was crying so I came and got her.'

'What happened to your house?'

'Gone, mate. All gone.'

'I don't understand. Where is Rose? Why are you sitting here in the dark?'

'Told you. She's gone. And . . .' His voice cracked.

'Are you all right, Tom?' Danny stepped closer. The face in the shadows was dark and old and broken. He took the baby from him, caught the scent of her skin, put a hand on Tom's shoulder. 'Why haven't you told them you're here?'

'I don't want them to know.'

'We've got to get food for the baby. We need to get her away from the fire. We need to find Rose. What are you doing?' It was like trying to extract important information from a small child without scaring him. Where's your mum? Why are you alone?

'I burned my house, didn't I?'

'Oh Tom. OK. Look, we need to get the baby food. They're going to know if you started it anyway, sooner or later. We might as well get it over with now.'

Tom nodded. 'You won't tell them . . .'

'We've got to tell them something. We've got to get help.' He tried to keep the irritation out of his voice, the rising panic.

'No. I was—meant to be in it. I'm sick, you see. No hope. You won't tell them that.'

Danny looked out across the river over the baby's head. Smoke was billowing from Tom's place under the fire barge's hose. The baby was beginning to let out little whimpers. 'Not if you don't want me to. You silly old bugger. Come on, we've got to go now. We need to find Rose before the baby gets hungry.'

Danny saw as he helped Tom down the steps that he was frail in a way he'd never noticed before. Even the meanest old buggers got old. Steve was standing on the barge, watching him, hands on hips. 'What you got there, mate?'

'It's Tom, with Rose's baby. She's not here. We need to get Tom to Alf's and find Rose.'

'OK, Dan. You want to take the baby to someone and I'll take Tom? I'll get one of the guys to have a look around behind the house. I'll call Alf on the radio.'

'OK.'

Tom's head was bowed. Under Danny's hand, he felt his shoulder tremble. 'It's all right, Tom. You'll be OK. We just need to find Rose. That's all anyone's going to worry about tonight. It was an accident.'

Tom looked into his face. He nodded quickly. 'That's right, Dan. It was that bloody grease trap. Should have cleaned it months ago. Shouldn't keep that metho there, neither. Wouldn't be told. You're a good man, Dan. Good son, too, I bet.'

Ha, Danny thought. Steve was walking over from the shell of Tom's place towards them. 'Off you go, Tom,' Danny said. 'You'll be fine.'

'He's always hated me,' he muttered, nodding in Steve's direction.

'He's a good bloke. He'll see you right. Listen,' he said quietly. 'Tell him the truth, about you being sick. He wouldn't drop you in it, if he knew.'

Tom nodded and shuffled away. Danny watched his frail old form disappear in the gusting smoke. As he walked back past Tom's decimated house he held the baby close against his body, hurrying carefully towards his boat.

You could never tell what was going to happen with pot. With Rose, it made her go to sleep. With someone like Kane, it might just as easily sharpen him up, galvanise him. He smoked it any time of day, while he was eating breakfast, fishing, whatever. He seemed to use it like other people used coffee. He passed her the bong. 'No thanks,' she said. Her eyes had adjusted to the dark. There was a half-moon out. His arm was pale, thin as he held out the little bottle.

'Take it,' he said. 'It'll relax you.'

Why would I want to relax? she thought. She drew from it as shallowly as she could, keeping it in her mouth for a moment, before breathing it out in his direction. His hand was in his pocket, fiddling with something. The knife? 'You know, I thought you were the prettiest girl on the river when I came here. Didn't mind about the kiddie. Why'd you start avoiding me? It's like you're embarrassed or something.'

She heard the complaint in his voice, the injured pride. She handed him back the bong. 'No, no. I should have talked to you, I know that. I'm just not ready for anything. I've had a—complicated time.' You bloody idiot, Rose, she thought. Why hadn't she talked to him as soon as it had happened? But there'd never been a need before. Her previous encounters, in the city—on the river, too, with James—were inconsequential. You'd be laughed at if you even bothered to try and let someone down gently afterwards. Or so she'd thought. What damage had she quietly done, without knowing it? She could see the wreckage now: Billie, Kane. Who knew what other litter lay in a trail, quietly strewn behind her? Shame nudged at her, but she resisted it. It would sap her energy to feel too sorry for him. He had kidnapped her. She would find out why; she would give him a chance to back away from the edge he'd pushed them towards. The pot was distracting her, taking her wandering off the path she needed to stay on. A mosquito bit her and she slapped it.

'I never took you for one of those girls that behave like a slut, Rosie.'

'I'm not, Kane. I'm really not. And I liked you—'

'Liked me?' he broke in. 'I would have given you everything you wanted. I still can. You don't know what's inside me. You all just make up your minds and then you're done.'

She was silent. Everything she said seemed to stir him up. He drew hard on the bong. 'We're going to get back to where we were. We were really good together, Rose. You'll remember. Tonight's about you and me.'

She shrank inside her clothes. She saw where he was going. No, she thought. Think, she told herself, ignore the pot. You are not tired. Then she caught it: a smell, a whiff of something new, beyond the grog, the pot, the rotting wood. It was wood smoke, but they weren't near any houses. You could pick the smell up from a way away if the wind was in the right direction, but no one would light their stove at this time of year, on a night like this. It was a bushfire. He hadn't noticed it yet, or if he had he didn't say anything. She didn't know what it meant for her, except that it was a change, something unpredictable. She said nothing. If there was a fire, where was it? She thought of Tom again: the bottle, the rag, then the baby in her cradle at the hospital, the smell of her when they bathed her. Why didn't I name you, baby? she thought. You need a name given to you by your mother. But she had to stop; these thoughts would take up too much space in her head, space she needed.

'I have to get back to the baby,' she tried again.

'Stop worrying about the kid and concentrate, Rosie. I've been talking to you.' He put down the bong and took a swig from the Bundy bottle. He held onto it for a moment, wiped his lips with his other hand, then slammed it down clumsily on the floorboards next to him.

She heard a crackle in the trees. He noticed it then, too. He peered groggily into the bush. 'Stay here,' he said. 'Let me check it out.' He was on his feet quickly and moving back towards the stairs. The smell was strong now; you could see smoke on the river, down through the black trees. She couldn't be sure if she imagined it, but she thought she felt heat, too. The bottle was right there. His back was to her. Now, she told herself. This is all you're going to get. She edged closer without standing. He took a few more steps down until his head was level with the deck. 'We're gonna have to move,' he called back to her. But she was already behind him, raising the Bundy bottle, heavy with liquid, in a swift action. He turned and his face registered shock briefly before she brought it down on his head. The impact reverberated through her hand and forearm to her elbow, but the bottle didn't break. He stared at her for a moment, then buckled and began to slip, but he'd grabbed hold of her shirt, and he took her with him down the last few stairs and onto the path where he fell on the ground, pinning her beneath him. She could feel his hot breath on her face. He ripped her shirt away from her, his weight heavy on her tender stomach, her stitches pressing into the dirt beneath them. He began to tug at her pants, his shoulders pinning hers to the ground.

She still had the bottle as well as freedom of movement in her forearms. She smashed it against the wooden step next to her hand. He turned at the shatter of glass and she swung at his back messily, the jagged edge connecting with flesh. He let out a cry, shifting his weight off her to grab hold of the wound. She stared at him, astonished at the chance he'd given her. It was like playing sport at school, at the moment you knew the ball was going through the hoop, or that you were crossing the line first. She saw the details of everything around her in hyper-focus: shards of broken glass next to her head, his face, clenched, furious as he clutched the wound, the black canopy looming above him. This is it. It's happening, she thought, and hit him across the back of the head with all the force she could muster while lying down. He collapsed on her, his weight crushing the air from her lungs. Her milk wet his shirt, her skin.

Above her, she heard the rush of the wind, the sound of

branches exploding. The back of the house had caught. She saw a towel hanging from the railing of the front verandah. She pushed him off her with a sharp groan and ran up a couple of stairs to grab it. Kane was lying still, his mouth slack. She wrapped the towel firmly around his waist and her hand came away sticky with blood. Her eyes were beginning to sting with smoke; she had to move while she could still make out the path. She grabbed his boots and began to drag him down towards the water, away from the burning house. The wind blew gusts of reddish smoke towards her as she struggled with him, the tatters of her shirt falling open. She was sweating and her eyes were streaming from the smoke. She had to keep stopping to wipe moisture from them, and she could feel that she was smearing blood and soot all over herself. She snagged the waistband of his jeans on a mangrove root and stopped for a second, waiting to see if he'd come to. He groaned but remained limp, and she wasn't sure whether to feel relieved that he was alive, or frightened.

It took her a good ten minutes to heave his body over the bumpy ground in the dark and smoke and heat to where the trees began to clear, close to the water. This is all I can do for you, Kane, she thought. As soon as she'd let go of his feet, she felt the urge to run. The smoke was thick on the path. She ran headlong into a tree and it smacked her squarely on the forehead. Trying to remain calm, she took the path more slowly, her head throbbing. She listened for him as she scrambled down through the mangroves to the water, trying to figure out where they'd left the boat. She couldn't hear him; she could hear only her breath, and the crackling of the forest. She had moved him, but if he burned she was still responsible. She didn't slow. She moved steadily down the path, looking for gaps in the smoke until she was there, at the boat. There was enough moon to see by, in the moments when the smoke cleared. She untied the loose knot, unwrapped it from the root. She tried not to think about what would happen to Kane if the fire reached him. She glanced behind her on the path, heaved herself onto the hull, breathing heavily, and pushed herself away with an oar.

Ten metres out she told herself to breathe more slowly. The smoke was hurting her lungs, stinging her eyes. She pulled at the motor. It started first time. She looked up at the moon and saw its grey shadows, its pale yellow light above the smoke. The fire was burning in a swath from over the ridge and down towards the shack in the bush. Fear squeezed her ribs. She had time to let the thought fill her head now. Where is it coming from?

# Chapter 22

The smoke was thick on the river and night had fallen. Danny pushed the boat slowly through the murk, holding himself back from opening her up, taking his chances. He'd fulfilled all the tasks that required no particularly difficult decisions. He had left the baby with Maggie, whose neighbour had a new baby of her own and had promised to make her up some formula and find some spare nappies. Maggie had called the police, then made the baby a little crib on the living-room floor from cushions and blankets, and he'd left Maggie and her kids sitting around her, watching her sleep. He had called Alf and told him that he needed to keep the boat for the night. Now he was just creeping through the gloom, headlights on, looking for a sign. It had to be Kane. He had no idea where he'd take her, but Kane had a boat, not a car, and so did Danny. This was all he could do. He'd been looking for an hour; had been peering into nothing, his blood alive, his skin layered with soot and sweat. Now he kept close to the foreshore, hoping for Kane's little dinghy to emerge from the fog. It was so thick he could have passed right by them a dozen times, though.

He was practically idling as he crept along the shore not a hundred metres from her house, the fire blazing above him in the bush. Just audible above the sound of his own boat, he picked up the whine of another motor. It disappeared for several seconds. Perhaps he'd imagined it. He killed his own motor and picked it up again, a high, whiny roar, a sick engine pushed too hard. Then there she was in his headlights, hair wild and something wrong with her clothes, a ragged, unhinged figure in the ghostly smoke. He waited for her to draw alongside. Her face was filthy with something dark and smeared. No sign of Kane. He reached down for the dinghy, pulled it close. He took her hand and pulled her up, her hair brushing his arm. It was blood on her face, and soot. As he pulled her onto the running board her shirt fell open for a moment. It was ripped. She didn't look at him. He smelled milk, blood, burned trees. 'Rose,' he said quietly. 'What did he do?'

'It's OK. I'm OK. Nothing, in the end.' He grabbed the rope from Kane's dinghy, threaded it through the railing on his own, tied it off. He considered for a moment setting it adrift, but decided it might be better if the cops didn't find it yet, just in case.

'Where is he? How'd you get away?'

She gestured behind her with her head, into the smoke. 'There was a bottle. I cut him. Do you know where the baby is? Did you take her from the house?'

'Maggie's got her. They got some formula for her. She's OK. Actually, Tom found her. It's his place that started the fire.'

'His place started the fire?'

Danny said nothing, but sat her down and wrapped a blanket around her. His fingers touched her neck. She held his eye. 'Do you want to go straight to the police?' he asked her. 'Or to the baby?'

'We should tell the police where he is. With the fire. And he's injured. He was bleeding.'

'Maybe. If you can find him again.'

'I can find him. I dragged him down to the water.'

'You could just—tell me where he is.'

'Why?'

'Because then you wouldn't have to worry about him anymore.'

The water taxi bobbed on the water. There was heavy traffic around her place, fire barges, police boats, Waterways. They'd drifted around the point, and she could see the dense smoke, the lights from the boats. Her house was obscured.

'No one knows him here. No one'll miss him when he's gone,' he said.

'What are you going to do?'

'We'll just make sure he doesn't come back here. Ever.'

He looked at her. 'Are you sure he didn't touch you? Do you want me to find someone for you to talk to? I can take you to the police, if you want me to. If that's how you want to do it.'

'No, really. I got away in time.' She paused for a moment. 'Can I trust you? Can I trust your friends?'

'What do you mean?'

'I don't want him on my conscience.'

He took a thin bunch of her hair in his palm, rubbed his dirty thumb along the silky shaft. He looked at her face in the dim light of the cabin. They were drifting close to the fire, up on the ridge; the smoke had cleared for a moment and it burned wide and red in the dark. Her face glowed with its strange light. 'It's got to be tonight. Maggie's called the police. They're looking for him.'

# Chapter 23

The smoke had mostly cleared now and the moon hung high and bright. There were three of them in dark clothes, creeping along the shore in Tom's barge with no lights. Danny wore a dark green beanie; sweat prickled in his hair. Alf handled the boat silently, his face blank, massive. Rob sat on the aluminium bench opposite, while Danny gave Alf directions as clearly as he could based on what Rose had told him.

Danny peered into the dark knotted bush, looking for the straight lines of the roof she'd talked about. The roof might have collapsed altogether in the fire; it had blown back on itself now and was burning more steadily back up on the ridge. We must be close, he thought. Perhaps Kane was dead. Perhaps he was gone. Danny's breathing was steady and slow, his body alert to the sounds of the bush burning above them, the smell of the river.

There it was—the corner of the deck, the tin roof in the moonlight. Danny tapped Alf on the shoulder and pointed into the trees. Alf switched off the engine, and Rob and Danny manoeuvred the boat into the shallows, using the oars as punts. They crept up the path in single file: Danny, Alf then Rob. He could see the house above them; it was partly burned out. They must be almost where she had left him by now. He slowed, then stopped. He was there, lying among the mangroves. He looked as if he'd fallen from a tree, his limbs at awkward angles. He was soaking wet, and he wondered if the river had somehow risen over him, lapping with the tide perhaps, but they were a good couple of metres above the river and the water was still. Then he realised the trees were glistening and there was water dripping from the leaves above. A fire helicopter had dumped water here. That was why the house was still at least partly standing. Even the water hadn't woken him. Danny thought: he's dead; she's killed him. But then the body groaned, and Danny stiffened.

Danny took a thick loop of rope from his shoulder and crouched by Kane's head. Alf took the feet. They tied his hands and feet up quickly, while he lay prone. He could have been asleep. Rob drew a roll of gaffer tape from his small backpack and ripped it open with a sound like metal tearing. Kane opened his eyes, took in the dark figures, his bound limbs, and screamed briefly before Rob brought a length of tape down over his mouth and the scream was muffled to a moan. Then it was all in the eyes. They were round in the dark, watering.

Danny put his hands under the armpits and Rob took the feet while Alf led the way back down the path to the barge. Danny heard helicopters above, dousing the last of the flames on the cliff with their enormous buckets. As they reached the end of the path, they caught a clear view as the whirling blades made a huge round dent in the water—a liquid crop circle. They hung back in the trees and watched the water bucket down into the creek. When the helicopter had risen and departed, they threw Kane in the boat and climbed in after him.

Alf started the motor while Danny untied. Kane had grown quiet, and watched them, Danny in particular, with large, rheumy eyes. 'What do we do with him, Alf?' Rob said.

Alf turned slightly. 'We dump him in the river, just like the old days. But first we have a bit of fun.'

'Well, I don't need to be home for a while,' Rob said. 'Wife's away with the kids. Got all night for an adventure. How about you, Dan?'

Danny said nothing, looked out into the blackness beyond the boat, wondered what was about to happen; knew that, whatever it was, he couldn't stop it.

As they rounded the point, he watched the mopping up over at the beach. You couldn't see the houses from this distance, only the lights on in some of them, but there was the fire barge, the helicopters overhead, the occasional shout just audible over their blades. They watched in silence as they made their way through the middle of the channel, past the island, towards the ocean. Kane tried to cry out from beneath the tape, but with the noise of the barge and the helicopters you couldn't hear much.

'Keep it down, kid,' Alf said.

Rob laughed. 'Who's gonna hear him, with all that going on?'

The swell increased as they left the wide basin containing the island and the beach. Alf picked up speed, and soon it was too loud for anyone to speak. You could smell the sea, feel its waves surging into the land, a black line on the horizon. They began to lose contact with the water as they sped over bumps, and Kane's body jumped and fell with each surge, letting out a brief moan on impact. Danny gripped the railing and sucked in the clean salty air beyond the smoke-filled basin of the river. His scalp prickled and he forgot briefly what he was doing here, about the body jumping and rolling at his feet.

Ahead of them, the rocky island loomed, black, silent. No lights, no houses. They passed an open bay; at its farthest end was the village Danny had walked to after he'd gone overboard on his father's fishing boat. The swell grew bigger, and Alf hunkered over the wheel, watching the shape of the oncoming waves so he could hit them square. Danny grasped the handles now with both hands, while Kane banged about in the bottom of the boat, his hard, sinewy body knocking against their feet and knees.

Alf turned on his high beams. The island loomed over them, a wall of rock. We're going to smash into it, Danny thought, staring at the face of stone glinting amid the gnarled scrub. But then the boat was in a tiny sandy bay, and they were ashore, the barge steady, the world righting itself.

Danny and Rob jumped down onto the little beach and dragged the boat up. Then they climbed back in and took opposite ends of Kane. 'What do you want to do with him, Dan?' Rob said.

'Put him down.' They dumped him on the sand and stood around him. He was moaning, his eyes bulging, staring at Danny. Danny felt the man's panic scrambling about his own body like confused blood. 'Check his cut,' Danny said.

Rob turned him over with his boot and shone a torch on his back. The towel Rose had tied around him was still there, dark at his hip. Danny peeled it away. The wound was wet and dark, but had stopped bleeding. He pushed him onto his side, took his fishing knife from his pocket with one hand and ripped the tape from Kane's mouth with the other. The skin stuck, his lips turning white as it pulled away. Danny brought the knife down to Kane's wrists. Kane stared at it as Danny cut the ropes away from his hands, then his feet.

'Stand up,' Danny said. Kane scrambled to his feet quickly, eyeing the knife. Danny handed it to Rob, and nodded back towards the boat. Rob put the torch on a rock, making a little pool of light that illuminated Danny and Kane to their waists, and he and Alf disappeared into the darkness.

Danny watched the man in front of him, tall, hurting, but still carrying a wary meanness, ready to spring. All the times he'd backed away, all this hiding on the river from the day he'd be found, all led to this. From the dark behind him came the slosh of water around the boat as Rob and Alf climbed back in. Kane leapt at him as soon as he heard it, his sharp fist connecting with the side of Danny's head. Danny's instinct was to cover himself, as he had as a boy, roll himself up into a ball until it stopped, careful to do nothing that would provoke his dad further. That urge was still there, to play dead. But he raised his fist while Kane was swinging for another blow and punched him as accurately as he could in the swaying dark on the chin. Kane slapped him a couple of times and went for a headbutt, but didn't hit him square on. Danny managed to jab him in the shoulder and then the cheek, and Kane staggered back, holding his side. Danny watched him for a second, waiting to see what sort of shape he was in. Maybe he was faking it with his cut, maybe he wasn't.

Danny stepped forward, put a hand on his shoulder to steady him, and Kane kicked him in the knee. Danny went down, the pain tearing through his leg. Kane grabbed the torch and hit him in the face with it. Fury exploded in Danny's head and he barrelled Kane over from his knees, slamming his shoulder into his gut, and sprang to his feet, standing over him. He couldn't see out of one of his eyes where the torch had hit him. 'Are you getting up?' he said through gritted teeth. Kane shook his head, coughing into the sand.

He waited for a moment. Should he drag him up, make him continue? But the fight had drained out of Danny; he felt as limp suddenly as the figure before him on the ground. You could only fight someone worth fighting. He heard footsteps on the sand behind him. It was Rob, throwing something onto the sand a few metres away from Kane's limp form: a thin red tube—a distress flare. He shrugged. 'Promised Maggie.'

Danny turned back to Kane, whose hand was over his face, his chest heaving. 'If I see you again,' he said, 'you come near me, or Rose, I'll kill you.'

In Maggie's house on the island, in her lamp-lit bedroom, Rose let her torn shirt fall open and held her sleeping baby to her skin. She kissed her and breathed in her smell. The little bald head against her cheek was smooth and hard but for the soft fontanelle, throbbing gently. She opened her tiny eyes and a bolt of electricity shot straight into Rose's body. The baby's gaze held her, frozen in position, filled with her presence. So this was how it was supposed to feel. There it was, a connection between them like a steel cable of many twisted strands. 'Emily,' she whispered. 'That was my mum's name, little girl.'

She lay down on the bed, carefully arranging the baby next to her, trying not to squeeze her too hard. The door inched open, and Maggie came and sat by them on the edge of the bed. 'I'm so sorry for all the trouble I've caused,' Rose murmured. 'I should have sorted this out myself.'

'Shush, love.' Maggie put a hand on her head, tucked her hair behind her ear. 'Let your friends help you. You've done enough on your own.'

Outside, there was a distant explosion, then a fizzing like a firework. Through the window they saw a plume of red smoke shoot out from behind the black hills and high into the sky, disintegrating after a moment, the smoke lingering for a second or two. Maggie nodded. 'Good,' she said quietly.

Rose pressed her face into the baby's hard, downy little head and closed her eyes. She breathed her in, her oaty baby smell, her whole body aching with gratitude and love.

# Epilogue

Danny had been working on his place for three months. It was still just a wooden frame on the hillside, but now that it was at least that, you could see what it would become. It'd be a while yet; he had to fit in the building between fares, with the odd day off, but it was happening in front of his eyes now. He was hot from hammering though there was a light rain and the air held the chill of autumn, and he sat on the rafters of his future deck and watched the clouds shifting quietly along the valley, the surface of the creek below blurred with rain. He watched as above the rise of the plateau a figure steadily appeared. It was her, Rose, carrying the baby in its pouch. They were still a good fifteen metres off but he could see the baby had grown beyond recognition, her legs hanging down below Rose's hips. Rose looked straight at him, shy but fearless as she approached. He'd waited, and waited—had known she was still on the river, Rob kept an eye on her—had accepted the waiting as calmly as he could.

He'd been thinking of her. The day before, he'd seen the River Baptists for the first time, up at the shallow end of the creek as he was having a swim. He remembered that she'd seen them, when he'd found her stranded on the river. She'd said they looked happy, and they did now, too; delirious they seemed. They were a sight, in their ordinary clothes, soaked to the skin—grown people being cradled by a big man, coming up smiling. He'd watched them from the shade of a tree for a while, then paddled home in his dory, shaking his head.

Now here she was, like they were a sign. It had been six weeks since he'd sent her the map, no signature, just a D on the little jetty in the creek. He'd resisted it for a while. Waited till he could wait no more. It seemed as he wrote her name on the envelope that he was staking everything on a hunch, a glimpse of a possible life.

He walked down to meet them, held his arms out for the baby. 'Give her to me,' he said. 'That's a bugger of a climb.' She unbuttoned the pouch beneath her coat and eased the baby out. His heart pounded as he took her, shielding her face from the rain with his hand. Rose said nothing, but she was smiling. He'd never seen her smile like that; she seemed to have shed something, the weight of her father perhaps, the stuff of the past. He smiled back. Her happiness was irresistible.

The baby in his arms was fat, warm, soft-skinned, still sleeping. There were children in his life now: he was beginning to know his own child, he wanted to know this one. Rose was watching him, waiting. He'd missed her face. There was so much she didn't know about him. But there was time now for everything, now she'd come, to lay himself out before her and let her decide. 'Want to see what I've done?' he said. She nodded, a tiny movement of her head, and he took her by the hand.

# Acknowledgements

Thank you Neal Drinnan, Caroline Lurie and Brad Shiach for reading and commenting on early drafts; Annette Barlow, Catherine Taylor and Ali Lavau for sensitive, patient and thorough editing; Catherine Milne for her work on this book and behind the scenes for *The Australian*/Vogel Award; Patrick Gallagher at Allen & Unwin, Alan Stevns at Vogel's and Murray Waldren at *The Australian* for running the award; the Vogel judges; Varuna—The Writers' House for a fellowship to work on an earlier novel that never saw the light of day; Gail Shiach and Hawkesbury River Child Care for taking care of my daughter so I could write. Thank you, too, to all at Allen & Unwin for their care and attention.

A final thankyou to Brad for his endless love, support and pride.